T0116959

It's Only Words

Keith McClean

iUniverse, Inc.
New York Bloomington

It's Only Words

This is a work of fiction. All of the characters, names, incidents, organizations, and dialogue in this novel are either the products of the author's imagination or are used fictitiously.

iUniverse books may be ordered through booksellers or by contacting:

iUniverse
1663 Liberty Drive
Bloomington, IN 47403
www.iuniverse.com
1-800-Authors (1-800-288-4677)

ISBN: 978-1-4502-5769-5 (sc)
ISBN: 978-1-4502-5771-8 (dj)
ISBN: 978-1-4502-5770-1 (ebk)

Printed in the United States of America

iUniverse rev. date: 9/1/2010

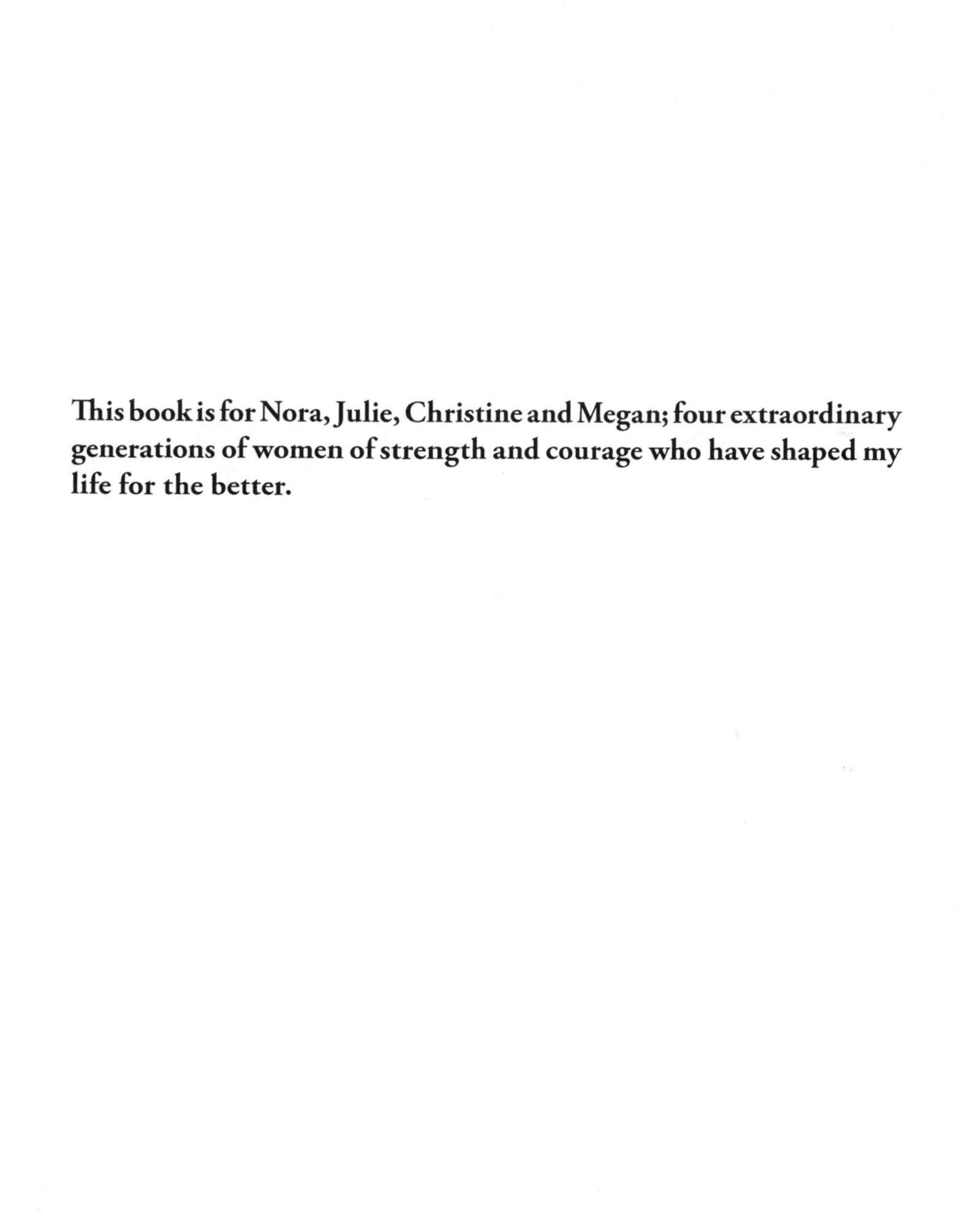

This book is for Nora, Julie, Christine and Megan; four extraordinary generations of women of strength and courage who have shaped my life for the better.

It's Only Words

There is no apparent cancer hovering about waiting to make its claim on him. His heart has never threatened to quit him. He is still able to move with relative ease and comfort for a man of his years and yet he knows that each day he dies a little more. He has lost family and he has lost friends and he has mourned the finality of these departures greatly and with acceptable and expected emotion. He understands that it makes little or even no sense to grieve for the little of him that dies each day but that is irrelevant. He knows that he is dying, but he has been dying for most of his life and his final passing may not come for many years. The body has withered – surely – but it is the promise that he mourns for. As the promise dims so goes all hope.

Chapter One

An elderly man calls through a screened door startling a woman carrying a tray. As the woman turns, a little too quickly, a glass falls from the tray and to the ground and shatters. In a corner of the room, in a wicker basket and lying on a blanket, a black cat with white feet is awakened by the sudden crashing outburst. The cat jumps up, visibly annoyed, stretches quietly and exits the room quickly through the screened door as the elderly man comes in from outside. Outside, on a field, the kitty spies a gray squirrel and goes speedily in pursuit, but her prey is too quick and it flees to the nearest tree and up high into its branches.

A golden leaf, drenched in the morning dew, is shaken and released in the gray rodents wake and begins to spiral heavily downward. A gentle breeze off the Delaware River interrupts the flight pattern of the leaf and carries it slightly off of its course and on down caressing the tip of the nose of Robert Montgomery before finally settling upon his lap.

Robert is suddenly alert. The cool moist leaf has brought him back from a dream or perhaps a momentary trance. He glances down at the leaf. The corners of his mouth travel further towards the east and west and somewhat towards the north. He takes it gently between thumb and forefinger and examines it more closely. He brings it up and under his nose and closes his eyes and inhales what is a pleasurable fragrance to him.

"The leaf," he says to the man on his left, "makes me think of Emily. Emily is my daughter," he explains. There is a slight tremble in his smile as he recalls Emily as a child. "She's grown up now," he continues.

He takes a handkerchief from his trouser pocket and wipes the dew from the leaf and then presses the leaf between the pages of a book that had been resting on the bench to his right.

"Emily liked to climb trees," he says. "Often I would have to let her stand on my shoulders," he says gesturing with his hands. "I would boost her up to the lower branches and then up, up she would go. It would upset her mother to no end. Her mother would always fear the worst. She was afraid that Emily would fall and get hurt. But I would catch her if ever she should fall," he says with strong conviction in his eyes. "I would be there to catch her."

Robert looks out across the river and reflects to that earlier time. "She would have climbed regardless of what I had wanted. If I had forbidden Emily to climb, I would not have been there to catch her. Kathleen didn't understand that." Once again his mind travels back to an earlier time. "Kathleen was my wife," he explains. "She's gone now."

Robert looks down at his feet and at the individual blades of grass around them. He picks up one foot and studies the blades that had been crushed beneath it. "Tell me something Toby, do you ever feel that we're all here just to pass the time?"

Toby says nothing. He sits staring out at the water. His face is hard and stern, but not lean as it had once been. There are lines that run deeply on his face, particularly around the mouth. He is an old man. He wears a black leather cap and a navy blue P-coat. He has a day or maybe two days growth of beard. Every now and again he reaches into a small crumpled brown paper bag and takes out one single cashew and places it gently onto his tongue.

"Don't worry, I don't intend on reflecting on the meaning of life," Robert says. "All of us ponder the meaning of life from time to time and then we move on." He speaks softly and unhurried. "We move on, I suppose, because pondering such things can become terribly tiresome. I get tired a lot these days." Robert looks at the old man for a time studying his face, but Toby stares straight ahead unfazed by Robert's close examination.

"I'm not alone in this, Toby. I see it all of the time. I think most people at times are doing one thing and feel that, or perhaps they wish that, they were doing something else. I'm sixty years of age, Toby." He speaks quietly. "Sixty years of age," he repeats mainly to himself.

He looks at the old man thinking that he must be somewhere north of eighty. "I suppose you don't feel obliged to commiserate with me?" Toby puts a cashew on his tongue.

The two men are sitting on a bench with a rather large elm tree centered behind them. It is late in the autumn and they are dressed appropriately for the season and the climate.

"I suppose that sixty isn't really so old," he says with a halfhearted attempt at convincing himself. "A great deal of things can still be accomplished provided that you still have your wits about you." Robert, still holding the handkerchief, looks down at his hands. He works the soft cotton cloth into those hands as though he had just changed a tire.

"I do a great deal of reading," he says emphatically. "Perhaps it's my greatest passion. It brings me an enormous amount of pleasure, but I suppose very little satisfaction. I mean it accomplishes nothing; at least nothing in a tangible sense. It's more of a mental exercise or even a spiritual one. Reading, for me, is a reward, but do I deserve to be rewarded? Can I sit down and enjoy a baseball game when the lawn needs mowing? Can I play a round of golf when my roof is leaking? I've always felt better about reading after some sort of achievement. Even trivial accomplishments make it justifiable. Keeping up," he says, "with the things that need to be done so that I can feel free to indulge in the things that I want to do. Isn't that how we're supposed to feel?"

A little boy is laughing heartily on the field as his mother chases him. On a blanket, with a picnic basket at his side, an old man wearing dark gray trousers, a sun hat and a cardigan sweater, sits embracing his knees. He watches as the young mother scoops up her child and swings him playfully in an arc giving the boy a thrill. She drops the boy to his feet and runs to the old man and kneels beside him, smoothing her dress against her thighs as she does so.

"My mother did not approve of my reading," says Robert. "Some people say that reading is an escape and I suppose there is a good deal of truth to that. Words, whether written or spoken, can be quite revealing.

I think they sometimes reveal more about the speaker or author than they do about the subject."

Robert looks to the child and to the child's mother with the old man and to the river and the surrounding trees and into the sky and to an airplane in the distance. "I like to read," he says, "because reading can take me to places that I could never possibly go on my own. As for my mother, 'its only words', she would say. 'It's only words on the page and not real life.'"

A surviving fly circles Toby's face for a moment and eventually comes to rest on his nose. It is content to sit still for a while and then begins to rub its front legs together. Robert smiles at the old man as he sits unfazed by the intruder upon his beak.

"She was right, my mother, as far as her life was concerned. And when she said such things to me it was not her way of scolding me. It was her way of telling me that there were better ways of living. Her way was better. Only she could understand that, though. It was her way, not mine. You see, I could never have possibly lived the type of life that had made her happy." Robert glances over to the woman with her child. "I did not approve of her way."

Robert is lost in thought for several moments before he speaks again. "I've only spoken so openly with one other person, Toby. Of course I have family and friends, but there is only this one other person I ever allowed myself to truly confide in on all levels. I hope you don't mind. You are most certainly a good listener. There is a great deal to be said of one who listens so selflessly"

Toby still says nothing. He looks at Robert only occasionally, but always with such intensity and seemingly with sheer concentration.

Robert speaks softly and gently, but always with assurance. "Please stop me if I begin to bore you with the details of my life. My mother was what people sometimes call a free spirit. She often proclaimed herself to be just that. I suppose it was in her nature and what and who you are is more often than not determined before birth. Blame it on genetics if you're a man of science or blame it on God if you're a man of religion or perhaps Lucifer himself. Be that as it may, my dearly departed mother was who she needed to be.

"My mother's husband, Robert Preston Montgomery was killed in England in nineteen forty-four during an air raid. He was not a soldier. Some sort of a defect in one of his legs kept him from fighting in the war, but did not keep him from dying in it. He was merely a working fellow. He delivered milk, as I understand it. I was born in Birmingham, England in nineteen forty-five just as the war was wrapping up. You may have picked up on the accent."

Robert closes his eyes and dabs the white linen in the corners on either side of the bridge of his nose. "All of my memories of that man came from a few scattered photographs and from some very brief words, when questioned, from some of my visibly uncomfortable aunts and uncles.

"None of the members of my family ever spoke about the early days. We never looked back as far as yesterday and I, speaking of the past with you, am breaking with a long family tradition. I'm sure you are honored by this, old man."

Robert stands up abruptly and stretches up towards the sky on tiptoe. "The early years of my childhood were a bit confusing to me," he says. His left hand grips his right wrist behind his lower back and he looks away into a vacant distance as he continues to speak. "I lived with my grandmother, my mother's mother, before she passed when I was four. After that I was shuffled around amongst four sets of aunts and uncles for a month or two at a time. My mother was the youngest of five children. She had three sisters and one brother. My uncle John, my mother's brother, liked me, but his wife did not. I could only have fun with him when my aunt was not around. They had no children of their own." He speaks to the old man as though his words are being recorded for posterity.

"On Sundays my uncle always took me out when I was staying with them. I remember that he always told my aunt that he was taking me with him on an errand and then he would take me to a park or a picture show and one time we went to the zoo." He smiles at the recollection. "He would always encourage me not to speak of it afterwards. In her presence he was severely quiet with me. I think it was because she resented my presence and he would rather not bring my being to her attention. I don't know if he did this for my sake or for his own. I think my uncle John liked to avoid any confrontation with my aunt.

"In the case with my other aunts, I always felt that I was a source of embarrassment to them and somewhat of a burden. They each had three children of their own, but my youngest cousin was eleven years my senior. For the most part when I was staying with any of my aunts and uncles I was the only child in their home. Their friends and neighbors always looked at me strangely. Even as a small child I knew that people were speaking of me as though I were of low class. Some were not very diplomatic about it. Perhaps they thought that a child had no mind for comprehension or perhaps they just didn't care. I suppose I felt out of place.

"All in all I can't say that I was treated badly by any of my aunts in that I was well fed and always properly dressed and well groomed. I was never sent to school in a shabby manner and I looked presentable in church on Sundays. As for my uncles, my aunts' husbands, I was treated with indifference by two of them and treated with great kindness by the other. My uncle Sean, an import from Ireland, was rather fond of me. He treated me as though I were one of his own children; included me in everything that was done. Unfortunately he died when I was six. A heart attack," he says somberly."

Robert begins to pace back and forth slowly as he speaks. His hands still locked firmly behind him forcing his shoulders back and his stance erect. He holds his chin up high and his eyes are wide allowing the daylight to energize him. He pauses every now and then to breathe in deeply.

"My mother's presence in my life was only intermittent. She was merely a woman who I was to call mother when in her company. She was virtually a stranger to me in my first recollection of her when my grandmother died. After that she would show up sporadically like a visiting aunt and always unexpected.

"She doted on me severely on those occasions, though. Showered me with such love and affection," he says almost dreamily. "She would talk of things that we would do on the following day, places we would go. She would sing to me and dance with me. She would tuck me into bed and cuddle with me and hold me tightly in her arms. She would play with my hair and kiss me behind the ears and make promises of tomorrow. And I would go to sleep with such delight and my body would shake with excitement. In the morning, though, she could be gone."

Robert returns to the bench, unlocks his wrist, and takes his seat beside Toby. He hunches over, places his elbows upon his knees, intertwines his fingers and rests his chin upon his thumbs. He again stares out to the little boy with his mother and sort of half smiles. "I would ask for her at first, but learned quickly that the asking was aggravating to my aunts and my uncles. In the beginning they would fumble with excuses and make gestures with their hands and then they would get angry. I used to think that that anger was directed towards me, but as I think about it, it was probably meant for her and for the situation that she had put them in. Soon I would learn to stop asking.

"Sometimes she would be gone for weeks and sometimes her absences would last for several months. Sometimes she would stay for a month or even two and sometimes it would only last a week or less. On any given night I would go to sleep and wonder if I would see her on the following morning. I loved her very much and I secretly hated her as well."

Again Robert is silent. His words falter and his light blue eyes are seemingly vacant. Toby, in much the same state, breaks the silence occasionally with the crinkling of the bag for the incidental nut. In the distance the mother and her child are helping the old man to his feet. They support him from behind while he claims his balance. In an instant the blanket is rolled and the basket collected and in another they are gone.

Up the hill and on the road a car waits at a stop signal. The drivers' head moves in rhythm with the beat of the music blaring from his stereo. Robert turns toward the sound and watches as the driver speeds off. His eyes follow the car until it is out of sight. He looks at Toby and then to where the woman and child had been picnicking with the old man. He hadn't noticed them leaving.

"Music", he says, "was important to her." He is again speaking of his mother. "Always, she would insist on playing the Victrola and she would play it much too loudly. Clearly it irked all of my aunts, but my mother paid no heed to their blatant attempts to shunt it. Soon they would ignore her and leave her be, because the more they tried to stop the music the louder she would play it. Even as a child I thought the music to be ear splitting and perhaps unsuitable as it was dance hall material.

"Still, I loved it when she played her music in those early days. She was so spirited and filled with good cheer. There was no denying her joy for life and even my uncles, who shook their heads and frowned upon her and her actions in the presence of my aunts, seemed to be more pleasant in her company. She was like no other person in our little world.

"She smoked cigarettes and drank alcohol and wore dresses too low in the neckline and too short in the hemline. She was a very sexual woman, Toby. Even long before I knew what it meant to be the way she was, I thought her to be, somehow, inappropriate. She danced with too much animation and with any man who asked. Men she barely knew would come to whichever home in which we were staying and she would leave with them in a moments notice and not return until the following morning. She was a mother and a widow and she was not at all proper. In her absence life was very quiet and most proper. In her absence, life was very lonely."

A moment passes and then Robert smiles. "I began learning to read when I was six and by the time I turned seven I became quite proficient in doing so. I read a great deal. *The Call of the Wild* was the first book that truly gave me a great appreciation for the written word. I remember that book putting me on the adventure of my short life. I read it several times over and slept with it under my pillow. None of my aunts seemed to mind my reading as it kept me out of their way. My mother was the only person to be uncomfortable, and visibly so, with my preoccupation. She would often pull whatever book I was reading away from me and drag me out to play. When she was around, I tried to keep my reading down to a minimum.

"She wanted me to be like her and for the life of me I could not understand why. I wanted her to be like the mothers in the movie pictures. I wanted a normal life as those depicted in the books that I read. I wanted to go to sleep at night with the expectation that she would be there in the morning. I wanted her to love me enough to stay with me." He sits quietly for a moment while his face defrosts.

"I believe that she did love me, Toby. In her way she loved me very much. She always left me behind, but she always came back to me. And when she did, she would cling to me very tightly. She would hold me so tightly as though she feared she would lose me if she did not. I felt that. Even then I felt that she was struggling with herself to hold on. Clearly she wanted a balance in her life. She wanted a path to stay on and yet she wanted to run free. She wanted to run towards the music.

"I gave her my book when I was nine. *The Call of the Wild.* I told her it was an adventure that she could go on without running away. I'll never forget the look in her eyes as I said those words to her. For the first time I felt that I had said something that had truly reached out to her. She stared at me for a time and then her eyes filled with tears and then she hugged me and wept. I went to sleep that night thinking that she would either change her ways or leave forever. When I woke the next morning she was gone.

"I was nine years old then and we had been staying with my aunt Bridget. She was my mothers' elder by only two years, but I remember thinking at the time that she was much more her senior. My aunt Bridget always wore floral print dresses that buttoned at the neck and hung down low over her shins. She wore her hair up in a tight, somewhat messy, bun. She always looked tired and perhaps even a bit defeated. The only resemblance she bore with my mother was about the eyes. They both had the same gray blue eyes. The eyes were the same color and the same shape. But even the eyes, while the same semblance, were different in that they saw a different world. It was quite apparent to even the most indifferent of strangers that these two sets of eyes saw an entirely different world. My aunt greeted life with great effort each and every day, while my mother saw nothing but blue skies and sunshine.

"Perhaps I describe these two people in a simplistic manner, but I was nine when I had defined their lives and I still view them as such. I know that each of them had experienced both joy and pain and I do not wish to diminish or to belittle their range of emotions. I simply illustrate the lives they chose to reveal. My aunt opted to be a victim and my mother, the victor. It may not have been by their intent, but it was most certainly what they had shown.

"After my mum," Robert pauses momentarily. "After my mother left I felt dreadfully ill. I was ill. The nighttime was the worst of it. I would get up from my bed, go to the lavatory and vomit quietly. I did this for more than a week. I was sure to clean up after myself very carefully and I did so with such meticulous care, as my aunt was quite particular about cleanliness. Although she was not one to scold me for being sick I did not wish to explain my illness. I knew it was no more than the pain of my loss for my mother and in particular the blame I put upon myself for her leaving when she had.

"I feared and truly believed that I would never see her again. Her leaving this time was very different from her preceding adjournments. I always remembered her to be rather jubilant on the eve of her previous disappearances. This time she had been crying. She had been crying over my words.

"I recall that I ate very little in the days and weeks that had followed. I even found it difficult to lose myself within the bound pages of an American western. She was gone and this time it was my fault. This time I could not lose myself no matter how much I had tried. And although I was nine and very much disapproving of the woman who was my mother, I dreaded the thought of losing the person she had chosen to be. She had been, up until that point, the only real light in my heart."

Toby pulls two cashews from his brown, crinkled paper bag and holds them in his hand, palm open. He turns his body towards Robert. Robert smiles and accepts the proffered nut and duly notes a hint of kindness in the eyes of the old man. "She came back to me, Toby," he says. "She came back six and a half weeks later and she came with intentions of staying. With her, she brought a man. Bernard Coltrane was the man and he was to be her second husband.

"Bernard was a smallish man with uncharacteristic features. In trying to describe him as I've tried to so many times in my head, I can think of nothing prominent that stood out about him except, perhaps, that he had very small hands. His hands were very soft and delicate and it seemed to me, even then, that he was an odd sort of candidate for a husband for my mother. She had always been a woman who had gravitated to more, shall I say, masculine men. The other men were always broad men with powerful hands and sharp tongues. Not vulgar per se, but with humor that was more colorful than dry. Bernard was nothing like that. He was soft spoken and I want to say genteel, but he was not that either. He gave the appearance of being well bred and polite, but only that.

"Bernard was humorless, much like all of my aunts and it was clear that he would fit in well amongst them, but he would not carry much favor with any of my uncles although that would be irrelevant. How he and my mother could survive as man and wife I couldn't imagine, but at the time I was happy to look beyond that and towards the possibility of having a home to live in and not just a house.

"They had a very small, very proper wedding. There were maybe forty people in attendance. Mostly it was just the immediate family. I would learn later on that Bernard had only acquaintances and not friends. The music was quite bland for a party and those who wished to dance never got a chance to do so. Also, there was no alcohol served. Bernard was not a drinking man and he thought it would be sloppy for others to be doing so on the day of his nuptials with my mother. Surprisingly, my mother had nothing to say about any of this.

"We moved into Bernard's home on their wedding night. It was a small, two- bedroom flat on the ground floor right on the canal. Bernard showed no interest in me whatsoever. Not as a father or as a friend. To him I was just another acquaintance. He did right by me, though, in that he provided me with proper food and clothing and I was given a room to call my very own and the things within the room were to be mine and that was something that had meant an awful lot to me. For so long a time I felt such a vagabond. I wandered from house to house with only a rucksack. And albeit they were the same homes that I had been wandering into time and time again there was no permanence. This flat was to be my home and the people in it to be my family.

"In the beginning my mother dressed more conservatively as Bernard would demand of her. He was a tailor and so the clothes she would now wear were all hand picked and fitted by Bernard himself. I thought it curious then, why a man would take a woman such as my mother to be his wife and to then demand that she be someone other than herself. I have since learned that this is not uncommon and it is perhaps why so many marriages fail.

"She still wore her make-up and hair as she pleased, much to the chagrin of Bernard, but the clothes made her different. She was no longer the cheerful, mirthful girl I knew her to be. She was a woman now. Much more like my aunts than like my mother and I wondered if they too had been like she in their earlier days; and I wondered if she were like this when she was wed to Robert Preston Montgomery; and I wondered then, if marriage sucked all the life out of those who once had life.

"I did not dwell on the changes she had made or had been forced to make, because it pleased me that she were married and grounded. I was pleased to have a mother who was there in the evening and who would be there in the morning. And so I did not hate Bernard. I was, perhaps, feeling as indifferent towards him as he was towards me. I understood very little about marriage at that age. I believed that marriage was some sort of a contract that bound a man and woman together for the rest of their lives unless, of course, one should expire prematurely relegating the other to an early release from said contract as had been the case between my mother and Robert Preston Montgomery.

"A year and a month after their union, the most wonderful gift one could ever imagine was given me. Elizabeth, my sister, was born. We were, for once, a true family. Elizabeth would be the tie that would bind Margaret, Margaret was my mothers name in case I haven't already mentioned her by name," he explains, "and Bernard together. I not only felt then that she was what they so desperately needed to strengthen their marriage, but also what I needed. I had my share of friends, but no one so close as a sibling and although she was ten years my junior I knew that we would be close for always.

"My mother seemed so pleased and proud to have a daughter and even Bernard seemed to have taken an interest in fatherhood. I supposed then that it was because the child was his own unlike me who was the product of another man. Still it made no difference to me. I knew that whatever it was that would make them closer, was something that I could benefit from. It was not to last, though. Elizabeth was not the cause of my mother's digression; her arrival merely sped up the inevitable.

"My mother tried so desperately to be up in spirit, but it was getting harder for her. I could see her struggling to remain steadfast and staunch, but I feared the worst as she went on. She did not greet the day with dread in the same manner as my aunt Bridget in that she had not yet been defeated. She had a nervous energy about her that was sure to explode. I could see in her eyes that she was looking for a way out. She needed to escape.

"Also, in this period I would never allow my mother to see that I had been reading. On one occasion she found me in my room with a book, she nearly went out of her mind. She took the book from me and tossed it through the window and screamed at me to go out. 'It's only words', she screamed as I ran from the flat. 'Live your bloody life.' I had never seen her like that before and I had hoped to never see her like that again.

"Within days her clothing began to change back to what she used to wear and this caused great unrest between she and Bernard. And although, I believe it to be healthy to express yourself as you please, I knew that she would eventually take it to the extreme. She was a free spirit and meant to live that way and no matter how many obstacles she had tried to put in her way it was only a matter of time before she overcame them. Only her obstacles were made up of people and people get hurt.

"Elizabeth was not yet a year old when our mother disappeared for the first time since Bernard had come into our lives. Once again my aunts came to the rescue by watching Elizabeth during the day while Bernard worked. I took over the housework as best I could and I became the primary caregiver of Elizabeth by night. Bernard paid the bills and I believe that was all he felt compelled to do. He came home at night, ate dinner, read the newspaper or listened to the radio and went to bed. I don't believe that we had ever shared a cross word. I did what I thought was expected of me and he did the same.

"My mother would show up after a week or two or sometimes a longer period of time and act as if nothing had ever transpired. Bernard would say nothing. He would go to his room at night and lock the door and mother would sleep on the couch. The arrangement had become more revolting to me than ever before. I was twelve years old now and I knew the meaning of the word 'whore'.

"It was a brutal period of my life," he says matter-of-fact. "Children can be cruel and when such merciless torment is put upon a boy where the subject is that boy's mother, life can become unbearable to say the least. I loved my mother and continued to do so, but I also hated her more than I ever could have imagined. She put me in a horrible position and I knew not how to defend myself. I fought some, but to little avail. They called her whore and in my heart I agreed with them.

"I would look at Elizabeth with dread. What would her life be like? How would girls treat her and when she approached adolescence what would boys expect from her?" Robert speaks faster now. His heart is accelerating and the anger is visible. His face reddens as he speaks and his fists are clenched. He breathes heavily as he continues. "Bernard was useless to her. To me, I could understand, but Elizabeth was his flesh and blood and he owed something to her. He knew the person my mother was before he married and took her to be his bride never the less. Elizabeth was his responsibility and it was his duty to protect her."

Robert looks to Toby. "What should he have done? You're asking," says Robert more audibly. "He should have pushed Margaret out of his home. He should have thrown her out on the street and not allow her to come back. He made a fool of himself by allowing her in time after time. The marriage was a mockery. The union disgraced. We were a laughing stock to all who were heartless enough to laugh, and there were plenty who did. Believe me, there were plenty of bastards who were amused by my… by our situation.

"My mother too, was getting on in years and there were not as many handsome suitors around to vie for her affections. Soon she took to slobs. Putrid, drunken slobs and the laughter got louder. The more time that went on the more disgusting life had been."

Robert settles down. There is the look of defeat on his old, tired face. "I said nothing. Through all of that," he says, "I said nothing. I was just a boy, but I knew better. Perhaps, I was no better than Bernard. Margaret could not suppress her bestial sexual desires and Bernard and I could not be forceful, or maybe courageous, enough to confront her with it. I hid more and more behind my books, but I no longer hid it from her. She would grimace when she saw me take to my books, but she knew that it was no longer her place to judge me. I did not confront my mother with words, but my face hid nothing from her. I only had courage enough to fulminate against her and her ways with a slight scowl. I looked at her sharply with unblinking eyes and contracting my eyebrows. When I was at my most boisterous, I would venture so far out as to adding a slight shaking of my head to show my disapproval." Robert lowers his eyes. "It still embarrasses me that I had failed to speak my mind. Perhaps by holding my tongue I was failing her as well as the rest of us.

"Again, my sin of what I had failed to do haunts me and will continue to haunt me until I die. I used to think that I would be able to bury those regrets along with my mother in her grave, but they remain with me. The worst of it comes when I have nothing to fill my time. Moments from the past come to me in great waves and they carry me out to a bottomless sea. It's overwhelming, Toby. It overwhelms me and I find it difficult to breathe." Robert inhales sharply, fighting the urge to lose his breath.

"Not far from here there is a boarding house. I've walked past it many times in recent weeks. I see these men there. Always the same men are sitting there and never any women. Perhaps this particular home only houses men, because I have yet to see a woman on the premises. I'm not sure about their mental health, but I do question it. It frightens me to see them. It's an old house," he says. "More than a hundred years old, perhaps as old as one fifty. You know, the type with the big old wrap around porch and deep wooden, gray painted, steps.

"Day after day I see them, always the same men sitting in the same place on the porch or in the garden and always sitting alone. One man sits in a chair by the screened door, another sits on a long wooden bench, and another sits on the front step second from the bottom. There is another man who sits on a bench in the garden and the last man that I see sits on a step on the other side of the house. These men are not old men. At least in my perspective and I assume yours as well, Toby. I suspect that at least four of these men are younger than I. Perhaps they are more than fifteen years my junior. Always they dress the same from one day to the next and all of them smoke. Cigarettes," he says. "Always cigarettes. I see them sitting there day after day. It makes no difference what time of day that I pass. Always they are there sitting in the same place drawing on cigarettes.

"I try not to stare at them, but I do. It terrifies me to see them in that state. It terrifies me because I fear that it could me. I don't want to be one of those men, Toby. They sit there all day long. Some of them talk to themselves quietly. I see them moving their lips. I don't know if they're mumbling incoherently or if they are speaking to ghosts from their pasts. I only know that… or I believe that having that much time with only your thoughts can be damaging to your mind.

"I want to shake my fist in their faces and tell them get on with their lives. Make themselves useful again." Robert's eyes shift back and forth as his mind begins to race. His heart pounds in his chest. He very suddenly senses a feeling of claustrophobia. It's a feeling that has been plaguing him for some time. He looks around himself, the endless sky of blue and white. He inhales deeply and embraces a mental freedom.

"How they sit there day after day in their self imposed isolation with an apparent lack of motivation, I cannot understand. A life without purpose…" He closes his eyes and ceases to speak. He shakes the images of the men and their boarding house from his head. Gone were the faces of the lonely men with cigarettes and moving lips that make no sounds. In its place are the faces of his daughter when she was a child and then as an adult, and of his wife, when they had first met, and of Elizabeth as a child and as she is now.

"I need so desperately to fill my time, Toby. I cannot survive with only my thoughts in my head. I dwell too much on the past. I no longer wish to live in periods of time that have slipped away from me. I've not always done that. I've made good use of my time. I taught young men and women and I've done it well. I truly believe that I've made a difference to a good many of them. I get letters from some of them, Toby." Robert gently smiles. It is a smile made entirely of pride and there is no shame in it. "I'll have to bring some of them around to you some time."

Robert leans back on the bench and stretches his arms along the back of it while kicking his legs out in front of him. His smile never dims as he once again thinks back to another period in his life. "I still get letters from one young lady… Actually she is not so young any more. She has two children in their middle teens. She's a single mother, widowed, not divorced or abandoned. She asks advice of me on occasion. I write back to her with the minimum amount of counsel. Mainly I try to assure her that she has the answers that she is seeking out and that she is simply trying to confirm what she already knows.

"She first wrote to me a little more than a year after graduating. I received a few letters and wrote a few notes back and then there was an absence of correspondence from her for some years. When I next heard from her it was after the death of her husband. Her children were still very small and for some reason she thought about me. It was, perhaps, the crowning moment of my career as an educator. Until that moment upon receiving that letter, I believed that there came a point in time when the years would erase me from the minds of my students

"I know that very few of them still think of me, but it gives me great satisfaction to know that there are some who, even after so many years, think about me in such a positive manner. I have gotten so many wonderful letters from people who have become solid and successful citizens. I suppose it would be more to the credit of their parents, but I like to think that I had a hand, even if only the slightest bit, in putting them in the right direction."

For a moment he is in another place where his pride has taken hold of him. His eyes are suddenly a lighter shade of blue and his mood is reflected in the lambency of his face. "My life," he says with determination, "has had meaning."

The sound of a laughing child catches Robert's attention. It is a little girl this time. She has in tow an elderly man who walks with reluctance unbeknownst to the child. "Hurry, grandpa," she says as she drags the man to the waters edge. "Hurry or he'll be gone."

The man says nothing, but picks up his pace as best as his frail body will allow. Robert can see that he is grimacing through the pain. Even through the man's trousers, Robert can see that his legs have been ravaged by arthritis. He looks at the man's hands. The twisted, bony fingers grip the little girl's hands gently. They stop a few feet before the water and the girl drops to the ground and studies that of a turtle a few feet in front of her. The man stoops to get a better look and smiles and rests his hand on top of the child's head.

"Elizabeth needed me then. She was the first person to ever depend upon me and it was important for both of us that I do right by her. I knew that if she were to grow up right she would need more than the dissolute parents that had brought her into the world. Yes, parents; the plural. Bernard was immoral in his lack of interest or his failure to accept his failed marriage or whatever you may wish to conclude by the facts. I never dwelled on Bernard's misgivings. I stopped caring long before I ever started. Elizabeth was all that mattered.

"We were brother and sister and due to the differences in our years, I was also her father. As the years went on, I deemed my mothers presence as intrusive. Her behavior was deplorable and I was quite clear about that fact with Elizabeth. I pulled no punches in that respect. Elizabeth was a bright child and she soon made up her own mind about our mother. She felt as I did, but she never discussed it. Not with me and... and I fear with no one else as well. She would not have me talk about our mother with any malice then and she will not to this very day.

"I'm very much the same in that way as I've explained before, but I am not so sure if our motives are the same. Even at my age now, I still am not quite certain of my own reasoning for silence on the matter. Do I wish to protect the integrity of my mother's character on the minds of others or do I fear the way in which her character reflects upon me? I don't like to think myself so shallow, but I need to be honest with myself. If I deceive myself, than I am nothing. I become a man mumbling to himself on a porch somewhere.

"I feel at a loss, Toby. I wish to revere my mother, but I cannot. There is love. I truly loved her, but it is a love without respect. I did not regard her with the deep and profound respect that I would have found comfort in. As for my father, there is no knowledge of him and so his character hangs in the balance. I can only look through my own eyes and cannot, knowingly, carry the spirit of him with me. I am not like her and I am left to wonder if I am anything like him. In essence, I do not know where I come from. I suppose that I feel much like that of an orphan."

The old man is holding the turtle in his crippled hands and he smiles at the little girl as she giggles and squeals. They walk together and settle at the first available bench where he lowers himself gingerly and not without tremors. The little girl kneels on the lawn and inspects the reptile more closely, but will not touch it. The old man is pointing out the marks and patterns on the shell. He holds it up and rubs its underbelly and encourages the little girl to do the same. She will not. She giggles and squeals some more and the old man laughs the delicate laugh of the very old.

"I was, perhaps, just a little bit better than that of a fair student. I worked to put myself through university and when I finished... I left. Elizabeth was only twelve, but she would, I knew, be all right. She was a bright child and severely responsible. I suppose it was unfair for her to miss out on a childhood, but circumstances would not allow her to be anything but a surrogate parent for her own parents.

"She was good to mother and Bernard. From a very early age she had taken on a great deal of responsibilities. In the beginning I played the surrogate and as I got older and worked longer hours, Elizabeth began to assume more and more of the duties that I had carried out previously. She did so, I dare say, in a more superior capacity than I. The transition was so smooth and seamless that I had not truly realized that it had happened until after I had graduated. It was then that I felt that it would be all right to leave. Perhaps, in retrospect, I was wrong.

"Nevertheless, I left mother and Bernard in Elizabeth's care and came to America to seek out the adventures that I had read so fervently of throughout my boyhood. Mother, at that time, was drinking heavily and Bernard, although living with us, was somewhat of a recluse. He barely spoke at meal times and without fail withdrew to his room immediately thereafter. To his credit, he continued to work and provide. Why he chose to live the way he did, I wonder.

"Elizabeth saw me off at the dock, I traveled by sea, and it would be the last time that I would see her as a child. A child was what she was and by leaving, I fear that I had failed her." Robert looks out once again to the vacant skies. "…And what I have failed to do," he says dreamily.

Chapter Two

"Elizabeth?" He called down the stairs. "My blue shirt, have you seen it?"

"You must have ten or so blue shirts, Robert. Can you be more specific?" she replied dryly.

He hesitated for a moment and then scratched at an itch at the back of his head that was not there. His gentle blue eyes looked up, for an answer perhaps, and then he said, "never mind."

"Happy Birthday, Robert," she called from below.

"Yes," he said simply. "Thank you."

He could hear Elizabeth's footsteps as she retreated from the bottom of the staircase as she walked back towards the kitchen. He had forgotten that it was his birthday. He was sixty today and just last week he had turned forty. The years were passing much too quickly as far as he were concerned and he had no penchant for celebrating yet another anniversary of his origin.

He returned to his closet and took down his tweed sport jacket complete with suede patches at the elbows; a brown pair of slacks that had been pressed with great care by his sister Elizabeth and a crisp white shirt with buttons at the cuffs and not suited for links. He carefully took these articles of clothing and draped them across his bed, which he had already made up, and proceeded with his daily ritual including a shower of five minutes with soap, (white soap devoid of any perfume), and water that was as hot as he could stand it followed by two minutes of water that was as cold as the climate permitted and finally a shave: A very close shave.

He looked closely at the face in the mirror. Younger than the one he had seen just ten minutes prior. The miracle of the water, he thought. It washes away more than soil. Temporarily softens the years and to the belief of many – cleanses the soul – also temporary. Still, there were lines in the face that were not there - not so long ago. Little web-like lines working their way into the eyes, in particular, like roads and highways pouring into a congested city on a road map.

His fingertips slowly inspected the top of his head. Still fairly thick, he thought. A slight frown overtook him as he crossed over the crown, but only slight. Not as thick as it had once been, but still dense. Dense and thick, he thought, and then he smiled. His wife had used those words to describe him many times. He took a closer look and examined the color of his hair. It had long since vanished. The black was now white. Faded like grass in the fall. The spring had long past from his own life and he had just realized that the summer too, was gone.

Sixty, he reflected silently. Not so terribly old, he told himself as he did each year at this time. Only every year he thought it with less conviction. He told himself that there were still many useful years ahead. Years to shape young minds and to give direction to lost souls. This was June, though, and with the end of June came the dreaded hiatus of the summer break for Robert. And so June, with the happy birthday and the beginning of summer vacation, made the season of spring less of a renewal and more of a termination. Not that Robert was a 'the glass is half empty' pessimist, but he did regret the end of the school year and dread the incremental notches of his age.

For the past thirty-four years he'd been a schoolteacher. The majority of which he had been teaching English literature and had been doing an admirable job in so doing as he'd been told. Quietly and with some modesty, he had always agreed. His students were of a high priority to him and at times so much so that his wife had blatantly suggested that they, his students, had been a detriment to their marriage. Robert, on the other hand, had looked at it in an entirely different perspective and had always felt that his relationship with his students had been quite a nourishment for his marriage as it had kept him in touch with the outside world and therefore made him an entirely more interesting person not only to himself but to his wife as well.

Robert, at sixty, resides in his three-floor brownstone house in the Park Slope area of Brooklyn with his sister Elizabeth. Robert occupies the top floor. There are three bedrooms, all fairly large, on this top floor and a comfortably sized bathroom with its original cast iron tub at the end of the hall. Robert had replaced the sink, toilet and tile flooring in recent years. In earlier days the rooms in the house were rented out weekly to migrant workers from Ireland and England. The previous owner had explained to Robert that all three bedrooms on the second floor and all three on the third floor had been rented out during the years of the "great depression" and that the basement too had housed up to six men at a time. The man, his wife and their four children subsequently used the rooms on the first floor to live, sleep and entertain.

When Robert and his wife, Kathleen, had bought the house they had kept on the three remaining tenants who had been occupying the third floor. All three men were decent, hard working people. They paid their rent in advance, never entertained and were generally very quiet. There was the occasional stumbling on the staircase in the middle of the night after some heavy drinking, but it was always followed with sincere apologies on the following morning. Robert and Kathleen were financially strapped in those days and the intrusion of tenants living under their roof was accepted. The rent was always paid in cash and it had been a great help in assisting them to pay the mortgage in those early years.

On the third floor Robert uses one room for a study, another for a small living room and the last as his bedroom. Elizabeth occupies the second floor similarly. The ground floor had a fairly large formal living room, a small dining room and a moderate kitchen. The décor of the ground floor had remained in tact from the time of Kathleen's death right down to the last picture frame. Elizabeth went to great lengths in keeping things the way they were. This had never been discussed with Robert, though. As far as he was concerned, Elizabeth could do as she pleased with the first two floors and he would gladly help her in making any changes. The top floor was his only concern and he made that floor to his fondness.

After dressing, he went into his study as he did each morning and opened the blinds of the oversized windows that went from two feet from the floor to about one foot from the ceiling. The study was a gentle room. It had been furnished to soothe. It was the largest of his three rooms by far. A little more than a year after Kathleen had died he had had all of the old furniture that had been used by the boarders in the early days of his marriage taken away. He tore up the carpeting in all of his three rooms and had stripped away the layer upon layer of various colors of paint from the woodwork to reveal its natural wood. He stained the woodwork, rubbed it down with steel wool and stained it again. The floors, too, had been sanded down and refinished by professional men. Area rugs had replaced the old carpeting in the rooms and a carpet runner had been tacked down in the hall.

One wall in his study was filled with some of his oldest and dearest friends including John Steinbeck, Ernest Hemmingway, William Shakespeare, William Trevor, Graham Greene and James Joyce to name just a few of them. There was a desk in the style of Chippendale. On it, at the right, was a teak wood pencil box that had been given to him by his granddaughter, Shannon. An old black rotary telephone rested on the left and in the center was a writing tablet.

The rest of the room had been dressed in cream white and chocolate brown. A cream white textured fabric sofa with chocolate brown trim and legs: A chocolate brown wicker coffee table that stored a duvet and pillows for the guests who would never be invited. Chocolate brown tape on the cream white venetian blinds covered the windows that overlooked Prospect Park in the east and his flower garden below.

There was an antique chair and ottoman with classic curves also in cream white with chocolate brown trim. The chair was positioned to face the windows and from there he was able to see the children at play in the park. He could see the dog walkers and the joggers; and he could see those who chose to eat their lunches under the shade of the trees or out in the sunshine. On those days in which he was able rise early enough he was able to watch the sun rising over the park.

At night, after dark, he would close the blinds and sit in his chair and read while Vivaldi or Bach played on his aging turntable. He would read his students papers. He would wince in September and would smile in June. He would be filled with great pride in their accomplishments and with his own. He would read his books and his newspapers and he would try not to be down in the summer months. September was his spring. In it held his rebirth.

In the summer he has his garden to fill his mornings. It is a small garden with lots of cutting flowers such as marigold, peony, lily, geranium, baby's breath and tulip. There is a small flagstone patio off of the back door with a little stone table with iron legs and matching chairs where Elizabeth entertains friends with tea and finger sandwiches in the early afternoons. The flowers go from the edge of the flagstone back to a low brick building. On the wall are climbing vines of white clematis and pink foxgloves. And then there are the roses.

In containers around the patio, Robert plants roses. Each spring he plants a different variety of roses. This year he has filled his containers with cider cup, golden sunblaze, red ace and Easter morning. Every morning, during the summer, he inspects his garden for weeds and pests and then cuts some flowers for Elizabeth to put about the house. He loosens the soil and fertilizes and waters them gently and steadily and this requires at least two hours of his time.

"Oh Robert," Elizabeth says as he enters the kitchen. "You're not seriously planning to wear your tweed sport jacket to the school?" She shook her head and rolled her eyes to express her distaste.

"No of course I'm not going to wear it to the school. I just thought it needed some exercise."

"For heavens sake, Robert, it's June. Dark brown trousers and tweed", she said. "Have you no sense for fashion at all?"

"It is fifty-three degrees outside, Elizabeth. When it was April and sixty-five degrees this very same semblance was perfectly acceptable."

"Sit down," she said with a wave of her hand as to dismiss their conversation. She walked to the stove and took a pot of coffee from it. "The world is collapsing around us, Robert," she said quite solemnly as she poured his coffee. Her face was tightly drawn and the intensity in her eyes explained that her remark was not to be taken lightly.

"Yes, quite so," he said as he opened his newspaper. "Kindly pass the toast, Elizabeth."

"Mrs. Wagner was robbed the other night, Robert," she continued. "She could have been killed in her sleep." Elizabeth waited, but Robert said nothing. "I do not understand how an educated man such as yourself can simply sit and read your paper as if I had said nothing at all, Robert. Mrs. Wagner lives three doors away from here. We are not talking about things going on half way around the world."

Robert added cream to his coffee and stirred it until the color was even. Elizabeth waited, tight lipped. She was determined not to speak. She would wait until her silence got his attention.

"Robert, for charity's sake put down that blasted paper and listen to me," she said. She took a moment to collect herself and exhaled softly. "I think we need to take precautions."

The hand that held Robert's paper faulted as did his eyes and then he looked up to his sister. "I thought we already had, Elizabeth. The locks on the doors and windows have all been replaced with the latest and greatest. You've had the place wired from top to bottom so that I can barely get into my own home. Mice can't by without central stations approval. Please, Elizabeth, let's just let this go."

"Mrs. Wagner has a similar house alarm and she lost many valuables without so much as a peep from her fancy system. The problem with you Robert is that you are just a little too passive sometimes. It is just plain foolish to sit by and believe that all will be well. Precautions need to be taken, Robert. Steps can be taken to prevent such things from happening." Her composure had taken hold and she seemed pleased with herself. Ownership of her emotions were as much a challenge as a necessity.

Robert looked more closely at his sister. Her gray hair was pulled back tightly making her face look all the more harsh. What had happened to her? He thought. Why was it that she never, not literally nor figuratively, let her hair down? "Mrs. Wagner has a son, Elizabeth. I understand from you and your extremely reliable sources of the ladies auxiliary that he's a son who uses cocaine on a regular basis with no means of financial support." Robert put the paper down and reached for the toast and butter. He wanted to end the discussion, but it would continue.

"You think Kenneth stole from his own mother?" Her eyes narrowed as she gently took her chair. Her hands settled demurely into her lap not daring to reach for anything.

"Please don't feed my remark to the gossips, Elizabeth." He spoke to her as though he were exhausting himself on some feudal argument that he hadn't a prayer of winning. He could see beyond her eyes into a mind that was working feverishly. "I only say it to pacify your concerns and because, quite frankly, it is a logical explanation. There are a lot worse places in the world than Brooklyn. This is a reasonably safe neighborhood. I agreed to this ridiculous burglar alarm system for no other reason than to put your mind at rest. Let's not talk any more of this."

He resumed reading his newspaper, but his eyes only passed over the words without comprehension. Perhaps the world was collapsing around him, but not in the manner that Elizabeth's ideals had subscribed. It was Robert's personal world that was at risk. He didn't like the feeling of being out of control, but emotional anxieties had been steadily maintaining a grip on him and the feeling was not easily shaken from him as it had been in the past.

"Perhaps you are right about Kenneth, Robert," she relented. She sipped her tea and her thoughts reflected. "What can we do about this?"

"There really is nothing that we can do about this. If you interfere you will lose your friendship with Mrs. Wagner; the fact that she lives three doors down will make life for you very uncomfortable. Trust me and say nothing more about this."

"I see your point, Robert, but what kind of a friend am I to be to say absolutely nothing about her troubles when I know the source?" Elizabeth spoke her words in the tongue of the self-righteous.

"You do not know the source," he said sternly. "You merely have suspicions that I myself have transferred on to you." His heart rate accelerated. "This is none of your affair. Do not step between a bear and her cub."

"But...."

"No. People see what they choose to see. Heed my words. People see what they choose to see." Robert delivered his words with conviction. "The world is not so obvious and you cannot presume it to be so."

"But Mrs. Wagner..."

"Mrs. Wagner does not wish to see the truth. She accepts what she accepts and perhaps she is incapable of opening herself up to any further truths where Kenneth is concerned."

"So I should say nothing?" She crossed her arms high up over her bosom. "I should simply listen to her go on and on about the intruder who could have killed her in her sleep?" she said as the though the very idea was preposterous.

Robert stared down at the white linen cloth on the table and spoke softly. "Allow Mrs. Wagner her delusions, Elizabeth. It may be the kindest gesture of friendship that one can offer."

Elizabeth nodded and without ceremony uncrossed her arms. "More tea, Robert?"

"Yes, please."

Breakfast concluded in brisk fashion and they each went on about their respective days. Robert gathered up his papers and folders and carefully placed them into his worn and scarred brown leather briefcase, a gift from students of another generation, and set out to work. Once outside, he inhaled deeply and felt the knots in his stomach loosen and untie. The air was cool and soothed him and as the sun shined down through the emerald green trees, he felt a sense of freedom that only came about on mornings such as these.

He stopped a moment and waited for the sound of a chirping bird to be heard. A few seconds passed and then he heard it. Somewhere in the distance was a bird that gave him the gift of a completed moment of perfection. He looked up and down his block and appreciated what was there. Small wrought iron fences around small gardens of grass and shrubs and flowers. Clean swept sidewalks and curbs and unmarred automobiles parked in front of every home. There were trees on his block: many trees that stood for many years.

While other neighborhoods had decayed, his had improved vastly. People with money came into his neighborhood and whilst he did not think himself to be a snob, he was pleased to have his surroundings restored to its original beauty. His home, too, had increased in its value and though he would never consider leaving it, there would be something of tangible value to leave to his daughter, Emily. Not that Emily would need it, but still, it was there for her nevertheless.

Three blocks from his home, he stepped onto a city bus and fifteen minutes later he transferred to another and ten minutes after that he got off and walked the seven remaining blocks to the school. He was greeted with genuine warmth and affection by many of the students as he climbed the steps and entered the building. He was a man revered in this building and felt embraced in its corridors.

A sixteen-year-old girl with plastic braces on her teeth made her way through a crowd of students towards him. She had dark hair and dark eyes and just a hint of makeup. To Robert she looked, as a sixteen-year-old girl should. She looked sixteen and not twenty. He thought back to Emily and the horrible years when she was a teen struggling to be older. "Good morning Mr. M," she said with a smile that was nearly a grin. It was Robert's observation over many years of teaching that nearly all-teenaged girls seemed to find it difficult to speak socially with any and all male instructors without the ear-to-ear grin.

"Good morning Miss Legori. You look particularly happy this morning. And to what do we owe this burst of sunshine from your face?"

She reached into a knapsack and pulled out the High School yearbook. "I would like a kind word and a signature from you, Mr. M."

"Of course," he said. "I'm always happy to oblige my fans with an autograph." He stooped down and looked into her eyes and spoke in a conspiratorial manner. "Should I be truthful or kind?"

She laughed out of a closed mouth and blushed furiously. "You better write something kind," she said. "Some day I'll be showing my kids this picture of the greatest teacher that I ever had."

"Ah, now it's my turn to go red in the face," he said, and in fact, he did. "You're being too kind to me." He took out his pen and wrote without having to give much thought. He was proud of her and pleased with himself and before he could say another word the first bell of the morning rang and she was simultaneously thanking him and running down the hall with her yearbook in hand.

He stood there smiling in the direction in which she ran until his attention was diverted towards the man patting him on the arm. Suddenly the hall was empty and it was only he and the schools principal, John McEntyre.

"Robert?" McEntyre put his hand on Robert's shoulder. "Are you feeling all right?"

Robert widened his eyes, as does a man fighting sleep. "Yes, I'm fine John." He looked down the hall and saw that it was deserted. "I was caught up in a moment of reflection." He felt shame and he wanted to move on quickly, but not with obvious retreat. "I must get to my class," he said a little breathily.

"Okay, Robert. I'll see you at lunch?"

"Of course," he said and moved away as quickly as his young student had before him.

He paused a moment before entering the classroom. Once inside, he felt himself again. He closed the door and the outside world with it. The students began to settle down, as did the incremental silence. "Good morning, class. Please put your books and your various toys and whatnots beneath your chairs while I pass out today's exam."

The class erupted in various objections and moans and pleas for mercy. "What test?" they cried in a baritone of angst. "You never said nothin' 'bout no test," from a boy in the back seat of the third row.

"Mr. Cabot?" Robert addressed the man at the back of the third row.

"Yeah?"

"Let us, for a moment break down your previous sentence."

Cabot hung his head down low. He was very much aware of how the next few minutes would go.

"I believe that your words, and correct me if I've mistaken, were 'You never said nothin' 'bout no test.'" Robert's imitation of Cabot brought on a raucous laughter from the class. He was pleased with himself and failed to conceal it.

Cabot stood up at his desk. He stood tall and straightened his imaginary tie and began to speak. "I apologize for my poor use of the English language, Mr. Montgomery," he said in a mock British accent. "I assure you that it shan't happen again."

There was great laughter from the class and Cabot took a bow. "Bravo, Mr. Cabot. You can speak the English language. Naturally, I'm offended by your accent and therefore I will add an additional question to today's examination."

The class was visibly taken aback. There was no smile on Robert's face and he was actually handing out examination booklets. They were suddenly very quiet. When all members of the class had a booklet in their possession, Robert instructed them to write down the first and second questions. "Question number one: What do you plan to do with the rest of your life and why? Question number two: What grade should Mr. Cabot receive and why?" Then Robert smiled brightly and the tension in the class subsided.

"This aint no real test," said Carlos Rodriguez.

"Et tu Mr. Rodriguez," said Robert. Once again the class erupted with laughter. "No, no this aint or, is not, as I prefer, a real test. At least it will not be counted against your final grade. This is for some well needed and, may I add mandatory, extra credit and more importantly for my own personal education."

"We all gonna be English teachers like you Mr. M." Carlos Rodriguez smiled brightly.

"God save the queen, Mr. Rodriguez and us from your, merciless brutality of the English language." Robert undid the buttons on his jacket and sat on the edge of his desk as he so often did. He smiled out at his class as he panned the room. "On second thought," he said, "why don't you put those booklets away and tell me, verbally, what you wish to do with your lives?"

"You mean we don't have to write these papers?" asked Letitia Webster.

Robert smiled at the eager faces of students who believed that they had been released from an assignment. "Oh, no Miss Webster the paper still needs to be written, but that can be done in the comfort of your homes."

Robert laughed at the collective sighs, grunts and groans. "Furthermore these papers will be graded. This will be your final examination." Silence immediately filled the room. "Have I gone deaf?" Robert asked.

"We can take our final exams home, Mr. M?" asked Candice Kowalski.

"Yes, Miss Kowalski. I think it would be more beneficial for all of you to take them home. Write the best papers of your lives. Do not write what you think that I want to hear, but write, truthfully, what you wish to be." He stood up and looked around at his students and then walked to the window and looked out. Tears began to trickle at the ducts and Robert inhaled deeply through his nostrils.

"Take your time," he said, still looking through the window. "Take your time. Give it your full attention. Be serious about what you wish to do with the rest of your lives." He turned to face his class. "I don't know what advice you get. I don't know what you believe. At the risk of depressing each of you in the most violent manner, I wish to tell you that life tends to pass you by very quickly once you pass through the doors of this institution. You leave here being all of eighteen years and you wake up one morning with the realization that you're three times that plus six. You wonder then if it is too late for you and no matter how much you deny it, you believe that it is."

Eyes of sympathy fell upon Robert and he could not stand it. "Mr. Cabot," Robert nearly shouted, "what will you do with the rest of your life?"

"Uhhh..."

"Very eloquently put, Mr. Cabot. I hope that you can do better." Robert stared into the soul of the young man. John Cabot had fair hair and green eyes. He was tall and lean and very popular with girls and admired by the boys.

"Come now, Mr. Cabot. Surely you have given some thought on the subject. In less than three weeks you'll be cast out there into a cruel and unforgiving world. What is your plan?"

"I'm going to college," Cabot finally said.

"Good for you," said Robert as he beamed over the boy. "Why is it that this is the first that I'm hearing of this?"

"You didn't get the memo?" said Cabot with his mock British accent.

Robert laughed. He was giddy and felt almost drunk. "No, unfortunately I must have missed it." He was speaking quickly now. His speech pattern always quickened when he was excited. "Tell me, son, what will you study?"

"I don't know," Cabot said. He appeared to have had the wind knocked out of him.

"Why not?" he asked.

"What do you mean?" Cabot was confused.

"You must have some notion of what you wish to study." Robert pulled an empty chair from a desk near Cabot's. He stepped onto the seat and sat on the back of the chair. They were talking one on one now.

"I spoke with a counselor and he told me that I wouldn't have to declare a major until my junior year." John Cabot sat back in his chair hoping that he had given his teacher an answer that would set him free.

Robert waited. Cabot shifted his eyes and then shifted in his seat.

"What else did he say?" He asked. His face showed deep concern. Is the patient going to make it doctor? What can be done for him?

"He said welcome."

Robert looked as though he'd been slapped in the face. "He said 'welcome'?" he repeated sharply. He closed his eyes and scratched at the back of his head. "Did he tell you to wander around for a couple of years and find yourself?"

"That's what you're supposed to do," Cabot replied. He looked to his other classmates. His eyes pleading for back up. The other students averted their eyes. They were unwilling to come to the aid of their friend.

Robert stood up and returned the chair to its desk. He walked to the front of the room. "Is that what they tell you?" he asked. He looked to all of the students and asked the question again. Letitia Webster sat up and spoke. "Yes," she said. "They ask if you know what you want to do and if you don't they tell you not to worry. We have time," she said.

Robert frowned. "I'm afraid they are not telling you what you need to hear." He was speaking to the class now. "I'm afraid you are all not hearing what you need to hear. You have time, but you have very little of it. You cannot muck about for two years before coming up with a game plan. Mr. Rodriguez?" he called.

"Yes?" Carlos Rodriguez sat up a little apprehensively.

"You play football, Mr. Rodriguez?"

"Yeah, I mean yes. Yes I do," he said sharply.

"Do you wait until after half time to come up with a game plan?"

Carlos laughed and looked around the room for supporters. When he didn't find any he answered the question. "No. Uh… No, Mr. M. We plan for the game the day after we play the previous game."

"A week between games, Mr. Rodriguez?"

"Yeah."

"Why not start preparing for the game at about midweek?"

"Because we wanna win the game."

Robert looked around the room. "Did you all hear what Mr. Rodriguez said?" He looked back to Carlos. "Do you think that you want to win the game or do you know it?"

"I'm pretty sure we wanna win it."

"Pretty sure or absolutely sure?"

"Absolutely sure," Carlos barked out like a soldier. "Absolutely, sir." There was soft laughter around the room, but it was pensive at best.

"You boys and girls are young men and women now. This is the big game. The one you'll want to win. They can tell you that you have time, but you don't." He glanced all around the room catching eyes along the way. "They may mean well, but trust me when I say that what they tell you is bullshit. Pure and absolute, bullshit"

For once Robert had actually stunned his class. They had never heard the man use a profane word and in fact, Robert had never used one in a classroom or even in a barroom for that matter.

"You have time to think, but not time to waste. You must use your time not only looking at things, but also seeing them. Have your fun", he said and then averted his eyes from theirs. "But plan your future."

There was silence in his class. Mouths hung open and some faces had lost their color. Robert had the attention of his students. "Think of yourselves as architects," he said. "You wish to create a thing of beauty. You'll want it to last as it will be your legacy." Robert took off his jacket and loosened his tie. "It will need to be structurally sound."

He opened the cuffs of his shirt and rolled them up over his forearms. "The foundation will support your legacy. The ground will need a geological survey. You will not wish to construct something too heavy upon a land that will not let it stand. You'll want to look at it for the rest of your lives and be pleased by its beauty and secure with the knowledge that the people who inhabit it are safe and secure and free to build on their own because of the foundation that you have laid and because of the fine work that you have done."

There were some blank faces staring at him and there were others that were clearly enlightened. "Miss Webster, what are you going to do?"

"I want to be a doctor, but I'll probably be a nurse."

Robert smiled. He had already known her answer as he had written a letter of recommendation for her. Letitia Webster had the mind to go as far as she would wish to go. "Both are very noble professions," he said. "You will succeed in either of those professions that you have chosen. I know this because you have not only the mind, but the strength, courage and determination to do so." His words were said in kindness, but he knew and believed them to be true.

Letitia smiled. Robert Montgomery was more than a teacher to her. He was a mentor and a friend who was always willing to listen. "Thank you Mr. M."

"Thank you, Miss Webster."

He walked to the window and peered out for a while. He focused on the traffic and then on the pedestrians. He followed a squirrel across the parking lot and up into a tree. "I am sorry", he said to his class without turning away from the window. The early sun colored his face gold and left his eyes a lighter shade of blue.

His students sat quietly. Some had wanted to say something to comfort him, but could not find the words. Others wanted to chime something humorous to lighten the moment, but did not. It wasn't much more than two minutes of silence from Mr. Montgomery, but the time passed painfully slow and seemed endless and the entire class felt an uneasiness that was unprecedented in his company.

A moment such as this with most any other teacher would have passed virtually unnoticed. It simply would never have registered amongst the majority of the students, but Robert Montgomery was not just any other teacher. He was a man apart. He had so very little in common with his students in the ways of popular culture. He did not relate or rather share in their tastes of music, movies or television programs and they, in turn, did not share his, but where fashion, art, music, speech and manners in general can keep most people at a great distance from one another, it did not, in fact, affect the relationship between he and his students.

These young men and women had great respect for this man; a respect that they did not necessarily show for other teachers and certainly did not feel. The basis for this respect was built on the respect that he had for them. His respect was genuine and not manufactured. He was open to their music, but did not pretend to understand or enjoy it. He questioned it without contempt or mockery. He questioned it with sincere interest and some authority. He wanted to know what they, his students, thought about the lyrics and what those words made them feel and by doing so it allowed them to think more deeply about their own music and for them to question it themselves.

In talking about his own choices of music, he too revealed how it made him feel and why. And with some of his choices he honestly couldn't explain why he liked it, but only that it made him feel younger. He explained that he did not have to like the music to appreciate its value and the power that it held over those who did; and at the same time, in the eyes of the younger generation, he never made a fool of himself by pretending to like it and fit in with them. He was who he was and they could trust that because they knew that the respect was mutual, and while some took that message as enough others were able to take it a step further. Some were able to open their eyes to a more valuable lesson in that they too should be able to be accepted as who they are so long as they were willing to respect others for their differences.

Robert Montgomery took great pains to open their eyes to literature whether it was written in modern times or several centuries earlier. While we may be separated from the past by speech, music, fashion, politics and above all – technology, the fact is, the thinking remains virtually unchanged; the emotional thinking, that is, and the way we deal with and rationalize our feelings. The lessons we learn are often too soon forgotten, if not lost on us altogether. It may be a cliché that history repeats itself, but if history teaches us anything at all it is just that.

In introducing his pupils to Dostoevsky's *Crime and Punishment*, Robert had to get them past their initial viewing of it as an overwhelmingly thick volume in small print with no illustrations. A book, written in a foreign land, more than a hundred an forty years prior, which may just as well have been written on the walls of a cave while dinosaurs roamed the earth.

On the surface these young men and women could not conceive of any possible connection between themselves and a character in a story set so long ago and so very far away, but the light came on to them so abruptly and pleasantly unexpected. Raskolnikov quickly became a contemporary of theirs. Raskolnikov, a young student, impoverished and feeling somewhat held down unfairly in the class system where he believed himself to be superior to those who had the wealth decides to show his superiority over the authorities.

This was a story that could very easily translate to modern times; a story that, for many, became personal and to some, emotional. *Crime and Punishment* sparked great discussion in the classroom. While many found the reading material to be difficult at times and even somewhat tedious, all of them had much to say about its content. And though there were no, and hopefully no, potential murderers amongst the classmates, there were some who admitted to having such feelings and others who knew a person or more who had carried out such atrocities.

Raskolnikov, coming unglued by the weight of his own actions, was intriguing to them. The fact that his punishment came from within and that the possibility of his redemption could come only from the aid of others gave pause for thought. The absence of technology mattered very little to them. Other than mentions of the use of gas lamps, Dostoevsky had had no reason to paint his mechanical world, as it was not a period piece to him. For Dostoevsky it was modern literature and in its day it was cutting edge stuff.

It was not lost on Robert that film adaptations had had to work very hard on the details of works written in various periods, but what had always mattered to him was how the story had related to the here and now. The grim settings of a world with no color or flavor, while not a distraction to an enthusiast, would most certainly deter most of those with energy, tastes and hunger for a world filled with vigor and passion. Raskolnikov had passion, but to look into his world with passing interest and to keep that window open long enough to hold that interest in an era, which moves at a furious pace, was asking for more than most are willing to give.

In literature you see only what the writer chooses to reveal. A director of a film, while having complete control over all that he shows, must show the landscape. He must show what is there, but also what is not. The viewer, if not seasoned, can easily get hung up on the bleak landscape as a reader can on its language. *Crime and Punishment* has stood up well to time and Robert Montgomery has always been able to take advantage of that.

Robert turned back from the window and looked through the tears that he had hoped to suppress. "I am sorry", he said again. "You do not need to hear my ranting and raving. I must sound like an old fool." He gave them a strained closed mouthed smile. "I am so very proud," he said. "I am inspired, actually."

Robert clasped his hands tightly and blinked the tears from his eyes. "You have all surpassed my hopes and expectations for you." He swallowed hard. "This is a very difficult time for me. I don't, and can't, expect you to understand this, but for me it is hard to let you go. I think of you, on some level, as my own children. And now I am a parent sending his children out into the world. I hope that I have not failed in preparing you."

As his tears became more pronounced so too did some of the girls who were willing to cry without shame. The boys, on the other hand, did not give in to sentiment; some, though, did fight it ferociously.

"I'm embarrassing myself," he said. "I teach English literature, which may hold very little value to some of you, but it holds the world for me. I can only hope that I've given you something to take away with you."

The girls rushed up to him first and, with false reluctance, the boys followed. They hugged him and reassured, without the use words that they were taking away a great deal. Robert smiled now and wiped the tears from his eyes. He grinned without embarrassment and after the bell had rung he could vaguely hear John Cabot asking if they still had to write the paper and then some of the girls slapping him in response.

In the teachers lounge Robert sat with the physical education director, Tom Higgins, and the history department head, Maria Scapelli. Both Higgins and Scapelli had been with the school for more than thirty years and had taken every available opportunity to discuss retirement for the past two.

"I'd like to be somewhere by the water," said Maria. Robert had heard these words from Maria at least a thousand times, but listened attentively as though she were only just professing these thoughts openly for the first time. "I love the sound of the ocean," she said dreamily. "I love the feel and smell of the sea. Miami is too pricey, though," she said with a slight frown.

Brooklyn has it own beaches, Robert thought, but did not say. He, of course, said it and said it many times over the years, but no one could compare what he or she has to what they do not have. "Could you pass me that salt, Maria?"

Maria Scapelli is, as far as anyone can tell, in her mid to late fifties at the very least. She had always been tight lipped about her age and far too sensitive to be teased about it even if done in a good-natured manner. Maria is generally very serious, but on occasion has been known to erupt in good humor. She is tall and very thin, but not at all frail. Perhaps it is better to describe her as being lean as opposed to thin. She is thought to be in excellent condition for her age, whatever that may be. She has the body of a dancer and in an earlier part of her life that is what she had been.

Maria has very large, expressive brown eyes. Her hair, once brown, is graying evenly throughout. She wears it short, combed towards her face, an angular face, and slightly curled up at the neck. A style that has not changed in all of the years that Robert has known her. As a girl she had studied classical ballet and had earned a less than modest income performing in regional productions of the *Nutcracker, Swan Lake, Sleeping Beauty,* and so on.

Shortly before her twenty-second birthday, Maria met, fell madly in love with, and married a fellow struggling dancer. Guillaume, or Guy as he was called, moved from his hometown in Toulon, France, which is on the Mediterranean Sea and where his bedroom window faced Mont Faron, to New York to follow his dream. Guy was tall and very handsome. Theirs was she had believed, a whirlwind romance that had died as quickly as it had begun. Guy was a passionate man. Passionate about many things, but Maria soon realized that she did not fit into his passions.

They parted after a little more than a year, but had not divorced. Maria was a devout catholic and her separation had brought shame to her family. Hers was the only broken marriage in her family and it had not been taken lightly. Two years after her separation she reverted back to her family name.

Guy and Maria had remained in contact and when he became ill in the early nineties, they connected in a way they had never been able to before. They were close then and their friendship was, while not romantic, honest. They confided in one another and for the first time in a very long time Maria felt that she was able to trust Guy. There had never been anyone before or since in whom she would permit such guardian over her thoughts. Maria was holding Guy's hand when he finally succumbed to complications that had stemmed from pneumocystis.

Maria, at her father's insistence, had minored in history, a subject that she had always excelled in and in which made her more interesting to him. History, like dance, he had explained, involves culture. Life, he would say, was so much more revealing when you understood its origins.

Maria, eventually, made use of her degree and became a teacher. The thought of being a single, aging, struggling artist did not appeal to her. She had, however, never completely given up on her dance. After abandoning any hope of a serious career as a performer, she had decided to give lessons and had hopes to one day opening a school of dance of her own. Presently, she occupied her free time with yoga, Pilates and as much tightly budgeted travel as she could afford.

"We're getting more serious about the Carolina's," said Higgins referring to him and his wife. "I'm leaning more towards South Carolina, but the wife is focusing more on North Carolina."

"Didn't Linda's sister and brother-in-law move to North Carolina a few years back?" asked Robert.

"Yeah," said Tom. "That's why I want to move to South Carolina." Tom Higgins was rarely serious and that, perhaps over all else, was what Robert liked about him. Robert knew Linda's sister and her sisters husband Paul. Tom was very close with Paul and it was hard on Tom when they moved away. If anything, Tom would be the one looking to live close to them.

"The taxes are very reasonable in the Carolina's," said Maria. "I've been looking there as well. I don't know anybody in the Carolina's, though. I have friends in Florida," she said thoughtfully.

"You have friends in Brooklyn, Maria," said Robert.

Maria looked at Robert closely. Her eyes trying to search his, but she found nothing of any deeper meaning as he bit into his sandwich. Her face flushed with disappointment. Her own eyes would have betrayed her feelings had he been looking for such evidence.

They were friends now as they had been for thirty years. They had a working relationship that had kept them together on a regular basis, but for that they would have lost touch, with the exception of

Christmas cards and on Maria's part a more personal birthday card. She, of course, would receive one on her own birthday with Robert's name, via Elizabeth who, now, was in guardianship of such matters and formalities that men are often forgiven for overlooking.

Maria had been invited to Robert's dinner parties when Kathleen was the hostess and the invitations continued when Elizabeth acted in her place. He, in turn, had been to her home for many such occasions with Kathleen and later with Elizabeth in tow. The occasions had never been intimate, though. Always there were many other people to distract his attentions. In the school lounge, Maria felt that she was a colleague and friend and nothing more and even now so many years later she feared that there was little hope of there being anything else. She had confided in no one. Confessing to her friends, even now so late in life, would prompt them to push her forward and for her to be the aggressor. That, however, was not in her makeup. A woman could never make such declarations to a man. There needed to be gallantry.

No matter how close in approximation, Maria would only be able to love Robert from afar. She had been in love with him for so many years and had to confess covetous thoughts regularly to Father McNeil and then later to Father Ianuzzi and finally to Father Alvarado of Chiapas, Mexico, who she found easiest of all to confess such matters as he had never questioned her. The good Father Alvarado, as English was not his language of origin could not understand much of her softly spoken confessions and was too genteel a man to demand that she speak up and speak more slowly.

"You never speak much of the future, Bob," said Tom. Tom was the only person to address Robert with such informality. Robert had always introduced himself as Robert and, in his own mild mannered way, managed to put a hint of finality into it.

"My present is my future, Tom. I've no plans for change. I like my life the way it is," he said thoughtfully. "I have my family, my friends, my work, my home and my garden, and I have my books. Why should I leave any of that?"

"Don't you ever wish for change?" asked Maria quizzically. "Don't you ever wish for a fresh start, a new beginning?"

"I've had fresh starts and new beginnings," he said. "I'm in a good place, Maria, and I don't feel the need or the desire to interrupt that place. I've made a sort of haven for myself," he said in earnest, "and I don't wish to venture away from it."

"Good for you, Bob," said Tom. "I need change in my life. I feel stagnant. I would love a change of scenery and something different to wake up to each morning. Unfortunately Linda plans to come with me." Robert laughed and Maria slapped Tom playfully.

The school principal, John McEntyre, a large man with a gregarious personality that had seemed to compliment his bulk, walked up to their table and rested his hand on Robert's shoulder. He gave Robert a gentle squeeze and then the follow up rub to express the warmth of friendship. It caused a slight shudder in Robert. "Planning out our summers?" he asked somewhat conspiratorially.

"Planning out the rest of our lives," said Tom.

"Good," said McEntyre jauntily. There was genuine encouragement in his voice. "It's always good to look to the future. At our ages we're lucky that we don't have to wait all that long to make good on our plans."

"Why you're just a boy, John," said Maria almost dismissively. "I'm afraid you're in it for the long haul."

"Don't rub it in," he replied.

"What is it with all of you?" asked Robert. "Why in such a hurry to get to the end of your lives? Appreciate each day as a gift because it is just that. I'm grateful for the years that I've had here and even more so for the ones ahead of me. Don't you see how valuable we are to these children? We have purpose here. The grass, I assure you, is not always greener on the other side of the fence. It may appear to be so from a distance, perhaps, but on closer inspection there are brown patches, scattered weeds and its share of barren soil."

"I covered my lawn with cement," said Tom. Robert and Maria both frowned. "What?" he said with defensive emphasis. "I put up a hoop and bought a leaf blower. Life is good. Green grass can be a real pain in the ass."

"Well, in any case," said McEntyre, "there is a big world out there and taking some well deserved time for ourselves is a welcome opportunity. There are so many other things to do, to accomplish, out there. Retirement is not the end of life; it's the beginning. It's the time to change the venue."

Robert grimaced at the prospect. "We're teachers," he said. "We have the time. It is money that we lack. We have plenty of time to accomplish other things. There's no place in this world where I would rather be."

"There has to be, Robert," said Maria almost pleading with him.

"Why is it so terrible for a man to be content with his place in the world, I wonder?" he spoke to no one in particular.

McEntyre, feeling that the question was meant for him, fell speechless and after a moment in reflection, exhaled without drama. "Robert, can we get together this evening? I have some things, school matters, to discuss with you and I thought we could do it casually over drinks. I wouldn't bother you with it after hours, but I'm full up and it needs a little time."

"This evening?" said Robert. "I would, only I have my daughter and grand-daughter coming in tonight and…"

"Today is Robert's birthday, John," explained Maria. "He detests any attention that it might bring and I am not supposed to make any mention of it."

"Oh," said McEntyre in that drawn out way that people tend to do when they are caught off guard and are uncertain as to how they should respond. "Your birthday." He slapped Robert on the back and wished him a happy one. "It can wait, Robert. It's nothing urgent." His face colored and the shading did not elude Robert. McEntyre tried to get away from the table hastily and at the same time he tried to mask that haste. He stopped abruptly and turned at once. "Tomorrow, Robert?" he asked somewhat gingerly and much too delicately for a man of his bulk.

"Yes," said Robert, nodding his head dully. "Tomorrow will be fine, John."

"Farrell's," said McEntyre. It was not a question. "Happy birthday again, Robert."

"Yes," said Robert wearily.

Chapter Three

Robert shifts a little, as the bench beneath him grows more solid. The comfort he had earlier delighted in has now deserted him. He is suddenly aware of each board that lies beneath him. The breeze is less gentle now and there is a chill to the air. He tugs at the collar of his coat to protect himself. Toby seems not to notice the wind or the drop in temperature.

On the field a young woman pulls at her coat tightly tying the sash and plunging her hands deeply into her pockets. She has longish hair, not quite red, but a very light shade of auburn. Her hair is not curly but there are kinks and waves, perhaps created by the use of hot rollers and cylindrical irons.

Robert smiles at her, but she is too far from him to notice. "Kathleen loved the cold air on her face," he says. "The rest of her body protested beneath turtleneck sweaters and heavy woolen coats." He smiles again at the young woman and sees her differently.

* * *

The smell of chestnuts wafted through the air and made Robert hungry for something else. It was after eight o'clock at night and he was cold and tired and feeling somewhat sorry for himself. It was Friday and Monday would be Christmas and he had no plans between now and then. He had left the school after an early holiday party that the faculty had thrown themselves. One by one the distinguished members disbanded from the festivity to be with their families and left Robert feeling very much alone.

He was twenty-four now and had only begun to teach in September. He'd arrived in New York two years earlier with a little money and a great deal of trepidation. Any romantic ideals that he may have had about his future in America prior to leaving England had remained in England. The shy young man who climbed aboard a vessel in an English harbor and sailed across the Atlantic would be, much to his chagrin, the same person to arrive in a port in New York.

Robert was not going to be the person he had wanted to be in this new world, this land of opportunity. He would, instead, be the same timid and awkward boy – possibly even more so – in this new land where he was isolated from familiarity. He found people to be friendly and polite, but too anxious and in a hurry to be moving on. He was not quick enough, verbally, to turn a phrase or utter a smart comment with strangers and strangers in this strange new land were, for all their gallantries, unforgiving or perhaps impatient with newcomers who seemingly had little to offer in the universe of social endeavors. He found silence better than stammering although he would grit his teeth in either event. Very often he found himself recreating conversations in his mind and altering the things he had said, or more likely and in most cases, the things he did not say. He would lose many hours of sleep in these futile exercises and his ensuing encounters would always be much the same until he had grown comfortable with his audience.

After the dispersion of the holiday party he had taken the train into Greenwich Village and had a cup of tea in a small café on Christopher Street. He read some pages from a paperback version of Dickens' *A Christmas Carol,* but found that every sound and movement around him too easily distracted him and lent him to realize that he would rather be a part of the world around him than the one in the pages of any book. Unfortunately, he was feeling much the same as old Ebenezer. The images around him were merely shadows, only these were shadows of the present and he was not part of it. He felt awkward and helpless in his present and wished to make a change, even in the slightest.

He left some money on the table in the café and smiled at the waitress as he exited, but she had not noticed. He crossed Bleeker to

Sheridan Square and then walked to Seventh Avenue and on to Times Square. He bought some inexpensive trinkets off of a few amiable street peddlers, but found that even they had little time to spare.

He walked over to Sixth Avenue and then up to Rockefeller Center and finally settled himself by the tall, lighted tree and overlooking the skaters who braved the cold and worked their way around the ice with loved ones. It was then that the smell of the chestnuts had woken his sense of hunger. He continued to watch the skaters for no other purpose than that he had walked for so long to be at this destination and felt that by moving on too quickly he would not have gotten his worth for his expenditure.

Eventually, he continued on and made his way to a delicatessen, much like the one in which he had worked upon his arrival in New York prior to becoming an educator. He sat at the counter, although he would have preferred a table, but that was frowned upon. Tables were meant for parties of two or more. In his earlier attempts at occupying a table he would be asked if he might be more comfortable at the counter and in some instances a bolder or even militant waitress might actually insist upon it. He had long given up on tables unless a delicatessen was primarily vacant.

It was just after he had ordered his roast beef with mashed potatoes covered in gravy and a side of string beans that he had taken notice of Kathleen. He had not been aware of her when he had walked in, but seeing that she had been sitting before a meal that she had not touched, he supposed that she'd been there for some time. At the very least she had been there when he had walked in.

She did occupy a table for two, but it was apparent that she was one. She sat by the window and pretended to look out, but Robert guessed otherwise. Her eyes were red and puffy and it seemed that she had been crying for some time. She was looking out, but she was seeing something that was in her past. The redness about the eyes had traveled about her cheeks, which were rather prominent. Her hair was shoulder length. She had thick red hair with natural curls. Robert surmised that the woman went to great lengths to keep her hair from curling up and covering her head like wild flowers. She was not beautiful, but he was attracted to her. She had blue eyes that were too small for her face. Beneath the makeup there were freckles. He could see them climbing out from where she had been wiping the tears so diligently.

His attraction to her may have developed more out of empathy than the physical. Her vulnerability was appealing to him as an element of danger or recklessness in a man can be attractive to some women, but there was the physical attraction as well. For the moment, while he was ignorant of her situation, he was quite astute of his own sensibilities. It was that time of the year in which it was almost criminal to be alone. He was alone and she also appeared to be so. He acknowledged, to himself at least, that he so desperately wished this to be the case. He thought himself to be cruel in that moment; seeing her sitting there looking so utterly miserable and he feeling less alone. Misery loves company, he thought. It was such a cliché, but it was truth. Like a fool he thought himself the proverbial knight in shining armor who could rescue her within a moment via a humorous observation of their doled out dilemmas. Yet he knew all the while that it was unlikely that he would pull himself away from the stool in which he sat.

The waitress delivered Robert's meal with a smile and a check. He resented being hurried and would not be so, although he felt uncomfortable and this made him angry. His meal was utterly ruined and he was yet to even taste it. He turned back hoping that the red-haired girl was still seated and was delighted to see that she did not seem to be in any hurry to leave regardless of the waitress hovering about her untouched sandwich. It pleased Robert that she was not in the least bit fazed, but there was also something disturbing in her detachment.

He ate his meal quietly and tried not to think of her and for a while he had succeeded. After finishing, and with a slight frown of the waitress, he ordered a cup of tea. He paid his check and slowly sipped his tea. He and the red-haired girl, coincidently, left at the same time.

Robert was content to just move on, but stopped when he realized that she was crying. Not just the tears, but outright sobs.

"Are you quite alright?" he asked. He hadn't considered this a moment to make contact with her. What he was feeling was genuine concern. He gently put his hand on her forearm and gave her a slight squeeze of reassurance.

"Yes," she said nodding her head. "I'm fine," she lied. It was clear, though that she was not.

"If this is you at fine, I would really hate to see you when you're distraught," he said, catching them both a little off guard and just like that she smiled. Robert had become her knight in shining armor. For a moment he was comfortable enough with a complete stranger to say something amusing and her smile, the smile that broke through the tears, had given him confidence enough to offer his name and ask her for hers.

"Kathleen," she said. "Kathleen Hennessy."

He took her proffered hand and held it a bit longer than necessary and asked her if she would like to get something warm to drink. She hesitated for a moment and then went against her nature by considering. After looking into his rather gentle eyes she surprised herself and relented and they settled on a café just a block from where they had dined separately just moments before.

He took her coat and scarf and folded them gently over a chair. They exchanged obvious comments about the weather and the crowds of people venturing into the city. Neither was very good at small talk, but they were not uncomfortable with one another and the frequent silences were anything but awkward. He was half way through his second cup of tea before asking her about the tears.

"I don't want to get too personal, Kathleen," he said, "but if you want to talk about it, I'll be happy to listen."

She pursed her lips and gave a hint of a shrug. "It isn't anything, really. I get like this sometimes. The season," she said. "The isolation." She smiled, though her lips had tightened. "I just get like this at times."

There was something in her eyes that he tried desperately to read, but there was no comprehension for him. She was holding back, perhaps. Or was it that she wanted to explain it to him more fully, but was unable to articulate it. Perhaps, he thought, it was expected that he should understand what she had meant, but he didn't. Perhaps it was the way of the woman. Understanding women was a field in which he would always be inept.

He thought of some of his aunts and although they didn't cry like that they did tend to just get a certain way sometimes. In any case he did not think that it was necessary to pursue it at this time and place and thought it better to just move on. "You're American, yes?" he asked.

"First generation," she said. "My parents came from Dublin the year before I was born."

"Did they go back home?"

She lowered her eyes and went silent for a time. Robert immediately regretted the query. He wanted to speak. He wanted to put the smile back onto her face, but the words were not coming. He was feeling the chink in his newly acquired armor. The moment was getting away from him.

"They passed," she finally declared. "My father was killed in an automobile accident when I was nine and I lost mum two summers ago to cancer of the bone."

"I'm so sorry. I didn't mean to open up old wounds." He clasped his hands and rested them on the edge of the table. She reached across and rested her hand upon his. He looked up and smiled weakly. "I am sorry," he said to her again. "Truly I am."

"Don't be sorry. You needn't apologize for such a simple thing as a question." She tightened her grip on his hands to reassure him. He was at once both warmed by the gesture and inept on how he should proceed. Eventually he removed his bottom hand and placed it on top of hers. Her smile returned and again he was put at ease.

The story of her parents flowed from her naturally and in a matter-of-fact manner that was typical of most people. He had been a wonderful father, she said and Robert could see in her eyes that she believed it to be true. She had loved him and he her. There were fond memories of her early childhood. They had taken trips to the shore and to the country. They all shared a love for music and dance. Her father played the fiddle while she and her mother did an Irish step.

It had been a happy home, the apartment they lived in. Their little place had always been filled with people who laughed and sang and danced well into the night. Her father was a gregarious storyteller and never let a glass go empty while her mother cooked and baked and kept an eye out for empty plates. Never was there a complaint from a neighbor because they were always invited to be there and usually were.

Liam, Kathleen's father, died tragically when a motorist passed a red light. Liam was in the passenger seat and was reported to be killed instantly, but years later Kathleen learned that he had died after several excruciating hours where he had asked for his wife and little girl. Kathleen's mother had been working and had not been located or contacted in time to be with him.

The years that followed were not as somber as some might expect. Kathleen's mother managed to keep their spirits bright and the friends they had had in those years banded together with love and support. Families were not made only of blood and Kathleen was never left behind. She and her mother continued to dance and to sing the songs her father had sung and his picture was always kept in a place of prominence in their home wherever that home may have been in any given year. And while her mother worked many hours to keep them fed and in comfort, she never seemed to be in absence.

Evelyn, Kathleen's mother, died slowly and her death was a mixed blessing as she had suffered immensely in the months leading up to her demise. "She was a beautiful woman," said Kathleen. "She was filled with love and faith and humor. She loved to laugh and to make others laugh. It was always of great importance to her that anyone in her space was made to feel cared for and comfortable. I was lucky to have her," she said. "I was truly blessed to have had both of them."

They talked well into the night. Robert, too, opened up, but did not bare all of the details of his childhood. His mothers' absences for example, went unexplained. Kathleen would make assumptions that it was the finding of employment that had taken Margaret away from him so much of the time. He had not told her this, but the simplicity of his telling would let her presume as much and he allowed it to be thought as such. For much of her life, Kathleen would sympathize with Margaret, thinking that her life was less of choice and more of struggle. She would think of Robert's mother's hardships in life and want to weep for her. Even now, after all of these years, was he still protecting his mother, or was he protecting himself? Freud would have a field day with him, he thought.

It wasn't until later, much later, after he had fallen in love with her, did he wonder about all of the people in her life, the friends that had given that early support, and where they had gone off to. She had spoken of them as family. They were like aunts and uncles and their children were like cousins. Some of them were like brothers and sisters, she had said. Where were they now, he had thought? But not even then, after he had asked her for her hand in marriage, did he ask her about it. As the years passed the question of their absence would burn in his mind, but to question her then would be to plant the seeds of his mistrust in her mind. The questions were awake in his mind early on, perhaps, but he certainly left them go unsaid. Robert found it best to walk gingerly around personal matters where Kathleen was concerned. Also, he was happy and did not feel the need to explore for things he did not wish to find.

Robert and Kathleen married six months after their first meeting. To the few friends, primarily colleagues, in attendance it was said to have been a whirlwind romance, but the truth was more that it had been two lonely people coming together so that they would be less alone. There was the love, of course, but it was never a love of passion or lust. The desire that they had felt for each other and for them to come together was a desire to quench the isolation that they had been feeling. Now they would have each other to brave that void, that emptiness.

It was a good time in their lives. They both had what they had needed so desperately for so long a time. They had companionship and they had a partner to work with to build a future. There were plans for a family and all that came with the family life. Robert had such optimism in that time. He thought about a house filled with children who he could adore. He would live in his own world now and not just the world of other peoples' imaginations. It would not be a world of words on a page. It would be a life. It would be a real life. He was confident in the belief that he had control over his future and that there would not be the mistakes of those who had walked before him. In Kathleen there was always some sadness that Robert could read. He could see it in her eyes and in the way she walked. He could hear it her breathing and in the way she would hold her head. She was fighting something and with his help she could beat it. Robert could not understand her demons or those of others. He could only work to keep those of his own at bay and deal with them in such a way that they would not destroy him and the people around him. His own demons, he thought to be harmless at any rate.

When Kathleen was down, Robert found ways to lift her and in that he prided himself. He was her knight and he found comfort in rescuing her. He would be her great protector. When she was at her most vulnerable, he was the rock. As for Kathleen, she saw things in Robert that she planned to change. She could make him a stronger man. She could guide him to be better and more productive. She would get him away from the things that he clung to and that she had disapproved of. She saw in him what she believed to be his demons, but she never commented on them early on. She had thought it best to nudge him into other directions. It would take time, but she could manage that. She was certain of it.

It was Kathleen who had found their home in Park Slope. Robert never believed that they would be able to make such a purchase, but Kathleen willed it to happen. She made the necessary inquiries with the banks and learned to ask the right questions. She pooled Robert's meager savings with what little she herself had saved and the little money her mother had left to her. She sold her mothers jewelry and what little pieces had been given her without Robert's knowledge. Robert, in the mean time, had taken on part time jobs to put together what was needed for the balance of the minimum down payment required.

Robert would look back on the months leading up to the purchase of their home as the happiest months of their marriage. The urgency to make it happen gave them such strength and determination. There was such little time to think of anything else let alone do anything else. They were fighting for a cause and they were fighting alone, but they were together. They had each other's backs. All of their energy was put into this one thing. The purchase of their home had become a living thing that had united them and that, unfortunately, would never happen for them again. Never would they bond on any other issue.

The home was a prize and in the first days they had celebrated with such joy, but the celebration soon wore thin. From then on it was just a matter of keeping the prize and after a while the prize had not lived up to its original promise. All the hard work led to more hard work and all of the struggling led to more struggle and there never seemed to be an end in sight. Work begets work. Struggle begets struggle. The tenants on the third floor, while being decent people, were eventually thought to be intrusive in Kathleen's world and soon she began to dislike them and dislike her dependence on them even all the more. She could not be cruel to them because of this dependence and so she would be cruel to Robert and Robert would not take it so well.

Soon she began to realize that there was nothing more and she would slowly give in to the depression that had always been just below the surface waiting to claim her. Robert would come home to find her sobbing, on occasion, in much the same way as she had on that first day when they had met. It was not so easy for him to pull her up as he had in the beginning. The depths of her depression were getting deeper and his resolve to lift her from them was growing weary. The depression was not constant, but it was there and for Robert it was unsettling.

Working at part time jobs would become his solace. For a time he would work weekend nights as a security guard just to get away from home allowing the work itself and the pay it gave him the excuse to be free from her without the need to feel the guilt of abandoning her. It also allowed him the privilege to get lost once again in his novels, the imaginary worlds of others. It was also at that time when he started to frequent Farrell's bar. With his many hours of work in several jobs he could justify a little recreation in the pub with the company of men. It seemed an age-old tradition amongst men and he felt a right to it.

* * *

"She was not very often happy, Toby. She cried a great deal when we were still young and less as the years passed us by, but that didn't mean she was any less melancholy". The wind was picking up again and the dead and dry old leaves circled about the two men on the bench. "Is that you, Kathleen?" he asks the field. He smiles, but he is not so certain that he is speaking in jest.

"I should have been more perceptive, Toby." Robert is speaking out loud, but his words are easily an inward reflection of his thoughts "First impressions should not be abandoned. They don't have to stand as testament, but should be noted and serve as a warning to proceed with caution.

"I was a young man in those days and if young men have anything over the older men it is energy. Unfortunately energy will often lead a man to do things before thinking them through. I quickly surmised that what had kept Kathleen so happy earlier on was having something to consume her fully. What I had failed to remember was that it had only been a temporary fix. Perhaps," he thought dully, "I was looking for a temporary fix for myself. Truth be told, Toby, I was tired. I was working many hours and I wanted peace at the end of the day. I found myself reading more. When I wasn't working or making feeble attempts at repairs in my house, I would look for escape into a novel or something historical and my mothers' words would come rushing back at me. 'It's only words'.

"Her words were getting to me, Toby. I was living in worlds that were not my own. For the first time in my life I wanted to go back to living in my own life and not that of someone else's. I wanted to have with Kathleen what we had had in the early months of our marriage and I believed that I could recapture those days by keeping her preoccupied. My suggestion was to have a child. Don't get me wrong, Toby, I never regretted having Emily, but I did learn that having a child is not the solution to any problem. As a teacher of high school students I have seen it far too often. I have seen girls and boys bringing children into the world with romantic and unrealistic expectations. Usually it was the girl who would want a baby. She would think that the boy would truly love her then and that it would make them a happy family. I often thought them fatally stupid and then one day I woke up with the realization that I had done much the same thing as an educated fully grown man.

"In retrospect I am glad that I had come up with the absurd notion of starting a family. Emily is by far the best part of my life and I thank God that I have her. As for solving problems between Kathleen and myself, I couldn't have been more wrong in my speculations.

"Kathleen was a good woman," Robert said with great emphasis. "I loved her most dearly. She worked hard in our home and made do with the little I could give to her on my teacher's salary. She did not ever complain, but always there was that look of disappointment in her eyes; pain behind the most rare of smiles and contempt for the day that lie ahead. Always I felt that I was letting her down and it took its toll on me. I wanted so very much to make her happy and I don't believe that that was possible. I used to think that it was, but eventually they said that she would need the medication to help her through.

"She was a good mother to Emily in the sense that she had always wanted what was best for her, but I don't think Emily truly appreciated her." Robert grimaced at these thoughts. "I pleaded with Emily to be understanding of her mother, but Emily was headstrong and had trouble hiding her emotions." A muted smile runs across Robert's face. "What is it they say, Toby? About women, that is. 'You can't live with them and you can't live without them.' Are there words any truer than those?"

Robert stands up abruptly and stretches his legs and arms. He pulls his coat around him more tightly. "Emily is the light of my life," he says turning to the old man on the bench. "She is very little like me or Kathleen. She's bold and can be brash. She's strong and willful and most importantly, she is so very independent. She doesn't need me," he says solemnly. "She hasn't for quite some time." Robert has a far away look in his eyes and behind the eyes his mind works to balance the emotions of what he felt and the importance of accepting what was and embracing that what was, for he knew what was, was better.

"That's a good thing. I know that in my mind where I presume it matters most. It's my heart that betrays me. I have conflicting thoughts about it. It was what I had always wanted for her, but still, I suppose, I feel less relevant to her. What's my place in her life? I brought her up to be her own person and Kathleen was almost brutal about instilling self-reliance into her. Kathleen taught Emily how to do something and expected her to take it from there. My part was less about expectation and more about theory.

"She married some years ago and that failed, but it did result in a beautiful little girl. My granddaughter," he says and smiles as though he is smiling down upon her. "Her name is Shannon."

Robert goes back to the bench with a hint of reluctance and sits next to the old man. "I would have liked to have played a bigger part in my granddaughter's life, but I didn't know how to go about that and I don't really know where I can go from here at all."

Chapter Four

Elizabeth checked inside the oven to see that the duck was still moist. Robert was late again and it upset her that this new development of his being tardy was becoming habitual. It had been unlike him in the past to be anything but unpredictable and now he could show himself anywhere from a half to two hours late. It bothered her all the more as this was his birthday and tonight they were having guests.

Emily had left work early, something she rarely ever did, to be there along with Shannon to surprise him. Henry Grifhorst, Robert's closest friend for nearly thirty years, was also there as well as Maria Scapelli. Together Henry and Shannon had decorated the dining room with streamers and balloons and a big sign that read 'HAPPY BIRTHDAY GRANDPA' while Emily and Maria set the table.

"For the love of God, I don't know where that man can be on this night," Elizabeth cried with anguish.

"Well this is one night you can't be cursing after me, Lizzie," said Henry. "I've my alibi tonight."

"I can still curse you yet, Henry Grifhorst. It was you who corrupted Robert with the taste for the local establishment."

"Me? I'll have you know that it was Robert himself who invited me to the local establishment on the very night that I arrived in Brooklyn." Henry made the little quotation marks with his fingers as he repeated "local establishment".

Elizabeth glared at Henry and her eyes darted from his to Shannon and back again. Her eyes were accusing him of a blasphemy against

Robert in the presence of Robert's granddaughter. Henry, at once, felt both small and irritated. Immediately he let the emotion pass. This was Lizzie and he loved her as if she were his own sister. "Maybe I ought to go over to..." he looked again at the glaring eyes of Elizabeth, "to the soda. Uhh...fountain shop and see if Robert had dropped in for a soda pop."

Elizabeth's eyes met his with approval. "That would be very good of you Henry," she said. "See that he doesn't ruin his appetite with an ice cream sundae."

In the corner Shannon stood with a balloon in her hand and looked at her mom and giggled. Adults could be so naive when it came to what a child could comprehend. Emily smiled at her daughter giving the child more credit for her understanding than she had deserved. Adults could also overestimate the comprehension of a child.

"I can't imagine what could be keeping him," said Maria. "Why just this afternoon he spoke of this evening. He knew that you would be making a fuss over his birthday, Elizabeth. I hope that he's alright."

The last of Maria's words irritated Elizabeth. She thought Maria a fool to put unnecessary fear and worry into the heart of Shannon. Maria knew full well that Robert had been a little absent-minded of late although she would not say it. In fairness, however, Elizabeth was aware that most of what Maria would say or do would act as an irritant against her.

Elizabeth had never thought of herself to be a petty person and had normally never given in to outbursts of jealousy or feelings of envy save for a few exceptions when she was but a girl. However, she could not help but to feel threatened by Maria Scapelli. It had always been obvious to her that there were in fact feelings for Robert on the part of Maria. If he had any such feelings for Maria he did not show it and if he was aware of Maria's affection towards him he had never let that be known either. In fact, Elizabeth surmised that he had always been an unwitting character in Maria's life and much to her dismay; Elizabeth quietly reveled in this fact.

In another world, she could imagine herself being a true friend to Maria as opposed to this world in which she could only make polite small talk and offer her false or half-hearted compliments. Elizabeth served a purpose in her world and she felt vulnerable in it. Her brother's happiness meant a great deal to her, but she realized, and ignominiously so, that his happiness may in fact threaten hers. If Maria, or any other woman, came into his life, what place would there be for her? She managed his household since Kathleen had passed. She had held this position for many years and she had served it well.

Of course since Emily had moved on to get married and start a family of her own there had been less need for her services or use as she sometimes thought of it, but she did still feel useful to him. He was, after all, just a man and in her learned opinion, a man was as helpless as a baby. Left to their own devices, men would live no better than pigs in a pen. A man, she had reasoned to any woman who would listen to her, needed a woman to push them forward or in some cases to hold them back, otherwise they would simply stay still or run amok.

A man needs a reason to get up in the morning. Hell, she thought, a man needs a reason to bathe. Women provided men with incentives to be useful to themselves and to others. Women guide men to live and to die properly and with dignity. Men needed to be looked after and that had always been her calling in life. First she had her father to look after and for a short while she tended to her uncle as well and then, thankfully, Robert.

Elizabeth had always been painfully aware of the fact that the attention of men came sparingly and usually came only from those whom she had found to be somewhat repugnant in either manner or appearance or both. Truthfully, remaining single had never been disturbing to her. It had always been irrelevant to her so long as she had someone to look after. Deep down and perhaps, not as deep as all that, she thought marriage to be a tether that cut too deeply into the circulation. She saw the pain in the eyes of her father and later in the eyes of Robert. She saw a lack of humility and an over abundance of desperation in her mother as she got on in years. For her mother, a man was as necessary as air or water. For Elizabeth, marriage was a road that need not be traveled. It was only important that she had purpose in her life.

In any case she often rebuffed herself when these feelings towards Maria came into play. She really did not need to worry as Maria had been holding on for decades without as much as a word of encouragement from Robert. Maria had been there when Kathleen was alive and to cut her out of the family after would have been reprehensible. No matter, Elizabeth would not have been able to live with herself to do so. On the surface Elizabeth hated herself for being so petty, but it was not on the surface where she had truly lived.

As Henry Grifhorst made his way to open the door, Robert was working the key into the cylinder. Henry backed away promptly with the aid of frantic whispers and hysterical gestures from Elizabeth. They stood there facing the door ready to surprise him as he came in. Only Shannon had the foresight to yell surprise and let the balloons in her hand break away from her grasp and fly and sputter and fall as the air escaped. The others stood silent and then, as an afterthought, yelled 'SURPRISE'.

"What's this?" he asked. Shannon was the first to greet him. She threw her arms around his waist and he pulled her in even tighter. He knelt down and kissed her and pulled her tighter still. The others gathered around him and there was a ridiculous group hug. "I love you all so much," he said as the tears gathered in his eyes. "Balloons and ribbons," he said as he got to his feet. "And what's that I smell in the kitchen?"

"That would be the remains of a duck," said Elizabeth dryly. "I'll just go and see if I need to serve it on a platter or in an urn."

He laughed as his sister left the room. "I do think she has gotten sarcasm down to an art." He looked at his daughter. "Emily this is such a surprise. I'm so glad to see you. What brings you here?"

"Now you're being sarcastic," she said.

There was a flicker in his eyes and then the ribbons and the balloons were suddenly registering again and he said "my birthday".

"Oh," said Emily. I know I haven't been around so much, dad, but work has been so brutal and…."

"No, no," he said quickly. "I didn't mean to imply anything at all. I'm just a little forgetful about by birthday today. Perhaps I am blocking something I do not wish to deal with?"

"You won't get any sympathy from me, Montgomery," said Henry with mock severity. "I've got more mileage on this chassis than you have on yours and I cannot be accused of whining about it. Nobody ever saw me crying into my…" he looked at Shannon, "into my pillow."

"Well I have nothing to cry about tonight, do I? I have all of my family here tonight." He put his hand on Henry's shoulder and offered Maria a hug. "All of my family," he said with great emphasis.

Elizabeth emerged from the kitchen carrying a platter. "The duck is not all that it could be, but I will not be responsible for it," she said, but Robert could see that there was not a hint of tension in her face and that the duck would be all that it could be and more.

"I am absolutely famished," said Robert. "I would like to wash quickly and destroy this beautiful feast and then to listen to the praise that you will all undoubtedly shower upon me. This is, after all, my day to shamelessly pilfer from the rest of you. I will take this day and keep it forever."

"No more soda for Robert," Henry said and then he winked at Shannon and again she giggled.

Robert turned and looked back to Emily while she fussed with a ribbon in Shannon's hair. "I won't be but a minute," he said. He turned on his heel and walked into the lavatory. He turned on the cold water and with cupped hands he pulled the cool water into his face and looked hard into the mirror. His face blurred and his mind traveled back to another place.

* * *

The sun was low in the sky and just breaking through the trees of gold and red and brown. The sidewalks were draped in these spectacular colors and the fragrance they emitted was as uplifting to him as any aroma in any kitchen that he had ever entered. The air was crisp and clean, but not yet cold. It was that kind of day for Robert in which he felt most alive. When all else was wrong a beautiful day seemed to offer him hope. The breathing came more easily and put him at peace. His students were beginning to take shape and that was very good for mid-October.

He walked into his home and immediately his spirits descended. His mood shifted eerily with the quiet of his house and its inhabitants. There was no music or television playing. There were no familiar smells from the kitchen or sounds of rattling pots and pans. All was quiet and quiet left for uncertainty and in this time of life that had never been a good thing in the Montgomery home.

With trepidation he made his way up the stairs and to his daughter's room. Emily was just nine years of age. She was sitting in a chair by the window. Her eyes darted quickly as he entered the room. For a moment she looked at him. Their eyes connected and messages were sent and received and nothing more need be said. She ran to him then and clutched him to her and her to him. "Don't be sad, daddy," she said. The pain that she had read in his eyes was more than she had wanted to bear. He was disheartened by her words and he felt distraught. He was failing her and it was killing him. He was her father and he was supposed to be shielding her from such things and here she was trying to protect him.

He grabbed her under the arms and pulled her up to cradle her in his. He smiled at her. The smile need not be forced. In that moment he loved her even more than ever before and that was something he did not think possible. He could feel the love from his daughter coming in waves of energy and again his hope had been renewed.

"I can't be sad, pumpkin," he said. "I can never be all that sad so long as I have you and your love for me."

"I love you, daddy. I love you so much," she said as the tears spilled from her eyes. Robert could feel her body trembling in his arms. He hugged her more firmly offering her reassurance. She was not alone in this, he was telling her. They were together in this.

"Don't cry," he told her. He wanted to say more, but all that could be said had been said in gestures and he knew that she had understood this. "Is mommy in her room, pumpkin?"

Emily nodded. "She's crying again, daddy. She just cries and cries and won't say anything to me."

"Did she pick you up at school?"

She shook her head hesitantly. He could sense that Emily felt that she was betraying her mother.

"You didn't walk home alone?" he asked fearfully.

"No, daddy," she said. "When mommy didn't show I asked Maggie and Jimmy Carver if I could walk with them." The Carver family lived on the next block. Robert knew the family well and was relieved to know that his daughter had the good mind to seek help. "I told them mommy hadn't been feeling well."

"You told them that mommy wasn't feeling well," he repeated mostly to himself. He began to feel the anger welling up inside him. He was disgusted that his little girl was being forced to grow up before her years. It infuriated him that she had felt compelled to cover up for her mother and perhaps more for her own embarrassment and then his own childhood and that of Elizabeth's came flooding back at him and he was helpless.

He would now go to his wife and he would talk and reason and he would get nowhere. He would plead with her for the sake of their daughter, but it would make no difference. There would be no reaching Kathleen tonight. It may be days before she is of any use to herself and then she would go on as if nothing had ever happened.

He would speak to her then, but she would not hear it. Determined, he would get into her face and demand that she get help, but she would turn it around on him. Her depression, she would reason, was a result of his failings. She would maintain that she was unhappy because he was not there for her emotionally and that she was in perpetual exhaustion by the constant struggle to make ends meet.

In the prosperous months of summer, while teaching summer school in the early hours and driving a cab in the afternoon and evenings or painting houses or working with a friend who restored furniture, the complaints of financial struggles had to be temporarily omitted from his faults, but no matter how hard he would try to be there for her "emotionally", she would not cease to put blame onto him for her depression and as the time passed he would feel less obliged to be there for her as he had been in the past.

He believed that she was incapable of helping herself. He could accept that about her and he didn't expect her problems to go away on their own accord. He couldn't, however, help but to resent the fact that she would not accept the help of others.

* * *

"I had all of my family there, Toby," he says to the man on the bench. "A small family we are, but a family nonetheless. I was very happy as I went off to the washroom thinking of Emily and Shannon being there with me. Of course Henry, Maria and Elizabeth as well, but they had been fixtures of my everyday life. Elizabeth shared my home,

Maria my work, and Henry was my very best friend and neighbor. It was when I looked at myself in the mirror in the washroom that I got that sinking feeling again. I hadn't the right to feel that way, but I suppose we can't really choose how we feel.

"It made me think about Kathleen. I wanted to understand her when she still had the gift of life, but for her that gift was a curse. I wanted to understand how she felt and why and I wanted to help her through it, but in my heart I couldn't and even though my mind told me she needed help and understanding I could not escape feeling resentment towards her. She was ruining all of our lives. She was ruining Emily's childhood as my mother had ruined mine. She was ruining her own life and she was ruining the balance of mine and to me it was inexplicable. I wanted to be supportive, and to a point I was. I was supportive in the physical sense. I was there for her when she needed me to be there. I held her when she needed to be held and I said the things that she needed to hear, but my words became mechanical, as did my movements.

"Inexplicable was the only word I understood. I just thought that there was no need for her actions or inactions. There was no justification for her moods. Life, I thought was not perfect, but one has to move on. Isn't that so, Toby? Lemonade from lemons and all that. I suppose what really bothered me was that I felt alone with her. I wanted her to tell me how she felt. I wanted to know what was bothering her. I was willing to work this out with her, but she shook me off. I felt betrayed by her. It took me so very long to learn that she did not know what was wrong with her.

"It was only later that the doctors would explain to me that she did not know. They told me she could not tell me because she didn't understand it herself. Again I wanted to believe that, but my mind and my heart were betraying one another. The mind to me seemed so much less complicated than the way in which others perceived it to be. My way of thinking was that everyone was over-analyzing. Some people thrived on the melodramatics and I just wanted to be simple.

"Simplicity, Toby, if you ask me, gets a bum rap. In literature the worst thing to be accused of is writing in simplistic forms. The human animal mustn't be simplistic. Simplicity is for all other life, but not for the human life. We are the depth to civilization. We are complex intellectuals and must be profound in our thinking. To be simplistic is to be a fool. To be happy is to be a fool. To be content is to be a fool.

"I wanted to be a simplistic intellectual. I chose not to over-think. I believed that you could be happy if you chose to be so provided that you had someone who was also a willing participant in such an endeavor. I felt that Kathleen's problem was due more to melodramatics than anything else. I felt that she liked being unhappy. I thought that was who she chose to be.

"I thought the doctors were wrong when they medicated her. It was true that she would cry less and she would spend less time in her bed with the shades down and the curtains drawn. They felt that they had taken away her blues, but the people who knew her saw that they had taken away her spirit. Again, Toby, I was lost. I felt more alone than ever and I didn't know what to do. I questioned the doctors relentlessly, but they swore that I would do her more harm than good by stripping away her medication. It was true, they conceded, that she was in some sort of a mental fog, but they felt she was safe in this purple haze and that she would be better in time. New drugs were on the way and they would be better and more aggressive towards the problem and less so on the rest of the person.

"All the while Emily felt that her mother was just a bitch - her words - and that taking drugs was just her selfish way of disconnecting with our world. I honestly tried to dissuade Emily on her thinking. I explained that she would understand it better when she was older. She was only beginning her teen years at this stage. She was so very young, but she was bright beyond her years and like most young girls of her age and intellect, she believed she knew more than most.

"I suppose that I was not very convincing because I could not be an actor. I held no strong convictions of my own on this matter. Secretly, so secret in fact I kept it from myself; I felt the same or at least similarly as Emily did. Kathleen was taking the drugs to disconnect from us. She was leaving us alone to fend for ourselves. It was just Emily, me, and some stranger who would cook and clean and smile a vacant smile. I would look into her eyes and I would see nothing."

Robert shudders there on the bench. He stands up and looks out into the sky. "God, forgive me. I had moments then that I wished that her body would follow her mind. I had moments," he said and the tears welled up in his eyes. "I had moments when I just wanted her to go away. Go, I thought and leave us be. It was too painful for me and for Emily. Emily turned all the colder towards Kathleen and in her own way she too disconnected from the family as well. All three of us were alone then and I could do nothing. Or I would do nothing." The tears in his eyes begin to blind him with its force and then his voice breaks. "I did nothing, Toby. Forgive me Kathleen," he says as if she were before him. "Forgive me."

* * *

It had taken a sharp rap on the door to bring him back. He grabbed for a hand towel and rubbed the water from his face and immediately regretted his choice of linen. It was one of Elizabeth's guest towels that she had always made clear should not be used. He patted the towel flat, folded it carefully and placed it back on the towel rack. He smiled mischievously knowing that Elizabeth would blame Henry and that that would help its offering of his night's entertainment.

"Good Lord, Robert, we were beginning to think you were going to retire in the washroom for the evening," said Elizabeth.

"Actually what Lizzie means to say," said Henry severely, "is …well we were beginning to think that you had perhaps nodded off on the john."

Shannon giggled and set the room off. Even Elizabeth couldn't refrain from a toothy grin.

"Was I gone all that long?" he asked with a feigned smile.

"Come and eat Robert. You've disrespected the great sacrifice that this duck has made for you enough for one evening," said Elizabeth.

"And what a noble sacrifice it was," he said. "Let's see to it that not a morsel remains left behind." He sat down, but still he was seeing the face in the mirror and the weight in his chest and belly was pulling him heavily to his chair. He smiled all around, but that too strained him.

After they ate, Shannon carried a cake from the kitchen, walking carefully as to keep the candles lit. Henry started the obligatory 'Happy Birthday' theme with enough audible force to make the more timid less reluctant to join in. It had been a task designated to him so often in the past that he no longer needed to be solicited to do so. Robert waved his hands around the room as though he was a symphony conductor and upon their completion he blew away the fire exhausting his lungs.

Mercifully no one had required a speech. Emily jumped up like a child calling for presents and before anyone could say a word the table before Robert was littered with packages. Socks and underwear from a practical Elizabeth; a fishing pole from an impracticable, but hopeful Henry Grifhorst, an array of shirts and ties from Maria which Elizabeth felt to be as wasteful a gift as that of Henry's. The shirts and ties were not to his tastes and Elizabeth saw them as just another ploy from a woman wishing to mold a man against his nature. Shannon presented him with a number of books that would not go unread and finally a package from Emily.

"What can this be?" he asked. "I've been spoiled enough for one year." He tore the paper away and squinted in confusion. "A computer?" he said almost incredulously.

"It's a laptop, dad."

"You must return this Emily. This must have cost a fortune."

"Don't be silly," she said.

"What would an old fool like me do with a laptop computer?"

"I should say a good deal more than fishing pole for a man who has no desire to fish," said Elizabeth.

"See here, Lizzie Montgomery. The man is going on vacation for two months and just why shouldn't he be expanding his horizons?" asked Henry. "Why, the old fool has worn the pages away on Ernest's "old man and the sea'. Why not live it and not just read about it?"

Words on the page, Robert thought. "Maybe I will try the fishing, Henry. Maybe the two of us can get out into Sheepshead bay on one of those fishing boats you're always going on about."

"That's the spirit, Monty," said Henry and then he stuck his tongue out at Elizabeth.

"Such disrespect," she said shaking her head. "And don't you be encouraging this old geezer," she said to Shannon while shaking her finger and scrunching up her face in mock severity.

"I thought that a laptop would be a useful tool to do something you always spoke of doing when you had some time," said Emily.

Robert lowered his eyes, but restrained his head from following suit. He knew that she spoke of his old dreams of writing a book. A dream that he always pushed off to the future and had, in recent years, shelved altogether. "I don't know, Em. I think maybe that ship has sailed for me."

"That's... what's the word I'm looking for?" she asked looking around the table. "I'm thinking b.s, but I don't think Aunt Elizabeth would forgive me anytime soon."

"I certainly would not," said Elizabeth.

"How about nonsense?" interrupted Shannon.

"Good," said Henry. "I was thinking poppycock myself."

"Why not tomfoolery?" interjected Elizabeth.

"Balderdash," erupted Henry.

"Drivel," said Emily. "That is just absolute drivel."

Maria wanted to join in, but she had never felt quite comfortable in these exchanges. At these times she felt more an acquaintance than part of the family. Henry, she had always felt, was more like family in this home and she envied him that.

"He's talking trash," said Henry. "Plain and simple bilge. Why," he said in mock British, "it's utter piffle. The man is talking idiocy."

"I may perhaps be biased, but I think I said it best when I said balderdash," said Elizabeth. "On the other hand, Shannon may have bested me with nonsense."

"Shannon trounced you, Lizzie. No contest," said Henry. "You were conquered, routed and thrashed."

"Thank you everybody," said Robert. "If we could all put away the thesaurus for a moment, I would like to say with deep affection that you were all much too generous with your gifts, but as I am such a wonderful individual I would like to accept these trinkets as graciously as possible." Robert lifted his teacup. "To a better family than a body deserves. I love you all so very much."

* * *

"Emily went to my den and proceeded to set up this new piece of technology. I was familiar with computers, of course. I had access at the school and in the library. I used them for the Internet and to type up my course requirements and to enter grades for my students and that sort of thing, but in my home this was foreign. It did not belong there. It did not belong there with me and again I felt that feeling, that sensation of sinking into an abyss. Emily was asking me to move on and I was struggling to hold on. Do you follow me, Toby? I was afraid that I would disconnect and there was Emily trying to plug me in to another outlet. The computer had a wireless card that put me on the Internet. The whole world came right inside my room."

Robert breathes the air in deeply and goes on. "Her gift was so very generous, but it became painful for me to have it about. How was I to sit down and put my thoughts to paper? Writing was something I believed I could do. To try now and fail would crush my spirit. To put words on a page and give them to Emily at this stage of my life could lead her to believe that there never was a talent. I would rather her believe that I had squandered a talent than to see that it had never existed.

"As a young man I had inspiration all around me, but that had faded into my past. Now I was an aged man with little passion and great despair. And while despair may do wonders for some it was purely destructive to me. This computer would be a constant reminder to me of my greatest fears, my past and future failures. And being afraid made me wish that my life were at an end.

"The computer would sit on my desk collecting dust and turning my little den, my haven of escape into a nightmare; a prison cell. A room I would avoid now and forever more. I didn't want to speak with Emily, because I knew she would ask me if I had been using it. Fortunately, she was always so busy; I wouldn't have to speak with her any time soon."

Robert is smiling. "Henry was another escape for me," he said. "Henry Grifhorst is my best friend in the world, Toby. I could confide in Henry and trust him to never betray me. As I said before, I never confided in anyone the way in which I confide with you now, but Henry came close. I can talk to him and I do, but something within me holds me back. I never fully let go. I never, at least not in any true sense, reveal myself."

Robert looks out to the river and says almost inaudibly, "I should think that none of us ever truly removes the mask entirely."

Toby stands up, surprising Robert and then sits down again without saying a word or even stretching. The old man barely moves on the bench. Robert wonders if birds ever landed upon his head or shoulders and if they did would he move or just sit there and let it be?

"I suppose," he continues, "you could say that Henry is a very complicated man, but most people who only think that they know him would say he was quite simple. Not simple in the mind," he explains as though he needs to defend his interpretation of the way others see Henry. "Just simple in the way he lives and has lived his life.

"Henry and I are practicing Catholics and belong to the same parish. Henry was born into Catholicism and I converted just prior to marrying Kathleen. Henry," he says with more than just a slight hesitation, "is what you might call a devout Catholic. He's a staunch member of the Saint Vincent de Paul society; he ministers to the poor and provides assistance to the needy. He collects food and delivers meals; he works the senior social club; he's an assistant for the sports league for boys and girls; he's an usher in the church at the Sunday morning mass and a Eucharistic minister for Sunday afternoon nursing home visits and he also assists for the Rite of Christian Initiation of Adults. Recently he suggested starting a prison ministry and pledged to govern that as well.

"Henry, you might say, lives for the church, but he differs from other devout Catholics in that Henry is an atheist."

* * *

It was the autumn of the season and the spring of their friendship. Robert and Henry were sitting upon barstools in Farrell's. They were each in the middle of their second pint of ale and talking on serious subjects. Henry was more forthright and it bothered him very little that Robert was less so. He was ready to be open and honest with a close friend and understood that it could be quite difficult to be on this plane for some.

Robert had known from previous conversations about where and when Henry had been born. It was in Duesseldorf, Germany during the war. The year was nineteen thirty-nine to be exact. "My father was a Nazi," Henry said. He was not looking at Robert. He held his beer mug close to his face and stared into it blankly. Robert nodded quietly glancing at Henry peripherally. He waited for Henry to resume or to change the subject. "I was six when the war ended," Henry continued. "I knew that my father was a soldier and that we children were to respect and to revere soldiers of the Fatherland."

Henry took a long drag on his cigarette and exhaled fiercely between his clenched teeth and nostrils. "We didn't speak of the war in my house. I was a child and so curfews carried no meaning to me. Air raid sirens, rationed goods and an absent father were a natural part of life. I knew no other way."

Henry gave pause for Robert to respond, but Robert waited furtively. "My mother kept us sheltered. In the aftermath of the war she attempted to keep the past at bay, but my father, struggling with his past, opened up those years to us."

"He needed to express his remorse?" asked Robert hopefully.

"No," said Henry. "He needed to justify what he had done."

Robert waited, but Henry held back. Robert looked into the mirror over the bar to see Henry struggling within himself. Henry needed to talk and Robert had to help him to do so. Robert felt somewhat hypocritical in playing that role, but Henry had something to get off his chest and he needed his friend to play that role. "What did he do?" he prompted.

"He led people into the gas chambers," Henry said stoically.

Robert closed his eyes feeling the horror. He took a deep breath and waited a moment searching his mind for the possibilities of a man in that position. "Maybe your father needed to justify his actions in order to survive the remainder of his life."

"My father was an ignorant man. I'm not interested in making excuses for him. He had charm and was considered attractive and I believe he had the ability to lead men, but only men like himself."

"Men like himself?"

"Strong men," he said, "with very little self-discipline to better themselves with hard work. They dedicated their lives to nothing and now they were going take by force what they couldn't merit through diligence. He could lead men with ambition only to take power and not to earn it. They were thugs, Robert and they had thug mentalities." Henry took a long draw on his beer and rested the glass against his forehead for a moment and then lowered it to the bar.

"You know the history as well as anyone. My father was just one of many ignorant men leading without a vision for direction. He was a big man, physically big, and powerfully built." Henry lowered his eyes. "He won the heart of my mother, but he was an ignorant man nonetheless."

Robert looked at his friend. Henry, too, was a big man. He was six feet four inches tall and he too was powerfully built. He had had blonde hair before it lost its color and his eyes were blue. He was the ideal prototype of Hitler's Aryan race. Robert could imagine Henry's father being much like Henry in his physical appearance. On only a few rare occasions had Robert seen Henry in a state of anger and although that anger had not been directed towards him, he would still feel somewhat intimidated by his bulk and by the explosiveness of that anger.

Robert wanted to speak, to console, but there was nothing to say that Henry hadn't already thought through. He simply nodded giving Henry his cue to continue.

"My father was a very young man when he and my mother married. He worked all sorts of jobs, but never moved up in any of them. He exhibited no aptitude and demonstrated even less patience. He joined the Nazi party because it was the simplest and fastest way to empowerment." Henry drew on his cigarette. "My mother explained this to me after his death," he said in anticipation of the question that Robert would not ask.

"He wanted to be an important man. He didn't understand the difference between fear and respect. He found it easy to hate people. He didn't understand the difference between fear and hate either I suppose."

"Most people find the line between the two a little blurred at times."

"I don't believe that. I think that they just wish to overlook the difference. In my father's case, though, I don't think he really did understand the difference." He paused a moment and narrowed his eyes. "Being a bully made him instantly superior."

"Are you really so certain about your father? Men of that generation were never very quick to express their feelings of that time."

"I wish I were wrong about him. I wish I had the slightest reason to doubt these feelings, but he always took me aside to let me know that he was on the side of the righteous. I never argued with him. What would be the point? He had to see the look in my eyes, though. He couldn't be as ignorant as all that."

"He was looking to provoke you?"

"Maybe he wanted a fight. Maybe he wanted me to confront him, but I never did."

"I think people like to turn their guilt into anger, Henry. I think that guilt eats away at the soul and that sometimes it's too difficult to confront it. Maybe your father needed to justify his actions to you. Maybe he needed you to tell him that he wasn't a bad man."

Henry looked at Robert and in his eyes Robert detected the slightest hint of hope. "Possibly," was all he managed to say in response.

Chapter Five

Robert woke earlier than usual in spite of the fact that his birthday celebration went on late into the evening with Henry being the last to leave. They shared the better part of a bottle of brandy and it had had little effect on him. His thoughts of the following day had kept him in check and the effect of that was somewhat sobering. He put on a pair of sweats and a tee shirt and went out to his yard carrying a tray with his tools and his teapot. Today was quite a bit warmer and he welcomed the morning sun in his eyes and its feel on his bare arms and face.

He set his teapot down on the little stone table and poured most of its contents into his cup as he did on most mornings. He took a small sip and then immediately went to work on his roses. He loosened the soil and plucked the few stray little weeds that had made their way up through the soil. He inspected the leaves carefully for any trace of spider mites and after finding a few he began to meticulously wash them off. Afterwards he pushed a steel skewer into the soil to make sure that the water had penetrated at least eighteen inches below the surface. When he was satisfied with this he began to prune them.

Elizabeth watched him from the kitchen window. It was something she liked to do. She liked that her brother was a gentle man. She appreciated his eye for detail when it came to his garden. Somehow he had managed to keep it in bloom throughout the spring, summer and fall and throughout the winter it had remained forever green. He made a little piece of the world a more beautiful place and she could use that place for her pleasure so long as she didn't interfere with it. It was his place and it was in his world and that world was his to mold. She learned along time ago not make suggestions or to offer opinions about the garden. He had been quite adamant about this. The garden and the third floor was his domain and she could do as she had pleased with the rest of the house.

When he was finished pruning the roses and the trees he took a little rake and cleaned the small clippings between the shrubs and collected them into a little pail. He then swept the patio and after, being satisfied with his labor, returned to the little stone table and reflected upon his progress. He would need to borrow Henry's car to pick up some mulch on the weekend and perhaps a flat or two of some mixed annuals. It needs more color, he thought. Also, he had wanted to experiment a little this season. His containers were different this year, but all else was pretty much the same and he thought that some change was needed to shake up his life a bit.

By this time his tea had grown cold, but it mattered little to him. He drank it down in one swallow and then just sat there admiring the climbing vines, which covered the low brick wall. The white and pink flowers on the vine were in bloom and his little yard cradled him now. He was at peace here and it felt good and today he would have wished to remain here in this little haven. He would like to have reread an old William Trevor novel that he had come across in a used bookstore a few days earlier, but that was not to be. He thought of the little laptop computer Emily had given him and he wondered if he could sit out here and actually write something that was worth the reading to someone else. He dismissed the thought as quickly as it had entered his mind. No, he thought, he couldn't do that.

"Robert," Elizabeth called from the kitchen. "You'll be late if you don't get washed up now."

"Mechanically, he glanced at his wristwatch, but the time did not register in his mind. He got up and made his way to the third floor and began his ritual shower and shave and when he came down the stairs Elizabeth saw in him the look of a condemned man. She said nothing about it to him, but she omitted the usual nagging and allowed him some quiet.

"I'll be late this evening, " he told her.

"Oh?" she said, somewhat surprised. Although he had been coming home later than usual, it was not like him to make an announcement. Typically his diversions had been unplanned and usually the doings of Henry Griffhorst.

"Yes," he said. "I'm going out with John McEntyre after work."

"Since when do socialize with John McEntyre?" she asked with more puzzlement in her voice than she had intended.

"John and I get together on occasion," he said almost defensively. "I've worked with the man for years," he said. "Why shouldn't we get together at the end of the school year?"

"I only meant that I had never heard of you and Mr. McEntyre getting together socially before. Not just the two of you in any case."

"Well it's not just socially, I suppose. He wished to speak with me on matters of the school and he uhh... we thought it best to do so more casually."

"I see," she said. She went to the stove and turned his eggs. She could see that he was troubled and chose not to persist in pointless questions. Robert rarely offered speech on his personal feelings and to pursue them usually meant pushing him further away. "What time should I expect you for dinner?" she asked furtively.

"I'll eat out tonight," he said. "John and I can grab a bite." He sat down then and ate some of the fruit that she had put out for him. "Don't wait up for me; I'll probably be a little late."

They ate quietly. Both were glancing at the newspaper, but neither read. They were both preoccupied this morning. He wondered about his future and she wondered about him. It was an uncomfortable silence for them and that was unusual because they rarely had been uncomfortable with one another before and silence had always played a large part in their time together. When he left the house she watched him walk all the way down the block until he turned the corner and disappeared from sight. She likened this moment to that of a mother seeing her child off to his first day of school.

Robert worked his way through the morning with as much spirit as could muster. He knew that he needed to be positive. It would be important today above all days to show the energy that he had always had for his position in the class and with the faculty. He believed that

John McEntyre would be offering him a package to leave and he knew that he would be turning that offer down. What he couldn't understand was why he had been going through such turmoil over this. He should have told John that he had no interest in retirement and that he should move on to someone else if he needed to make room. There were plenty others who would kill for this opportunity.

In the back of his mind, however, he could not understand why John would even come to him, above all people. He had made himself clear, many times over, that he had no interest in leaving and so why would the board even waste their time with him? Perhaps, he thought, John had other plans on his mind. Maybe John was looking to alter his position in some way. Maybe he was looking for Robert to take on more responsibilities. That was it, he decided. He'd been making himself sick for nothing. He'd been doing this to himself all of his life, he thought. He would let his mind, that ridiculous and vivid imagination of his, go off in tangents and assume the worst and then something totally unexpected would turn the tides and all would be well. More responsibilities, he thought. He could handle that. He would welcome that.

Robert had had many ideas concerning the program and how he believed it could be improved. He had spoken with some of his former students about coming back to tutor some of the freshmen and sophomore students. This did not only pertain to English literature, but to all subjects. He hadn't gotten any commitments, but he believed that to be a mere formality. When help was needed there were always people ready to step up and make the pledges needed. He spoke with John about this a year or perhaps two years ago and there had been real interest, but up until now nothing had transpired. That was my fault, he reflected. I dropped the ball on that.

He would spend his lunch making notes and working out a plan for the fall. It had been a very long time since he had been making preparations to make such changes and he now saw that it had been long overdue. He would look through his records and make a list of names of some of the people he believed would come through for him. He would make a long list knowing that most of them would have other commitments that would impede their desire of community service. He needed to discuss junior and senior programs to get these kids moving in the right direction towards college or into the workforce if continuing education was not an option. This could all be done through a student alumni program; a program that he had considered long ago, but had somehow gotten lost in time. There was much to do now and he only wished that he had gotten started sooner.

In any case, he thought, he would have the summer to work on his ideas and he would do it all on his time. He could use his office in the school and perhaps that laptop would come in to some use as well. Robert could feel that great weight lifting off of him and he was now able to breathe again. He had allowed himself to be down, but only for a short while. There was always hope, he believed, and only you could bring yourself down and only you could pick yourself up again.

Although Robert's office door was open, Maria knocked and peered in at him. "We missed you at lunch," she said.

He had been flipping through folders and making notes at a frantic pace. "I'm sorry," he said barely looking up at her. "I've quite a bit to do here."

"Anything I can do to help?" she asked.

He pulled his reading glasses from his face. "Yes," he said. "If you are willing."

"I'm willing," she said.

He told her of his plans and what he'd hope to accomplish in the short and in the long terms. He was excited in a way that she had never seen before and she would be happy to be a part of it. While he spoke with passion of what they could do for these young people, she could not help but to think what it could do for them. They had never worked together before and this seemed a project with such ambition that they would need to spend countless hours together.

Immediately she had offered the use of her home office and that of her high speed internet connection. She suggested that they correspond with all would-be volunteers and students alike via email. She would set up an account for each of them for this sole purpose and suggested that she maintain it. Maria also suggested that they design a website link through the school that would enable them to make announcements and offer directory assistance.

Singularly, Robert's mind worked quickly, but together with Maria the ideas multiplied faster than they could record them. It had been a short brainstorming session that would be interrupted by the class bell, but not before she would voice her concerns of an early meeting with John McEntyre. "Put him off for a day or so," she urged. "Let us first get our ideas into writing. You can come over to my place tonight and we'll put together a syllabus with our objectives and the main points that will aid in achieving them. We...," she said and then hesitated, "you need to show John that you're serious and that you've done the work to prove it."

"I don't know that I can put him off," he said. "I told him that I'd meet with him this afternoon."

"We have to put him off," she said. She took his hand and squeezed it gently. "You have great ideas and there is still so much you can offer this school. We need you here, Robert. We all need you very much." She let his hand go and stood up. "I see what you mean to those kids. They don't look up to any of us as they do you, Robert."

"That's not true. You..."

"It is true," she interrupted. "They need you as much as you need them. You must put John off another day at least." She turned her back to him and faced the window. "You have to be prepared or..." She stopped abruptly, at a loss for words. She could feel his eyes on her back and then mercifully the bell rang. "I have to get to class," she said.

"Or what?" he asked.

She looked at him then. "Put John off for another day," she said. She was pleading with him. Her eyes betrayed her and he knew then that he had been right. It had astonished him that she, too, had had her suspicions. He did not know at that moment whether or not he would be able to carry on, but his options were limited and the alternatives would leave him stricken.

"Yes," he said forcefully enough to startle to her. She jumped a little as he stood up. "Yes, Maria, I will put him off for a day at least. Perhaps you could tell him that something had come up and that I would be glad to meet with him tomorrow or whenever is convenient to him." The second bell rang which meant that classes had begun. "Wait until after classes are dismissed, will you?"

"Of course," she said. She smiled and hugged him briefly. "I'll see you tonight?"

"Yes," he said. "Six o'clock alright?"

"Six," she said and hurried off to her class.

Robert sat down and then remembered his class. "Oh," he said to the empty room. "I'm late for class."

His last two periods went well enough, but he had been a little tense. He was afraid that John might, at any moment, appear at the door to confirm their appointment. When the last bell had rung, he picked up his briefcase and immediately left the school without stopping in to his office, as was his usual routine. He started off for home, but then thought better of it. He had no desire to explain himself to Elizabeth and was in no mood for the exchanges that would inevitably take place if he had made any attempts to dodge her line of questioning.

He stopped in a little bookstore that he had frequented over the years, but felt no solace in the rows upon rows of bookshelves. While perusing the titles he found that he had already read all that was of interest to him and had, in fact, already possessed many of them. In any case he felt that this was not the time to get lost in another world and yet he was in desperate need to find a comfortable distraction. Farrell's was out of the question as there was the possibility that John might appear and so he left the bookstore and made his way to a pay telephone on the corner.

Henry answered the phone on the third ring and agreed to meet with him at an alternate pub. He was not one to press his friends for explanations when they seemed a little hesitant and not quite forthcoming. He knew that Robert would have his reasons and that he would reveal himself in his own good time. He said that he would be there in twenty minutes and to have a cold one waiting for him.

Twenty minutes later and they were already in deep conversation. "Do you ever miss the work, Henry?" Robert asked.

"It's a little complicated," he said. "I do miss the work. When you're good at something and follow through the way I did…" he stopped. "What is it?" he asked.

"What do you mean?"

"Never mind," he said. "I started my own company and it grew into the millions when millions still meant something. I was smart and tough, but it took its toll on me. I put a lot into that company and took a lot away from it, but I lost something there." Henry swallowed down his beer and gestured to the barman for another. "I didn't like who I was," he said. "I was mean in the business world. I was sharp and efficient and ruthless. The more the company grew the less tolerant I became. I wasn't apt to give second chances and found myself berating people for their shortcomings. I paid well and demanded more. I didn't want to hear about family obligations," he said. "My people learned quickly not to seek time off for the class play or the dance recitals or the little league games of their children. I paid them well to be there for as long as it took and that meant a lot of hours."

"They didn't have to stay, Henry."

Henry looked at his friend. "That's what I told them, Monty. That's exactly what I told them, but I knew better than that." He shook his head. "Once you get used to making that kind of money it's damned near impossible to go back. The money pays for the biggest house on the block and the nicest car in the driveway; it pays for the private schools where the kids are safe and well educated; it pays for the dance lessons and the personal hitting instruction; it pays for the country club and the green fees; it pays for wardrobe and all its accessories. The money feeds the ego like a drug feeds the nervous system and once you get hooked on it you find yourself perpetually chasing that high.

"It wasn't the money for me, though. It was the power that drove me. I liked wielding that power over my people. I liked growing the company and crushing the competition along the way. A game I played, Monty. It was a game that I played, but people got hurt in my game. The money was a necessary tool, of course. Money motivates people," he said. "It makes them ugly; it makes them do ugly things." Henry turned and slapped Robert on the back. "That's why I like you," he said with affection.

"Because I'm not ambitious and have little motivation?" he asked.

Henry laughed. "Yes, I suppose that's it, my old friend. "You have principles, Robert. You live by a code of ethics and money never played a role in your life."

"Perhaps," he said, "I was just a little too apprehensive to reach for the brass ring."

"Is money all that important to you?" Henry asked

"No," he answered honestly, "but it would be nice to have."

"You're talking about survival money. You're not talking about keeping up with the Jones' or keeping the Jones' in your rear view mirror." Henry took a long draw on his beer and motioned for another and one for his friend. "I liked the power," he said getting back on track. "I only had men in the top positions. It wasn't because I thought them superior to women, on the contrary. I found that it was easier for me to manipulate men. I had their wives on my side."

Robert was puzzled. "How do you mean?"

"On the one hand the women wanted their husbands' home at night. They expected them to make the ball games and the school plays and the dance recitals; they expected them to own up to the family obligations. On the other hand, they too got addicted to the money and they had more time to spend it. All but one of my top people had domestic help to tend to the housework, garden and for some even the children. They would make their husbands feel guilty for being an absentee father and husband and charge that to them being career driven workaholics. The men, though, had little choice. They needed the money to pay for all of the things that they never truly needed. They had become slaves to lives they couldn't enjoy and I never failed to let them know that they didn't have to stay. If the schedule was too tough or if the work too demanding they were free to leave at any time of their choosing. I wasn't holding them there.

Henry pushed his beer away from him. "I would even offer them a good reference. Nice guy, ha? I was playing with them," Henry said with disgust in his voice. "Over time, for the women, the men became nothing but a paycheck and a false sense of security and for the men, those poor bastards, the job became an escape from the homes that they had earned."

Robert looked at Henry incredulously. "That's horrible, "he said." He wanted to say more, but he was stunned. Instead he finished the beer he'd been drinking and reached for the one that Henry had just ordered for him.

"It was horrible. One day I was fortunate enough to realize just how horrible I was. That was the day I decided to sell off all of my interests in the company and start my life again."

"How, exactly, did you come to this realization?"

"I had gotten into a heated argument with an employee of mine. You see I had him place a rather large order for some machine parts with a small company. This company had to go into deep debt to finance the equipment to make said parts. I pulled the order when a competitor of theirs made a last minute better offer. My guy made the deal on a handshake and now the little company was going to go under. My guy liked this man and knew his family well. We'd done a lot of business over the years and after a while he'd done more and more work for us. His company was still on the small side in comparison to mine, but it was flourishing. Unfortunately he had put all of his resources into supporting us. When I pulled our business, he was virtually ruined. I maintained that it was his fault for putting all of his eggs into one basket. My guy saw things differently. He maintained that a deal, whether it was on paper or on a handshake, was a deal. His word, he said, meant something. He lectured me about honor, morality and integrity. He said he couldn't just stand by and watch a man and his people be ruined by my greed. I told him that he was being weak and that business was business and not to make it personal. I pointed out moments in his life where his greed had prevailed. I could see that these truths hurt him. He stood up to me and I shot him down."

Henry pulled his beer back in close to him. "Then," he said, "he told me he quit. Just like that, Robert, after thirteen years with me, he quit. He had no other prospects that I knew of. He was in debt up to his eyeballs and he quit." Henry drank down half the beer and said, "he told me he wouldn't work for a nazi."

It was a little past six before Robert took notice of the time. He apologized to Henry for rushing off, but did not explain. He simply left Henry sitting in a strange bar where he was not surrounded by friends or familiarity. Henry would stay and have two more beers fighting the desire to sulk and wonder why it was that Robert had brought him there in the first place and why he had left him in the second.

Robert left the bar and walked to a car service office on the next block. He reached Maria's apartment building ten minutes later. He was forty minutes late, but still entered hesitantly. He did not know her apartment number and subsequently rang three other bells before he was directed to 5B. There was no elevator in this building and so he had to climb the five flights to the top floor. The climb was three flights more than he was used to and they proved difficult. He found himself struggling after three flights and feeling that he was in need of oxygen by the fourth. On the stairs between the fourth and fifth floors he tried to regain his composure, but his efforts were futile. Two apartment doors opened to peer out at him and he quickly made for the fifth floor.

Maria was waiting with her own door open and after seeing his state; she ran down the last few steps to offer him assistance. "My God, she said, are you alright?"

"Yes, yes," he said fighting back the urge to gasp for air. "I'm fine. I was just admiring the architecture. Is that the original crown molding?" he asked pointing up to the crumbling worn wood that bordered buckling and cracked plaster walls.

"I suppose under the forty coats of lead paint it might possibly be," she replied. Another door opened and a woman peered out and then she, too, closed her door.

"People are a bit nosy in my building," she explained. "Let me get you inside where you can catch your breath."

He wanted to protest the help, but his body wouldn't allow him to do so and upon sitting down heavily in an armchair he exhaled through his mouth and inhaled through flared nostrils. He took the proffered water from her. She had always kept a glass ready upon the arrival of her guests.

"I'm used to the climb," she said with pride. "Most people might have trouble with it so I don't often entertain."

"I should imagine that it might be difficult for some," he said sputtering through gasps of air. He drank some more of the water and rested it gently on a ceramic coaster on a little sideboard. "Beautiful place you have here," he said while attempting to take it all in.

"Thank you," she said almost grimly. "It's a bit smaller than the old place, but I'm comfortable here," she said in a matter-of-fact tone that justified the apartment. "It's inexpensive and practical for someone in my situation."

He knew that she was explaining herself and he thought it funny how people, even he, often felt the need to do so. To tell her that there was no need for it would be considered insulting and so they both must be uncomfortable for a moment until other words would grant them an easement. "I appreciate your help," he said. "I know you have better things to do with your time."

"No," she protested. "I have nothing more important than this. We can do a lot of great things together. You have great ideas and I have some skills that will get them implemented. We can do this," she said.

"What did John say?" he asked.

"He said tomorrow would be fine," she said as she walked towards the kitchen. "I chilled a bottle of Merlot if you're interested."

"That would be great," he said. He got up and followed her into the kitchen. "Let me help you with that."

Maria carried the glasses into the living room and placed them on a glass table. Robert opened the bottle and followed her. He did not take notice of her lighting the candles while he filled the glasses. He sat down on the sofa and became all business. He did not leave her apartment until one in the morning.

* * *

"It was a wonderful evening, Toby. Maria and I shared ideas well into the night. She's a very bright woman, you know. Her mind works so well and with such clarity," he says with a sparkle in his eye. With pride he says, "I was pretty sharp myself that evening. I will be forever in her debt. She really wanted to do this, but I don't think it was as much for the school as it was for me and I suppose that was my main objective as well. I feel ashamed of myself, now that I think back on it. I had never been a self-serving man in my estimation, although if I were to be honest, I suppose living in a frequent state of escape can be considered somewhat self-serving. In any case our ideas were good and constructive and would benefit many people other than me for years to come. Maria and I were like politicians that night and we were building a campaign for a better future. I was running for reelection and she was my top advisor, campaign manager and personal aid.

"The time had passed so quickly that evening that I just couldn't believe it. Not in so very long a time had my mind worked so well. I tell you, Toby, I was drunk with happiness. I was as giddy as a schoolboy and never had I felt so positive and optimistic about life. I was a new man and instead of greeting the following day with dread, I was going to embrace it."

Toby stands up and, to Robert's surprise; he expels a significant amount of intestinal gas. He then proceeds to adjust himself and then sits back down and reaches into his bag for another nut. Robert starts to laugh and after a while his entire body shakes with its intensity. "Are you trying to tell me something?" he asks. It is a while before he can get the laughter under control. "I must admit for a man with such an economy of words, you do tend to get your point across. A gesture, too, is worth a thousand words."

* * *

When Elizabeth woke, she was greatly surprised to see Robert tending to his garden. He did not get in until well past one o'clock in the morning. She knew this because she had been reading in her bed for part of the night and when she was too sleepy to read, she began to pace the floor in her room. Upon hearing the front door open, Elizabeth turned out her light and got into her bed and pulled the covers up to her chin. She could hear the floorboards in the old stairs creak tenderly as Robert went up on tiptoe.

"Good morning," she said as he came in through the back door and into the kitchen.

"Good morning to you," he said and kissed her gingerly on the cheek. "Smells good," he said referring to the sausage in the pan. "It's a beautiful day out there, Elizabeth."

She looked out of the window. "It's quite overcast," she replied. "They say rain and I dare say they'll be right for a change."

"I think a little clouding over makes everything appear a little greener," he said jubilantly. "The rain will make it so."

"What time did you get in last night?" she asked. "I drifted off rather early in the evening."

"I'm not really sure," he said. "I suppose on the late side. I hope I didn't wake you."

"No, not at all," she said. "I could sleep through a train wreck. You," she said to him on close examination, "look rather merry this morning. Did your meeting with John go well last night?"

"Actually, I'll be seeing him this evening," he said. He was not quite telling her a lie, but his omission of the facts was misleading and he felt somewhat deceitful. He decidedly let the feeling go and chose to move on. "I have some ideas to discuss with him and I'm rather eager to put them out there."

"Well don't be staying out there all night again," she slipped. "You need your rest. You're not quite as young as you used to be."

"I am young," he declared forcefully. "I'm not yet dead and I won't lie about waiting to die."

"I just meant…" she started, but went back to the turn the sausages in the pan. Her face went flush. "I did not mean to imply that you were old, Robert," she said testily. "I just meant that…"

"I know, dear," he said. "I wasn't really snapping at you." He put his arms around her and gave her an uncharacteristic hug. Elizabeth, caught a little off guard, hugged him back, but more gently and almost non-committal in her manner.

"I'll try not to be so late, but I can't promise. Please don't wait up or worry about dinner." He turned and started for the stairs. "Why," he said stopping sharply, "don't you get out tonight?" he asked. "Call up some of the ladies and make a night of it. You haven't been out in a dog's age."

"Maybe I will," she said to his back. "Don't dawdle," she said. "Your breakfast will be ready in a few minutes." She shook her head and exhaled sharply. "I just don't understand the male mind," she said to the sausage. "You would think that a man of his years would know his place in the world by now, wouldn't you? Frightful bunch, the lot of them," she said. In frustration, she pulled hard on the refrigerator door and the eggs went flying out of their little compartment. Elizabeth frowned at the mess on the floor. "We'll be having our eggs scrambled this morning, Robert," she called up the stairs.

At the end of the last bell Robert again had asked Maria to accompany him in his meeting with John McEntyre as he had the previous evening and again during lunch, but she declined. "It'll be alright," she promised. "Speak with conviction as you did last night," she said. She grasped his shoulders and fought the urge to shake him. "You were so passionate in your plans and so sure about your strategy last night and it gave me great confidence in you. You must," she said fiercely, "move John the way you did me." She released him from her grip and adjusted his jacket. She tugged lightly at his lapel and smoothed out any wrinkles over his shoulders and sleeves. "Convince him of your clarity, Robert."

"My what?" he asked.

"Clarity," she stammered, "clarity in your vision. You see it all, Robert. You see the future for these boys and girls and you can help them to improve upon it. Believe in yourself and others will believe in you."

There were tears in her eyes and Robert looked at her curiously. "Alright, Maria, I will." He smiled and gently wiped the tears from her cheeks with his thumbs. He brushed them gently to the sides of her face and then kissed her on the forehead. "This work," he said, "is as much yours as it is mine."

"No," she said. "This is all you. I just helped you to get in on paper. You've drawn up these blueprints in my head for so many years that they are imbedded into my mind like an old favorite song."

"Is that true?" he asked.

"Yes," she said.

"Why haven't I done something like this before?"

"I don't know," she answered.

Robert turned away from her and stared out of the window in his little office. "Why am I doing it now?"

Maria lowered her head a fraction of an inch. "I don't know," she lied. "I am glad that we are doing this now, though."

"Necessity is the mother of all inventions," he said still looking out of the window. "Look how green everything looks in the rain," he said. "My garden will be pleased and I'll be well rewarded."

"Will you bring me a rose?"

He turned to her and said that he would. "I should probably get going, Maria. I told John that I'd meet him there at three-thirty. Are you sure…," he said and stopped. "Thank you," he said and touched her shoulder. He stepped around her and walked out of the office and out of the building and into the street. It would be all right, he thought to himself. I'll make my case.

When he walked into Farrell's, John McEntyre was already sitting at the bar. He had a scotch in his hand and was engaged in a conversation with the bartender. Robert wanted to turn and walk away and this made him feel a fool. He felt like a child in a doctor's office. "Hello, John," he said hastily, denying himself any chance of retreat.

McEntyre turned to face him and smiled. "Robert," he said haughtily as though his appearance was a surprise to him. "I was afraid you'd forgotten me."

"No, not at all," he said. Robert looked at his watch and saw that it was nearly four. I do apologize for being late," he said. "A few pressing matters at the school kept me later than I realized," he lied.

"It doesn't matter," he said dismissing the need for Robert's apology. "You're here now and that's all that really matters. Would you mind if we took a table?" he asked while gesturing towards one in a corner.

"A table would be fine," he said and followed the big man to the back of the bar. John McEntyre seemed an even larger being when presented from the rear. He had huge shoulders, a very broad back and legs like tree trunks. He was a wall of a man, Robert thought. It was only his face that made him seem non-threatening. He was a kind man with a warm smile and a gentle disposition. He would have been well suited for politics, Robert thought. He was a proven administrator and a very articulate speaker. He was still a young man, but he ought to move quickly, otherwise, Robert thought, he would grow old fast and his time would pass.

"Robert," McEntyre began, "I speak for the whole board when I say that you have been a tremendous asset to our school and to your students in particular."

A politician, Robert thought. "Well I appreciate that, John." He picked up his briefcase and began fumbling with the clasp. "It's the students that must come first," he said.

"Your service over so many years, dedicated years," he added hastily, "has been most generous."

"Well it did come with a paycheck," he said. "There we are," he said more to the briefcase than to McEntyre upon releasing its clasp. He began to retrieve the syllabus that he and Maria constructed the night before.

"Robert, I am please to present to you a package..."

"This, John," Robert said as he handed the syllabus to McEntyre, "is my plan for the school." It was a bad beginning, he thought. He was tired now and wished he had had time to think more about what he wanted to say. It was all in his mind, but speaking out loud was unnerving. He needed to practice in front of a mirror as he did when he himself was a student preparing for a speech for a class or a mandatory debate. He had been moderately successful in those appearances, because he'd prepared so diligently. Now he was ill prepared and it was at the wrong time. He needed to step up and put the pressure of it aside and move ahead. All this was going through his mind and he thought it silly.

"Robert," McEntyre said, "I have this package plan to discuss with you."

"Yes," Robert said dismissing McEntyre altogether. "I too have a plan and if you have a moment, I'd like to discuss it with you."

McEntyre looked at the proposal in his hand. He was somewhat stunned and at a loss for words. "A plan?" he asked. "I don't..."

"Yes, a plan," he said.

"Actually, I was here to present you with a plan and..."

"I understand, John, but before we discuss your plan, I'd like to discuss mine. I have several key points in there that ought to be addressed. It will take a bit of time and, perhaps, some funding, but I think very little of the latter. The time will come mostly at a voluntary expense and the funding can be done through fundraisers. It's all in my proposal."

"Robert, I think we're getting ahead of ourselves here." McEntyre shifted uncomfortably in his chair. The barman, bringing over two scotches, was a welcomed distraction. He made some light chit chat with the two patrons and then moved on. John and Robert were left facing each other with little to say, although much dialogue was well needed.

"It's all in there," Robert persisted.

McEntyre looked wide-eyed at Robert and then down at the syllabus. It had been presented nicely in a hard plastic slipcover. He opened it up and perused the pages quickly and without his full attention. Robert sensed this and put his hand on McEntyre to stop him. "We need to go through this carefully, John. You need to fully understand what it is that I'm presenting to you. I need for you to believe in this and in me and to take it up with the board."

"Okay, Robert," he said. He understood Robert's position in that moment, but still he needed for Robert to understand his position. "We'll discuss your plans, but I also need for you to hear me out."

"Agreed," said Robert. "I hope you're not in any hurry tonight."

"No, Robert," he lied. "Just let me make a phone call and then we'll hash all of this out." McEntyre excused himself to call his wife and explain his situation to her. His wife, already being privy to her husband's dilemma, was sympathetic and encouraged his benevolence. "He's a good man, John," she needlessly reminded him.

"I know, Carol," he said.

"Isn't there...," she started and stopped.

"I'll see you later, honey," he said and hung up the phone. He went back to Robert who'd already started on his second scotch. "I really need to get a cell phone," he said. "Most of the students have them and I'm still looking for pay phones."

"I know what you mean," Robert agreed. "Pay telephones are getting harder and harder to find. On the other hand I should think a cell phone to be somewhat intrusive. I find more and more often that while engaged in a conversation other people tend to drop you, albeit temporarily, to answer the bloody thing."

"It's also a little harder to go into hiding for a few moments," McEntyre added. "With a cell phone you can always be tracked down. It's good for parents to have their teens carry them about, but when I was a teen I know I wouldn't have been too happy to have my parents know where I was at every moment. I liked getting lost," he said conspiratorially. McEntyre shifted a little in his chair and sat up a little taller. His manner, while still congenial, also shifted to a more serious demeanor.

"Robert," he said, "you are at tier one status with more than thirty years of service under your belt. This means that in addition to the two years of service credit that you're already approved for you also get an additional one month of service credit tacked on for each year of service that you have given us. That's nearly three additional years plus the two that I had mentioned. The board is also offering you a number of local incentives that we can discuss." It was now McEntyre's turn to fumble with his briefcase and the papers within it. "I have here a formal offer from the board, Robert, for you to look over. Of course I don't expect you to sign it tonight, but I would like to go over it with you step by step so that you can be comfortable with your eventual decision. There are also more learned people down on Water Street whom I urge you to discuss this with in the event that there is something that I overlooked. Believe me, I wouldn't fully trust my own judgment concerning something this important," he said with a curt laugh.

"I appreciate all the time you've taken on this, John, and I will look through this briefly out of respect to you, but I must say and I believe that you already knew coming in to this evening that I have no desire to retire my position in the school."

"Robert, I don't want you to retire either," he said. "I think we need more men like you."

"Then we can put this part of the evening on the shelf and move on to the more important part of improving the school."

"Not quite," said McEntyre wearily. "I'd like to, Robert. There's nothing that would make me happier, but I'm not really here on my own behalf." McEntyre rested his head in his hands. He rubbed his face vigorously and pulled at his collar. "I'm being pressured into offering these retirement incentives in an effort to cut costs, Robert. With your accumulation of years and status, you are at the higher pay scale and that is where they are determined to cut. The package that's being offered won't put you at any financial disadvantage, but it will shift funds for the board. They can offer a young teacher less pay."

"If that's the problem, John," Robert said solemnly, "you can make this pitch to a number of other qualified tier one status employees who would kill for the chance to take an early retirement."

"There will be others, Robert. Unfortunately I don't make the final decisions. That's up to others."

"The powers that be," said Robert.

McEntyre averted his eyes away from him. He motioned for the bartender to make two more and then stood up to retrieve the drinks. Robert sat motionless in his chair and looked down at the file that John McEntyre had laid before him. When McEntyre returned with the drinks, Robert asked about a reduction in his pay. "The union would never allow that," he replied.

Robert searched his mind for a solution. "What about my plan?" he said jabbing his finger on the table.

"You're plan?" said McEntyre visibly taken aback.

"Yes," he said motioning McEntyre to look at the syllabus before him.

"You're plan," he said almost with glee. "Of course, yes. Forgive me." McEntyre welcomed the shift in subject matter and began reading through Robert's document. He began reading quickly and then slowed down to scrutinize it more carefully. "There's some good stuff in here," he said. He continued to read, his face a studied look. "I see you've given this a lot of thought," he added.

"A great deal," Robert assured him. "I believe in this, John. I think there is always much to do and perhaps we've become complacent in deference to routine. I want to do more," he said.

McEntyre lowered the pages to the table, but kept them in his grasp. "Robert, this is not about your work ethic. If anything, you've given more to your students and the school than most, if not all, of us. It is a matter of politics and number crunching. I don't want you to think…"

"I'm beginning to feel like a jilted lover. 'It's not you, it's me.' I can read between the lines, John, but there's plenty I can do."

"I know that."

"Those words," he said, again gesturing to the syllabus. "They're not only words. They represent something bigger. I can do a lot of good," he pleaded.

"I'll take this up with the board," he said. "I can't promise anything, but I'll fight for you. I believe in you." McEntyre looked down again at Robert and Maria's power-point presentation. "Do you really think that you can get the volunteers to come in and make this program work? People get busy," he said doubtfully.

"Yes, John, I think I can. People do get busy, but when something greater is at stake they come together. If there's anything I've learned in my life it is that people bond for two reasons," he said. "Love and hate," he contended. "They'll come together for love, John. They'll come together for the love of a past life, for love of their fellow man and for their love of me, John. They'll come to make a difference," he said passionately. "I do believe in this."

* * *

"And I did believe, Toby. I think people are fundamentally good and that most, under the right circumstances, are willing to extend themselves to make a difference in the life of another. I know that I was struggling," he said. "I was grasping at something and John, also a fundamentally good man, would have loved to have thrown me that life preserver. His back, I knew, was against the wall, but I also knew that he would go to bat for me."

Robert stands up and watches the water in the river rushing by carrying twigs in its current. "I could see it in his eyes, Toby. He read those pages and saw the possibilities. I felt as though I'd been in some way vindicated. Perhaps I would be given a stay for at least a while. It was my plan to hang on. No quitter am I, old friend," he said and smiled. "The plan was to survive and to make a difference along the way. I don't deny that my motives weren't somewhat selfish, but a man needs a reason to live."

Robert squints at the sun, which has been fighting its way through the clouds. "I believed, Toby. I gave John the ammunition to fight for me and believed that I would come out victorious."

* * *

Chapter Six

A light rain started to fall as Elizabeth made her way into the restaurant. Damn, she thought as she peered through the glass pane. I should always go with my gut and not with what they say, she thought referring to the weather forecast. Clear skies had been promised for the evening, but now there was rain and the sky above had been growing increasingly sinister.

"Elizabeth," called Doris Gladstone from a table in the rear.

Elizabeth turned and smiled and then squeezed her way through the snugly placed tables and made her way to Doris, Elsa Brightman, and Nettie Tubman. "Hello ladies," she said gaily.

"We took the liberty," said Nettie as she gestured towards the bottle of red on the table.

"You took the liberty of liberating three quarters of the bottle as well," retorted Elizabeth.

"It's the early bird that catches the worm," snorted Elsa.

"You've drained a liter of tequila as well?" said Elizabeth. At that they all laughed a whooping and oft chirping sound that evoked many smiles in the quaint dining room.

Elizabeth poured herself as tall a drink as her glass would allow and then proceeded to compliment Doris on her hat, Elsa on her blouse and Nettie on her handbag. Similar acclamations were, as was expected, showered upon her and then the usual niceties about a recent sermon, a superb meal, or good movie were exchanged before getting down to the real business of the dirt. The dirt was the gossip on all those not in attendance and it had always started out as guarded and furtive whispers before the eventual full blown discussions punctuated with noises and grunts of revolt and disapproval. The eyes would roll, but never would they fail to register and record the look of those before them.

Sharing the dirt and provoking the disapproval of the others was quite gratifying business and if one could make the eyes of another widen and have their jaw drop simultaneously, their work was done and done well to boot. Each would strive to hold the juiciest of tidbits for the last, but that was not so easy a task as there was no certainty of who else may be holding the very same ace. Each in turn had to keep the others in check and test them gently with hints as to the subject matter lest they be bested on material. Doris Gladstone had the best material of the evening, but she would not reveal it until the meal was done and the coffee served.

Elsa Brightman believed that it was she who held the evening's gem, but she could not hold off any longer. Nettie had ordered the chicken breast and she was notorious for picking it clean in what seemed like an insurmountable amount of time. Elsa watched as Nettie scoured each bone with the tine of her fork until she could stand it no longer. "Mrs. Fenton," she said, "is struggling with the urge to have an affair." Elsa proceeded to scour her own finished plate with an air of nonchalance, but as expected the others would have none of it.

"Is this true?" intoned Elizabeth.

"It is," said Elsa with certainty.

"Who is your source?" demanded Nettie who had now abandoned the chicken breast.

"My source," Elsa said and leaned into the table, "is myself."

"Mrs. Fenton confided such a thing with you?" Elizabeth asked doubtfully.

The others waited as Elsa squirmed a bit in her chair. "Not exactly," she admitted. "I accidentally overheard her telling someone else."

"You were eavesdropping, Elsa Brightman?" Nettie chastised.

"As if you've never done that, Nettie," Elizabeth rebuffed.

Nettie gasped and then shrugged as if to accept the rebuff. "Well?" Nettie asked, "Who was it that Mrs. Fenton was telling?"

Elsa looked about the room conspiratorially. "This does not leave this table."

"Of course not," they all agreed.

Elsa looked at the others suspiciously and then revealed herself. "It was in the church," she said.

"In the church," said Elizabeth. "She was talking about such a thing in the church? Who was she telling, Elsa?"

"It was Father Donovan," she said and gestured to the waiter for some coffee.

"She was telling that to her priest?" asked Doris. "Is that a normal practice for you Catholics?"

"It is if it's in the confessional," Elizabeth said in Horror. "Is that what you're telling us Elsa? You eavesdropped in the confessional?"

"Well," said Elsa as her face reddened. "It wasn't on purpose. I walked up to cleanse my sins and Mrs. Fenton was in the box. I didn't even know it was she until she came out from the curtain."

"We have doors now, Elsa."

"Yes, but there's the curtain in between," she reasoned. "It echoes a little," she explained. "I wasn't trying to hear, you know. It just happened."

"Should you be telling us this, Elsa? I mean the confessional is private," said Elizabeth.

"The confessional is between God, the priest and the sinner," said Doris. "There really isn't any precedence on Elsa," she resolved to the others. "What else did she say, dear?"

"Enough," said Elizabeth. "Leave Mrs. Fenton be. It doesn't mean she's cheated on Mr. Fenton in the physical sense. It merely means that she's cheated in her heart as even former president Carter has admitted to. There's a difference," she said. "I suppose, though," she continued, "it wouldn't hurt to keep an eye on her."

Doris and Nettie acted surprised at Elizabeth's last remark, but their eventual and mischievous smiles proved that the act was just that. The busboy came and cleared away the remaining dishes while the waiter served the coffee. "I think I'd like to try the pecan pie," Doris said to the waiter.

"Apple a la mode," intoned Elsa in her singsong upbeat voice.

Nettie couldn't decide and said she would have whatever Elizabeth was having until Elizabeth ordered an apple crumb. "No, no," Nettie protested. The crumb is much to dry for me."

"Hence the apple," Elizabeth objected.

"I think I'll try the key lime pie," she said. "No, no," she said, halting the waiter in his tracks. "Maybe I'll go with the chocolate mousse cake instead."

"Are you crazy?" Elsa objected. Don't you remember the last time you had the chocolate mousse cake and what it did to your stomach?"

"Let her eat her cake," Doris snapped. She had something to say and she would wait no longer.

"I'll just have the shortbread," said Nettie.

"Because it's so moist," Elizabeth said under her breath. Nettie gave Elizabeth a curt look and then sipped at her coffee.

"So Elizabeth, do tell us," said Doris sipping her coffee daintily.

"Do tell what?" Elizabeth asked suspiciously and with all due caution. She didn't like the way Doris was sipping her coffee. Doris was one to slurp at her coffees and teas and now it was obvious that she was putting on airs and considering that Elizabeth was whom she were addressing, Elizabeth had every right to be concerned. This was the set up for Doris and the meal had just been cleared. This was her playing field and Elizabeth had just been made the opponent.

Doris lowered the cup to its saucer and took her napkin from her lap and dabbed at the corners of her greedy mouth. "About Robert," she said coaxing the moment along.

"I don't follow," said Elizabeth. "If there's something you wish to say Doris, I suggest that you just say it."

"There's really no need to get defensive, Elizabeth. Truly I think it's wonderful and I'm honestly quite happy."

"I'm not following, Doris," said Elizabeth sharply. She was now quite annoyed and considered to let some things that she had kept quiet about in the past to be revealed.

"What is it, Doris?" Nettie said sounding almost as perturbed as Elizabeth. "Don't play this game with one of us."

"I don't what you mean," Doris said defensively, but of course she did. "I'm only referring to Robert and that nice school teacher, Ms. Scapelli," she said. "I think it's nice for them to have found each other after all of this time.

Elsa and Nettie raised their dyed eyebrows high up on their foreheads. "What's this?" they both inquired and turned to Elizabeth for lore.

Elizabeth's face went white and she felt a sensation of paralysis going throughout her body. "I haven't the foggiest," she managed to say as she struggled with her composure. "You might like to fill us all in, Doris."

"Oh dear," she said narrowing her eyebrows to exemplify her concern. "I hope I haven't let anything out of the bag."

"Well you know damn well that you can't put it back in, Doris," said Nettie with assured sarcasm. "You may as well fill us in with the details."

Elsa leaned in a little. She was aware of Elizabeth's discomfort, but all the same this was good stuff and Nettie too wanted more. Elizabeth's face, however, was a virtual blank; it lacked expression and was devoid of color.

"Well," Doris explained, "it's just that last evening Robert was seen going into Ms. Scapelli's apartment after six and staying very late into the evening."

"From that you get some kind of whirlwind romance?" said Nettie.

"They've known each other for years. They're friends, Doris," said Elsa. "Friends get together. They sometimes talk over dinner," she continued and spread her hands over the table they were sitting at.

Elizabeth said nothing, but strained to listen. She could feel beads of perspiration collect at her neck and hairline and in the palms of her hand. What the others were saying was true, but why had Robert not told her. She was reminded then of his upbeat mood of this morning despite his lack of sleep and of his plans to be out again this evening with Mr. McEntyre.

"I agree," said Doris. "I didn't mean to jump to any conclusions, but when he was seen going into her apartment again this evening…"

"Again?" said Elsa confirming her own suspicions to the others. "Where do you get your information?"

"From Mrs. Tully, of course," she said. "Mrs. Tully lives just one flight down from Mrs.…. Ms.," she corrected herself with a little roll of the eyes, "Scapelli. She called me again this evening just as I was leaving the house."

"Well," said Elsa. "This is exciting news." She glanced at Elizabeth furtively and then cast them down upon her coffee.

"It is indeed," said Elizabeth. "I am so pleased that Robert has decided to move on with his life." The others were quick to note, however, that Elizabeth's face contradicted her words. Clearly they had wanted more from her, but she was not going to be of further assistance.

There was a moment of silence as Doris, Nettie and Elsa had waited on each other to break it and get the gossip back into gear. The waiter returned with the dessert and Elizabeth thanked him graciously. "I'm going to have to walk this off tomorrow. So late," she said, "to be eating such decadent foods."

"Yes," Elsa agreed. "I've put on at least five pounds this passed winter."

"More like ten," said Nettie looking over her sharply.

"You're one to talk, Nettie Tubman. If anyone's gained ten pounds it's certainly you."

"Are you out of your senses, woman? My bathroom scale says I've lost seven pounds since the holidays," Nettie contended hotly.

"Your bathroom scale lies, dear," Elsa said softly.

"Do you believe what you're hearing from this woman?" Nettie asked Doris.

"I think both of you ladies ought to drop this now," said Doris. "And I think you might wish to make an investment in a new bathroom scale," she said to Nettie. "I have a twenty percent off coupon at…"

"My scale is quite accurate, I can assure you," said Nettie.

Quietly, Elizabeth finished her dessert and swallowed the last of her tea. She reached into her handbag and retrieved more than enough of her share of the bill and placed it on the table. "I really need to be off," she said and stood up.

"So soon, dear?" asked Nettie.

"I'm really rather tired and it is getting late," she replied. "You three stay on and continue with your barrage of insults," she said dryly. "You can use the exercise," she muttered under her breath as she departed.

Outside the rain had stopped and Elizabeth began her six-block trek home. Until now, she had truly thought of Robert's home as hers as well, but with a few passing words and innuendos, she suddenly felt out in the cold. Where will I go? She thought. What will I do? Her lower lip began to tremble as her mind carried her back to a day long, long ago. Again it was in the late spring of the year as she watched and even helped her big brother to pack his belongings into a suitcase. She had been horrified as she watched him dismantle his life before her. He gave away things that had been dear to him for so long. "It was all dead weight to him", he had said. He had dismissed everything in his life in order to move on. He did not want to be held back then and he would not want that now, she thought.

She quickened her pace and was nearly struck down by a car as she crossed the avenue. She heard the screeching of the tires on the wet asphalt and the horn blaring at her. The man behind the wheel screamed some obscenities at her and gestured an additional one with his hand. It did not matter to him, she thought, that she had the right of way. For the first time in her life she lifted her hand and saluted him in the same manner. The man sped off with a final word. He was determined to get in the last obscenity.

Chapter Seven

"Tell me everything," Maria said to Robert as he came through her door. The twinkle in his eye gave her credence to make positive presumptions. "It went well," she said before he could utter a word. "I can tell," she persisted.

He opened his briefcase and pulled a bottle of champagne from it. "It must have lost some of its chill on the way over here," he said. "Will you join me?"

Maria smiled, but it wasn't one of glee or joy, but rather one of affection and or maybe even one of seduction. "Let me get the glasses," she said. Her voice was more throaty than usual, but that was lost on Robert.

"He was impressed, Maria," he shouted to her from the living room. "He really needs to know that this is our work, though. Both of our names should have appeared on that paper." He removed the foil from the top of the bottle and twisted off the metal fastener.

She came into the living room with a small tray. In addition to the glasses, it contained a small plate of caviar and toasted triangles. "I had a feeling we would be celebrating this tonight," she said. Her voice was still throaty and this time it had registered with Robert.

He stood there dumbstruck. He noticed now the robe she was wearing. It was not like the robe that Elizabeth wore around the house. It wasn't like anything that Kathleen had ever worn. This was a satin robe trimmed with lace. It was of a black and white floral pattern and it stopped at mid-thigh. Robert was sure that the robe had been closed at the neck when he came in, but now it was open at the top and revealed a plunging neckline. He had never seen her like this before. Her breasts were fuller than he had ever realized and her legs were good. The legs of a dancer, he thought.

The look in her eyes and the quality of her voice stirred something within him. She evoked feelings in him that he thought was long dormant. The cork in the bottle exploded and the foam from the champagne ran down the bottle and over his hand on down, finally, to the floor. He looked down at mess that it had created and began to apologize profusely.

"Don't worry," she said and smiled. She took the bottle from his hand and placed it into an ice bucket on the sideboard. He hadn't noticed the ice bucket before. She untied a towel from the handle of the ice bucket and dropped it onto the floor.

"Allow me," Robert said. His throat was dry and he very much wanted to drink straight from the bottle. Instead he bent down and mopped up the champagne. "I'm such a klutz," he said. "I hope this doesn't leave a stain in the wood."

"Leave it, Robert," she said. "Come over to the couch and tell me all about it."

He looked up from the floor. "About it?" he asked. He could think of nothing outside of the immediate.

She sat and smoothed the satin robe over her thighs. "Tell me about your meeting with John," she said and gently patted the sofa cushion on her left to indicate where she expected him to be. She shifted a little and crossed her legs revealing more thigh than before. Robert tried to avert his eyes, but he was having trouble. He tried to maintain eye contact with Maria, but he was failing miserably. Finally he looked away and concentrated on the task of cleaning the floor. He rubbed furiously, insistent on drying the wood thoroughly. "Come here, Robert," she said.

"I'm afraid this will leave a stain," he said.

"Really, I'm not worried about it. That floor has more marks and scars than I can count. It needs to be refinished anyway," she said. "Come over here and talk to me, Robert." The way she said his name was foreign to him.

After he had left her apartment on the previous evening, Maria had spent much of the night surfing the Internet searching for clues as to how one might achieve attracting a shy man. Most advice, however, was focused on attracting shy men who you did not know. It illustrated in great detail how to lead in conversation. It maintained that you should go back to your shy man two or three times before giving up as a shy man needs to be drawn out more than that of an outgoing man and that it would take more time before you may hit upon a topic of conversation that will comfortably engage your shy man. The advice was little more than frustrating to her, as it offered nothing to women who had known their shy man for thirty years.

The following morning she sought the advice from her friend Sue who had been more seasoned with experience in relationships with the opposite sex and decided to follow her words of wisdom when she told Maria to get noticed. "Give him the milk for free," she had suggested. "There's no use in letting it pass the expiration date."

"I'm not playing hard to get," Maria retorted. "He can have all the milk he wants," she said. "I just want to know how I can get him to reach for it."

"No offence," her friend had prefaced, "but you're strictly skim milk."

"What the hell does that mean?" Maria demanded into the phone. "I'm still in great shape," she said looking herself over in the mirror. "Pretty good shape," she said with less confidence while looking at herself from different angles. "I look pretty good," she said. "Don't I?"

"You look great, honey," she said. "I just mean that maybe you should dress it up a little. Maybe your man wants a little chocolate in his milk."

"Chocolate?"

"Skim milk is good for you, honey, but whole milk tastes a whole lot better. Add some chocolate syrup and now we're talking. A scoop of ice cream and maybe a little soda water with some whipped cream will lock him up for sure."

"What the hell are you talking about, Sue?"

"No offence, babe, but…."

"Don't start with 'no offence' if you plan to offend me."

"You're a little bland, Maria."

"I still turn heads," Maria objected.

"You can turn a lot more heads than you do."

Maria pondered that for a moment. "I'm in my fifties, Sue. I'm not interested in being a tart."

"That's exactly what I mean."

"What?"

"You're too uptight, honey. Relax it a little. This Robert of yours has seen you in the same light forever. You're too safe for him. Put yourself out there."

"I don't want to be out there. I just want him."

"Put yourself out there in front of him. He's a man, Maria. If you want him to respond to you, you should give him something to respond to. Unwrap the package a little and show him what's inside, babe. A burger doesn't look too enticing without a great set of buns and some cheese dripping out the sides, but if you keep it in the bag it has no appeal"

"Are you hungry, Sue?"

"I'm always hungry, honey. Go and put a fire in that grill and don't call me again until you're cooking."

"Thanks," she said and they hung up simultaneously. Maria went into her closet and perused her wardrobe as objectively as was possible. Skim milk, skim milk, skim, skim, soy, she thought. No chocolate here all right. I guess I need to get some chocolate milk in the house. I hope Robert likes chocolate milk.

She had done a little shopping after school and had spent more than she had planned on. She purchased the chocolate and then picked up some other flavors that she thought might be enticing to him. She had always dressed in what she considered to be a sexy-conservative way. Today she was wearing her first push-up bra and matching thong. The bra she kind of liked, but the thong was something she would have to get used to. Robert, she thought, would either go for it or go running for the hills. She was uneasy about how it would play out, but she was more troubled thinking about not giving it a try. Too much time had already passed.

Now she was here in her little robe and underneath was nothing but her push-up bra and thong panty. Perhaps she had gone too far, she thought. It wasn't her intention to dress so scantily, but as she tried on her new things in the mirror, she became increasingly more excited. She liked the way she looked. The cut of the panty climbing so high on her hip gave her legs new length and accentuated her small waist. Her breasts, now cradled in this new technology were higher and fuller than they had been in years. She looked younger. She was like the women in the TV commercials. Well, she thought, maybe not like them, but better than anything a sixty-year-old Robert Montgomery could ever hope for.

She was proud of her body and had never shown it off like this before. She had not even exhibited herself to Guy in this manner, but that would have proved fruitless in any event. She reached across her body to the sideboard and picked up her empty glass. Her robe fell open a little more to reveal her very flat midsection. "Come fill our glasses, Robert," she said. "I want to celebrate." Her voice was still throaty and more sensual now than before.

"Of course," said Robert. He picked up the bottle with his hand trembling slightly. He was feeling a little weak at the knees. He was staring at her without meaning to. Her skin was so utterly flawless. The smooth olive complexion had no visible marks that he could see and there was a silky glow to her that he had never noticed before. She was a strikingly beautiful woman, he thought. He did not know what to make of this. He had known Maria forever and had never had feelings for her in any sexual way.

"I shouldn't have barged in here unexpectedly," he said. "I just wanted to let you know how it went this evening with John."

Maria pulled her robe in to cover herself. "I'm glad you came," she said. The confidence in her voice was fading. The throaty, sensual voice was now timid and reserved. She uncrossed her legs and adjusted herself back on the sofa. She covered her legs as much as possible and sat stiffly in her seat. "I wanted you to come tonight, Robert," she said, but she was no longer making eye contact with him. "Why don't I just go and finish getting dressed," she said. She started to get up.

No, he wanted to say, but didn't or couldn't. He just stood there as she walked past him closing her robe all the tighter. She closed her bedroom door softly and struggled to suppress the tears, but failed miserably. Robert was lost in confusion. He did not know what had transpired in the last moments. He did not know what to do. Should he leave? No, he thought that would be bad. Did he want to leave? No, he did not. Did he have feelings for Maria? He could not be sure. There were strong physical feelings for the moment, but that was not clarity. He had never felt a sexual tendency towards her before and now they shared this awkward moment. Had she offered herself to him? Yes, he believed she had. If he were to knock upon her door and act upon it, would that mean commitment? Yes, he thought, it would. Could he act upon it if he so desired? Yes, he realized, he probably could.

Robert began to pace back and forth in the little room. He was like a caged animal with no place to go. His heart was racing and his face was hot. He loosened his collar and without thinking he opened the window. What do I do? He thought. And like too many things that had befallen him in his life, he would let it be decided by others. In this case Maria would decide his options. She returned to the living room wearing a pale blue blouse and charcoal gray slacks.

"Would you prefer a beer, Robert?" she asked. Her manner and motions were now perfunctory. She was putting up a wall.

"No," he said. "Let's drink the champagne." He was looking at her in a new light. It was as though he had been seeing her for the first, or at least the second time. Her slacks were tight at the hips, waist and buttocks and hung loosely down her slender legs. He had seen her dressed like this on countless occasions, but now he was noticing her and it made him a little uncomfortable. They were, after all, friends. His friendship with her was now being interrupted by feelings that would leave their future uncertain. Without ceremony, he poured the champagne and they drank without toasting.

"Thank you," he said. "Thank you for being so supportive, Maria."

"Of course," she said and smiled, but the smile was strained. She was embarrassed and felt rejected and therefore betrayed. Her strained smile was a mask to her emotions, but the mask was nearly transparent and Robert read her well enough to know that they were forever changed.

They stood face to face with their glasses in hand. Should he move in and kiss her now? What would that do to salvage their friendship? "I should go," he said.

"Yes," she said. "Perhaps you should." She took the glass from his hand, but did not see him to the door.

* * *

"It was very disconcerting for me to leave Maria that night, Toby. I was so very confused," he says. Robert is standing now and he paces the length of the bench and returns. "I walked for hours trying to make sense of it. She must have thought me a fool," he says. His head is hanging low and eyes are cast downwards. "I thought of going back, but it was too late. She threw herself at me and I embarrassed her. I also didn't know if that would be in my best interests. Should I have embarked on a new relationship at my age?"

Robert shakes his head vigorously. "I didn't know what I wanted then, Toby. I had seen Maria in this new light. She was beautiful. She was a very attractive..." he begins to say and stops. "She was sexy," he says almost whispering. "What could I offer her," he says pleading to the man on the bench. He makes his hands into claws and raises them between heaven and earth. "What did I wish to offer her?" he asks.

"When Kathleen died I didn't give any thought about other women. Despite the troubles we had, I was so stricken with grief and guilt that for so very long I had shut myself off from such feelings. Over time I was comfortable being alone. Not alone," he corrected. "I still had Emily and of course Elizabeth had come after a time to help me with her. But I was alone as far as a truly intimate relationship was concerned. I don't think that that's such a terrible thing, Toby," he says looking for the approval of the man. "I find women to be very complicated. Maria is a lovely and intelligent woman. I must be honest and say that I desired her immensely that evening, but should I have thrown my way of living out completely for an evening of passion.

"I couldn't have just had a one night stand with Maria. I don't think it was what she was looking for. I don't believe that she was the kind of woman that could accept a man under such terms. If I had had the courage to give in that evening I would have been trapped. I don't know," he said wrestling with himself. "Possibly that could have worked out. I just couldn't see myself with her. She had everything, but there was something missing. Truthfully I believe that she was better than I deserved, but who can tell a woman that? Still there was something missing. I didn't have feelings for her. Sexual sensations existed, surely, but not the emotional connection that I would hope for. Until then, though, I had not even been aware that I still had hopes at all."

Robert walks down to the waters edge. The cold air stings his face and eyes. "Maria had awakened something in me that night, Toby," he says out of earshot from the man. "She startled some dormant thoughts and stirred some past hopes and yes, some dreams."

* * *

Elizabeth sat quietly in her room. It was passed three in the morning and Robert had only just come in the front door. She did not make for the light or her bed. She sat there waiting as he walked up the stairs. He was not so quiet tonight. He walked up as he would at a normal hour. His shoes were heavy on the stairs. His pull on the banister gave way to its grunts and protests. She waited for him to notice the light and step in to see her as he usually did at odd hours, but tonight he passed her door and continued on up to his rooms. Elizabeth closed her eyes. Tears began to run down her nose and over her lips. With her tongue she tasted the salty liquid. It was a bitter taste and a painful reminder to other unfortunate times.

She had encouraged him to go. America, she exclaimed, how very exciting. It was the right decision, she had assured him. Even the Beatles had gone to America. Some day, perhaps I too, will go to America. She rambled in exaggerated excitement and Robert, in his own genuine fervor, failed to pick up on her deep sense of loss and disdain. She had helped him to pack his things, although there was so little that he had put into his bags. He would be leaving most of his things behind. He would be leaving her behind as well. Never did she ask him to stay with her. Go, she said to him. It was the right decision, she repeated over and over again.

She smiled from the pier and waved furiously. She knew that from this distance he would only detect her smile and fail to see her tears. She wept as the ship sailed out of the harbor and she continued to weep as she turned away and wept all the way home. She would cry on and off for months and then she would stop crying for years. Elizabeth was only twelve years old, but already she was long past her childhood. She did not know if she would ever see her brother again. Robert was the only presence in her life that furnished any amount of stability. He was her brother, father, mentor and best friend. He, she knew, was probably unaware of his importance in her life.

When he told her that he wanted to go to America, she bit her tongue and smiled. She knew that if she had asked him to stay, he would have. In truth, she knew that she did not need Robert. She did, however, want him to stay around. Robert was the one bright spot in an otherwise gloomy world. He too, however, lived within his own dismal world and she did not wish to hold him to it. His freedom lent hope to hers.

From an early age she believed that America had more colors than Birmingham. Her part of England seemed always to be so gray. The America that she had come to love was fabricated in Hollywood and presented in Technicolor. Even Robert, she believed, would have more color in his otherwise pallid cheeks once he had crossed the Atlantic and reached the shore. The sun shone a little brighter in America. Of course they were just coming off of a long winter in Birmingham. The winter seemed to go on forever and ever for her. She much preferred the summer months.

She was not the best student, nor was she the worst. She was no better than average. She was not considered pretty nor was she considered average looking. Elizabeth was opined to be plain in her physical appearance by some of the more charitable individuals who felt it necessary to make such observations and thought to be somewhat ugly by others who believed in being honest to a fault. Although no one had ever actually articulated these rather harsh judgments to her personally, she had never been so dim as to not pick up on the snickering, smirking or furtive whispers that went on around her. She was quite capable of seeing herself in the mirror as she was. It was as plain to her as the sharp and pointed nose upon her face.

Early in her life, Elizabeth found sarcasm to be a useful tool against those who would challenge her. She could quickly cut a boy or a girl off at the knees with a mere passing comment. She would only use this tool as a defense mechanism and use it well enough to keep would-be challengers at a safe distance. She had made many friends in this manner, as others would appreciate her quick wit. The friends she had made, however, were never truly admitted to penetrate the wall she had built around herself. Elizabeth, for the most part, had isolated herself from the others. She never quite allowed herself to put her trust in another person. She would not allow herself to be vulnerable where her emotions were concerned. Even now, in middle age, Elizabeth was still the frightened girl she had been on the pier so many years ago and although the years piled on, the little girl continues to struggle and fight her way to the surface while the woman she has grown into fights desperately to reinforce and maintain the wall she had built so many years ago.

Elizabeth lay on her side and curled up into the fetal position and pulled the blanket up to her chin. Her eyes strained from their sockets and with her eyelids she reined them in and expelled several droplets of water. She put her hand up to the light switch, but failed to make contact and so she pulled the blanket over the top of her head and sought the sleep she so desperately needed, but would not find.

She knew, and she believed, that she did not have the right to begrudge what was perhaps her brother's last chance at happiness, but begrudge she did. Her only true pleasure in life had come from a sense of stability; tomorrow, for her, needed to be much like today. There had been very little in her life in the manner of adventure. Coming to America had been her sole account of that. She had had a brief encounter with romance, but it had been one-sided. The man she had befriended so many years ago was at a loss for words when she revealed, and only slightly so, her fancy towards him. He had left her on that night with poor excuses and had made himself scarce forever more.

Perhaps she had seen much of herself in Maria in that way. Maria, however, was attractive and she thought that some day her brother might actually discover that. The day has arrived, she thought. Her somewhat absentminded older brother has finally opened his eyes to what was before him. Maria, she thought, was worthy of her brother's affections, but that realization had been much too painful for her to consider. It had been easier to leave Maria in the distance and not to act on her behalf as a matchmaker. In hindsight, perhaps it would have been better to do so. She had never been particularly warm towards Maria and, she knew, it had not gone unnoticed. Now it would be good for her to have an ally in Maria, but that was not to be.

For the sake of pride, she would have to go, but where could she turn? She had some money saved, but very little of that. She had no skills to offer other than being hard working and efficient. That, she thought, would surely count for something in a world where she felt had been becoming increasingly complacent and lazy. There was no time for school, she thought. At Robert and Maria's age, they would move quickly. There was little for them to plan for. They had all they needed to set up house and there would be no children in their future. They would rush, she thought, to make up for time lost. They would speak endlessly of the years that had been wasted and the need to remedy it in the future.

Elizabeth shuddered under her blanket. Her fists were clenched in the folds of the goose down. It will be a struggle, she thought, but I will fight and I will make a life for myself. I have always served others and now I shall serve myself, she thought with staggering vehemence. I'll not be petty, she whispered as though in prayer. I will welcome Ms. Scapelli in as I depart. She swallowed hard and squeezed the goose down a little harder to counter the pain in her throat. She closed her eyes and thought of it no more. Sleep came to her shortly thereafter.

Robert crawled onto his bed fully dressed and lay above the bedclothes. He lifted a pillow and slid his head beneath it and with both of his hands he pulled the ends of the pillow down as hard as he could. He wondered how his life had gotten so difficult in such a short span of time. Had the house been empty he would have screamed into his pillow. It was all he could do to keep from screaming now. It would be a help to him, he thought, if only he could scream out freely. He desperately needed to release some of his pent up frustration. Instead he punched and kicked his mattress furiously rocking the bedposts across the hardwood floor. He was completely oblivious to the racket that he was making.

On the floor below, Elizabeth awoke. So startled was she that she could barely move. Frozen in her bed she lay there wide-eyed in horror. Her eyes were transfixed on the ceiling above her. Gradually her mind began to thaw and process the accounts of the evening. Slowly she allowed herself to put the pieces together and arrive at what must be the obvious conclusion. Above, Robert grunted a muffled scream into his pillow. Elizabeth sat up and the shock in her eyes began to dim with the darkness of anger. "That son-of-a-bitch", she mouthed, but made no sound. She shook her head slowly and gritted her teeth. Her eyes took on a cold indignant scowl that was too fierce for her to ever conjure for the sake of pretense. Right above my head, she thought. Such insolence I have never witnessed.

Robert's fit of frustration ceased as his energy depleted. He moaned a final moan and sat up in his bed. He was drenched in sweat and it took him a few minutes to catch his breath. He felt better, though. Somehow he had managed to shake off some of how he had felt without actually changing anything at all. He would survive this, he thought. He would get past this and he would move on. There really was no other choice. Maria, too, would get past this. She would, he thought. There really was no other choice.

He climbed out of bed and removed his clothes and made his way into the shower. Down below, Elizabeth could hear the water running. The old pipes began to clang as the hot water made its way up from the cellar and it made her all the more angry. She sat up on the edge of her bed and stomped her feet on the floor. "I'll not be making breakfast for them," she said aloud. She reached up to the light switch and darkened the room. She was determined to lose no more sleep.

Chapter Eight

The early afternoon had turned suddenly dark. The pinpricks of light that had penetrated the clouds and streamed onto Emily's desk had just ceased to exist. She turned to look out of her window. The sky was thick with black clouds and its affect on her was, as always, soothing. She could never understand why, but she had always felt most comfortable in the darkest and dreariest of all weather. The heavy clouds that blanketed the sky were, in a way, a security blanket for her. In the past she had never given poise to such emotions. She had merely accepted and even embraced such comforts, but now she stopped to think about such things.

Four weeks earlier she had begun therapy with a man she called Dr. Freud. His name was actually Hiller, but she preferred calling him Freud and that had been considered to be of much interest to the man. They spent a good part of that first session defining her motives for doing so. Emily learned that there were deep reasons in her psyche that emitted such behaviors of thought. The fact that she was a senior VP at Hiller & Brandt publishing Company was of little relevance to her therapist.

Whether or not she took the therapy or the therapist for that matter seriously was something that she would decide later. For the mean time it was good for her just to talk. She was not altogether interested in looking for answers to any particular questions, it was just that she had always been painfully private and that had been somewhat of an obstacle in her life. She had always been angry towards her mother for keeping everything bottled up inside to the point of what she deemed a useless eruption. Her father, too, had not opened up all that much, but his demons were gentler and even non-intrusive.

Emily was now thirty and was looking back on a failed marriage and other failed relationships. She was an admitted workaholic with a daughter who she feared would be hurt by her long absences and lack of attention. Shannon, for all intents and purposes, seemed to be a well-adjusted child, but Emily realized that she too might be bottling up and oppressing thoughts that would change her for the worse. She supposed that what she feared most was that she, herself, might some day turn into her mother.

She did not know all that much about her mother's beginnings. For Emily, Kathleen had always been a volatile person. To broach the subject with her mother about her earlier life, she felt might be pulling at a thread that would completely unravel her mothers' very existence. As a young girl, Emily wanted only peace and quiet in her home. Her excitement could be gotten anywhere else. Her therapist suggested that somewhere down the road, Emily could bring her father in to search for some of those answers, but that would come later. Emily had no desire to put her father under such scrutiny, but Dr. Freud need not know that.

In the first two sessions they discussed her work and her need for perfection in that area of her life. When her therapist suggested that she take it down a notch or two in order to explore new avenues in her personal life, she went on the defensive and had asked the doctor if he was taking his professional life down a notch or two while in her employ. The doctor became silent and let her vent, but he did take notes and that infuriated her all the more.

She talked about her relationship with her daughter, but was vague in reference to Shannon's personality. She did not want Dr. Freud analyzing her daughter and let that be known. The doctor would let the subject of Shannon go for now, but there were notes taken and he would come back to her in the future. Emily would have to be coaxed along and that would add length to her treatment. That much he had explained to her and she merely shrugged and said that it was her dime. All in all she liked having Dr. Freud to talk with. He could listen to her, but he couldn't talk about her behind her back. She was paying him a considerable amount of money and did not feel badly about verbally smacking him around. It was a good relationship and she was in no particular mood to put it in her past. The more she talks with him the less she worries about him passing judgment on her. Overall he lets her talk and on occasion he pulls more from her than she had been willing to give. He does not say 'how does that make you feel'. He obviously watches enough television to know that that would sound too cliché, but he does prod information that answers that question.

Much to her surprise, she had subsequently grown to trust Dr. Freud and at this point in their relationship her calling him Freud was more like a term of endearment than an act of scorn. The doctor was gentle, yet firm. He kept her on track and that she admired about him as she too was in the habit of keeping people on task. Digression was a sin in her business and, she supposed, his as well. When he did let her stray there was usually a reason. In the beginning her own digressions was a distraction to her. She would periodically stop her speaking to do a little self-analysis to just peek ahead at where she might be going and whether or not she wanted to take Dr. Freud along with her.

By the fourth session she had relented herself and surrendered to him nearly with complete trust. She had come to terms with the fact that no matter how private she wished to remain, her secrets were not all that impressive and there was really no interest in her beyond that of man who was salaried to be intrigued by her. Her life, in a nutshell, was dull. Perhaps that was why she had sought therapy in the first place.

"Why am I dull, Dr. Freud?" she asked almost playfully.

"Are you dull?" he replied. He was looking at her over the tops of his glasses the way her father had always peered at her when looking up from his newspaper or one of his books.

"I'm afraid I am," she said with less tongue in cheek.

"Afraid?"

"Just an expression," she said.

He waited.

"I'm not really afraid that I'm dull," she said with very little certainty.

He waited.

She looked up at him. For the first time she was very much aware that his chair was significantly higher than hers. At this very moment she felt as though she were shrinking deeper into her own chair. "You're expecting me to elaborate on that?" she asked.

He waited.

"All right," she conceded. "I am a little dull and that frightens me. Maybe I'm going through an early mid-life crisis. Suddenly life seems to be passing me by and I guess it's not all that I had hoped it could be."

"What's lacking?" he asked.

"I don't know," she said and gave a slight shrug. "I have more than I have a right to."

"Explain."

She looked up at him a little perturbed. "You're an intelligent man, Dr. Freud. Fill in the pieces."

"You fill them in for me."

She exhaled sharply through her mouth; her face looking much like that of a blowfish. "I have a great job," she said. "A career," she corrected. "I'm young and have gone very far in my profession. I have a wonderful daughter. I'm comfortable in my home and I know that I can afford to send my daughter to the best schools."

"You have money," he said. It was a statement.

"Yes," she said. "Yes I do. You know that because I've been giving bunches of it to you each week."

"You have stuff."

"Yes. I have stuff," she said with sarcasm on her face. "I have lots of stuff all over my place. My daughter has lots of stuff too. I am able to buy her lots of stuff," she said.

"This makes you feel good about yourself?"

"It doesn't make me feel bad."

"You're sure about that?"

She looked up at him again, but she did not feel small any more. She was taller in her seat now. "What the hell does that supposed to mean?" she demanded.

"You said that you had more than you had a right to," he iterated her own words.

"Just an expression," she said with very little certainty.

He waited.

Emily took a bottle of water from her bag and took a small sip to wet her dry mouth. "I'm very fortunate," she said.

He waited.

"I used to think that money could solve all of the problems in the world. Money buys food and shelter," she said. "It buys the best possible health care and education. Money gets you into the best restaurants and the best seats for any show in New York. It puts you in first class on the airlines," she said. Money makes life comfortable. It buys stability." She looked up at him and waited for his assurance to her position.

He waited.

"What?" she said after a moment.

"Was money a problem in your childhood?"

"It was a problem for my parents," she said.

"Were they so poor?"

"No."

"No?"

"I didn't think so," she said. "I never felt as though we were poor. We lived in a big house. There used to be tenants on the top floor, but only for a while after I was born. I think my father was able to make enough money to let the tenants go after a while," she said.

"Did you ever feel in want of anything?"

"No," she said hesitantly.

"Nothing?" he asked.

"Not things, Dr. Freud. I had nice clothes. I always liked nice clothing and I always had nice clothing. There was always plenty of food in the house and as far as I can remember we had never gone without paying the utilities."

"Birthday and Christmas?" he asked.

"My parents were very generous," she said.

"They were generous with you?"

"Yes," she said. "They were very generous with me."

He waited.

"They were generous with each other as well," she said anticipating the look on his face.

"I thought there was a money issue?" he said.

"There was a money issue. It was my mother's issue. My poor father worked all of the time back then. She complained if there wasn't enough money and she complained when he went out to get more."

"Tell me about your mother," he said.

"She was difficult and then she died," she said flatly.

He waited.

Emily turned her head toward the window. She was holding her ground and would not face the therapist.

"How old were you when she died, Emily?"

She continued to look out of the window, but she was not really seeing anything at all. The tears that rarely filled her eyes since childhood were coming now. "I was twelve," she said.

"Was it a long illness?" he asked.

"I suppose it was in sorts," she replied cautiously. "I'd rather not talk about it," she said with a rather harsh finality in her voice.

"What about your father?" he asked.

"My father is a good man," she declared defensively. "He's kind and gentle and very supportive."

"Was he there for you?"

"Yes," she said angrily. Her look and tone suggested that Dr. Hiller should have known this, as though it were common knowledge. "My father did everything for his family."

"Okay," he said softly.

Emily nodded. She knew that her temper was flaring unjustly and she was taking a moment to step back and compose her emotions. She nodded again as if to say 'I'm all right now'.

"What do you want to talk about?" Dr. Hiller asked.

"Read any good books lately?" she asked sarcastically.

"Yes, as a matter of fact I have. Some of which were published in your house," he said.

"Good," she said, but she did not ask him which titles he had read nor did she seek his opinion on them. Normally she would not only query for thoughts concerning titles in Hiller & Brandt's catalog, but she would go as far as to, in the opinion of those close to her, interrogate readers for specifics on these titles. She would want to know what they thought about the style of the author and what emotions erupted from certain passages. She would want to know not only what they saw, but also what they did not see. In effect, she sought the very same things that Dr. Hiller sought. She wanted to know 'how it made them feel'. Her mind was not on her work right now. Her mind was in the past, but she was not ready to bring that past into her present. Dr. Hiller sensed as much and begged off.

"We're just about out of time, Emily. If you need more time from me before our next session..."

"I won't," she interrupted.

"Okay, but if you do..."

"I'll call you," she finished. She stood up and looked at her watch. "There was a time when an hour meant sixty minutes and not fifty," she said.

"I'm not busy," he said. "I'll give you the other ten."

"I can't," she said. "I've got to get back to work, but thanks." She picked up her purse and left his office unceremoniously.

Fifteen minutes later Emily was back at her desk trying to busy herself within the torrents of paper that surrounded her. Her father could never understand how she could possibly manage to focus amongst such chaos. 'A cluttered desk is a cluttered mind', he would say. He did not take credit for these words, but he did understand and live by them. His own desk, and office for that matter, was meticulously neat and orderly. Her father could not function in a messy and cluttered environment. Often he would spend much of his time getting organized before embarking upon any task.

Her mother, she reflected, made her life's work organizing herself and her surroundings. She did little else, but what she did filled her time and left little voids for personal matters of pleasure. Emily differed from both her parents in her disorganization and for some reason she felt comforted by this departure. It had, in a way, made her unique from them. The difference, she believed, was not deliberate nor was it rebellious, but just a natural distinction presumably inherited at birth, but from whom, she did not know.

She looked away from the pages before her, realizing that she had comprehended nothing at all. She turned towards her window and comprehended as much beyond the pane. She was tired and lost and frightened. She needed to open up to someone, but could not do so. Little by little she revealed herself to Dr. Hiller, but it was too little and mostly irrelevant. She talked about her marriage and how it had failed. Most of the blame she had put upon her husband and his insecurity at her success. In part that was true. It was also true that he had been somewhat immature and irresponsible, but there was more to it than that and Dr. Hiller pressed her on it, but she stood firmly

She had been running her entire life without traveling very far at all. She married to get away from her life and she married a man who was not yet a man, but a boy. Richard was still being called Ritchie at that time and he tried desperately to please his first love, but she wore him down with demands that were unrealistic to his nature. At first he thought that she wanted to be married to a man that he could never be and later he decided she did not wish to be married at all. He confronted her with his speculations, but she dismissed him on this as she had on so many other issues. She decided that having a baby would make things right and wanted to have that baby right away. He did not wish to have a baby at that time, but he consented and had regretted the decision as soon as he had made it.

He was a husband and a father, but he was ready for neither. He liked to cook and wished to work as a chef, but Emily dissuaded him from this path. After a little research she came to the conclusion that he would make very little money in this field particularly since he had no formal training. Even if he were to be formally trained his future would be uncertain at best. His only real hope for success would be to open his own restaurant, provided he possessed such talents in the kitchen which she heartily doubted, and make his money there. Restaurants cost money and that kind of money they did not bear. If they did have the money, she would never consent to gambling it on a restaurant let alone a restaurant that Ritchie was to take charge of.

She explained this to him in a manner, which she believed to be soft and loving. She explained with the aid of statistics that she had downloaded from her research on the Internet on failed restaurants across the nation. She spoke of his lack of experience in the field. When he protested bitterly, she rebuked him sharply and suggested that he 'grow up' and that he consider his responsibility as a man with a family. She did not wish, she said, to be married to a short order cook. He turned away from her angrily and thanked her for not trusting him with their hypothetical bank account.

Emily guided Ritchie into an insurance office where she believed he could, with some work, succeed. She suggested that he begin to call himself Richard and to get used to wearing a tie and a jacket. If not for the arrival of Shannon, Ritchie would have left. He did not voice his feelings on this; he kept that much to himself. Instead he decided to take the job in the insurance company and to wear the jacket and tie and be known as Richard to all those in his peripheral world.

In the mean time Emily worked at making herself a name in the publishing world. Her firm offered day care for the children of its employees and Emily took full advantage of this service. Throughout the day she could peek in on Shannon and go back to work. If she needed to put in some extra hours, Richard could come and take Shannon home and handle the dinner, bath and bedtime. It did not take long for Richard to grow weary of this arrangement. While he truly believed that he loved his daughter, he began to resent her as the tie that bound him in a life not of his choosing.

Emily's growth at Hiller & Brandt was rapid. She had by far exceeded the expectations of her superiors and quickly made a name for herself. There were promotions and there were raises in pay that would alleviate Richard from much of his responsibilities. He would shortly thereafter take this opportunity to bolt and to do so with little regret from Emily. It would be Shannon who would pay the price, but as she was so little at the time, little consideration was given her.

Emily was able to afford domestic help. She had a woman named Clara Billings, much like Elizabeth, to come in and take care of Shannon and the household. As Emily was scarce in the home, Clara was able to manage her duties with little effort as the apartment in which Emily had secured had few rooms to superintend and only one small child to pick up after. Clara performed her task well and was considered more like a grandmother to Shannon than a paid employee.

Richard, subsequently, followed his heart and took a path in the culinary world. His commitment to that, however, was not as determined as he had imagined it would be and after muddling about for a year and a half, he found himself working as a short order cook in a low scale diner and struggling to keep up with its demand. Eventually he abandoned this as well and made for the west coast. Emily and Shannon had not heard from Richard in over four years and prior to that the contact was minimal at best.

Emily knew that she had not been fair to Richard. It was she who had pressed for marriage and it was she who had pressed to have a child. The awareness of what she had been doing, however, was never so very far from her grasp. She had taken a man whom she'd found to be aesthetically pleasing and tried to transform him into something other than what he was intended to be by nature. She knew that it had been wrong, but at the same time she believed in earnest that he would benefit all the more by her efforts. His current life, although unknown to her for more than four years, was, she believed, impeded by his poor judgment of vision and his lack of self-discipline and fortitude. In short, Richard was a failure, but it was his right to be one.

Emily had come to terms with these faults of her aggression, but had not yet revealed them to Dr. Hiller. She knew that in time, if she were serious about therapy, she would have to open up. In her core she believed that realizing ones own faults was the most important part of psychotherapy. It was the dealing and working with these truths that left her confused and in want of guidance. If she were to keep these truths to herself, she would never get where she needed to be. On the other hand, however, she did not know where she needed or even where she wanted to be. In truth her only certainty was that she did not wish to be like her mother. She feared it in her acts of aggression and in her slight bouts of depression.

It should not have been a bad time in her life, but it was a bad time. She had realized many of the successes that she had believed to be everything and now with these realizations she continued to sense a void that persisted to eat away within her. The void was an emptiness that seemed to expand all the more as she conquered her goals of success. Perhaps the realization of these goals had been making it clear that these objectives were not at all what she was in search of, she reasoned. As the successes piled up so did the emptiness. Emily shook off the thought. Dr. Freud would be better to make such suppositions.

She went about her work for another minute or two, but knew that it would be to no avail this afternoon. It was a rarity for her to lose focus, but when she did it was better left unchallenged. 'Even discipline needs to be rested', her father had told her so many years ago. She did not understand him then, but it made perfectly good sense now. "Lydia?" she said into the intercom.

"Yes Ms. Walsh?"

"Clear my schedule for the rest of the day. Something came up and it needs my immediate attention," she said.

"I'll reschedule everything and confirm it with you for your approval."

"Thank you, Lydia," she said. Emily stared down at her desk for a moment and then picked up the telephone and then hit number one on her speed dial. "Clara," she said into the phone. "Can you have Shannon ready to go out in about a half an hour? We're going to visit my dad this evening." She listened to Clara for a moment and then thanked her and hung up.

Chapter Nine

Elizabeth had no intentions of preparing dinner that evening. She had already written a note for Robert stating that she had last minute plans for dinner and a show and would not be home until very late that evening and to make do for himself. She had planned to be vague on the subject when asked the following day and to appear somewhat suspicious and even a little mischievous while attempting to change the subject. Her plans, however, would have to be left for another day. Emily had called and said that she would like to stop in with Shannon for a visit. She offered to bring in some take out food, but as was Elizabeth's nature, she refused the offer and said that she was already in the middle of preparations for dinner and would have plenty to spare for two more.

Robert had come directly from the school that afternoon which had been both a pleasant surprise to Elizabeth and also the source of some minor irritation. Her plan would have been quite a success on an evening when he would have been home at the very earliest of times. She had feared, prior to Emily's call that she would have been out and about trying to liquidate the afternoon and evening and beyond only to find that he had not been home to take notice. She had, in fact, no plans at all and would be unable to make plans with anyone that he might know which would be anyone that she happened to know. It was not in her nature to be out all night on her own and she could never be comfortable under such circumstances.

She said hello to him as though nothing were amiss. He replied in kind, but his manner was one of disorientation. This was not lost on Elizabeth, but she would and could not query his disposition. She would have to let it go.

"Emily and Shannon are coming for dinner this evening," she said flatly. She had her back to him at the kitchen sink and was washing vegetables with a little brush that she had always used for just that purpose.

Robert looked up sharply at the back of her head. "What's the occasion?" he asked with a bit of concern in his voice.

"Need there be an occasion?" she replied.

"Of course not," he said. "It's just not like Emily to pop by out of the blue like this. Is everything all right?"

Elizabeth, in her confusion, believed that he was picking up on her insecurities. "Everything is just fine, Robert," she said with too much verve to suit him. It left him a little suspicious and filled his heart with worry for his daughter or perhaps his granddaughter.

"Did she say anything to you,?" he asked.

"Why would she say anything to me?" she said abruptly. And then she was confused. "Whom are we speaking about?" she asked indignantly before she could realize that that would make matters worse.

The force of her comment startled him into a clarity that had evaded him all day. The day itself had been trying for him. It was not what had been presented to him, but more that nothing had been presented to him. He had left that morning dreading the day before him and struggling furiously with what words he should choose to alleviate the discomfort of the night before. Maria, though, had other means of dealing with her discomfort. She chose not to see him at all that day by calling in sick. A thought that he had considered before relenting to his will of courage under fire. It was important for him to deal with this problem head on and get past it. Maria had perpetuated the hell that both he and he supposed she had been going through. How he could face her would not be answered for at least another day and the very thought of it was churning within his gut to the point of his constant desire to vomit.

"We're speaking of Emily," he said softly. "Is she all right, Elizabeth? Tell me if there is something wrong."

The very look on his face was sobering to her. She dropped the vegetables into a colander. She had not considered that Emily might be in trouble. "I'm sure she is," she replied as softly as he. "She sounded just fine on the telephone. She offered to bring in some food, but I wouldn't hear of it. I thought she sounded rather well," she continued with more confidence in her voice. "She said she missed us and wished to drop in for a visit was all." Elizabeth dried her hands on her apron and looked up again at her brother. Her mouth hung open. "It is rather unlike her," she said mirroring his concern. "Do you suppose that there is something troubling her, Robert?"

"I'm sure she's fine," he said, but his mouth had gone dry and he found it hard to swallow. "What time are we to expect them?"

"She said five. She sounded well enough. She sounded quite well," Elizabeth said hopefully.

"Can I help you with the food?" he asked.

"No," she said without hesitation. "We should like it to be edible this evening. Let me get back to my work." She looked up at the clock on the wall. "It's half past four as it is. If you wish to be of use you might try and set the dining room table," she said. "And do be careful with the good china."

"Very well," he said and set off to do as he was told.

Elizabeth immersed herself in her work and would think no more of anything but her task at hand. Focusing on a particular task had always been a means of defense against a pending nervous breakdown. She was aware of this and oddly enough, she was comforted by it.

Robert was on the porch as the car pulled up carrying his daughter and his granddaughter. It was a black Crown Victoria that had carried them from New York City. The driver got out of the car to open the door, but Emily was already climbing out onto the curb and Shannon was just behind her. He stood there frozen and waited anxiously as they made their way up the steps. Shannon was in his arms before her mother could even get to the first step. Both mother and daughter were smiling brilliantly and Robert began to breathe easily. He clutched the little girl in his arms dramatically and a tear of relief escaped his eye. "Are you well?" he asked his daughter over his granddaughter's shoulder.

"I'm fine, dad," she said casually.

With only a subtle movement of his eyes, he asked her the same question of his granddaughter. "Fine," she mouthed and added a reassuring nod. He exhaled and kissed them both.

"What brings you here?" he asked.

"Can't we just come by to tell you we love you?" she said.

"Of course you can," he said suspiciously. Come in and put your aunt at rest. I'm afraid I've got her riled up for no good reason."

The four of them shared a pleasant dinner. Shannon would have preferred the take-out, but was much too polite to say so in front of her great-aunt. "I'm afraid that I did not have time to prepare dessert for this evening," Elizabeth said with a frown.

"I'm sorry Aunt Elizabeth. I didn't think to stop along the way."

Elizabeth looked conspiratorially at Shannon. "Is it too late for the two of us to go into the kitchen and bake some cookies?"

"It's never too late to bake cookies," she responded enthusiastically. "Mom and I baked cookies last week."

Both Robert and Elizabeth were taken aback. "They came in a tube and I sliced them onto a cookie sheet," Emily confessed.

"It's a start, dear," said Elizabeth with false praise. "Come," she said to her grandniece and together they moved quickly into the kitchen.

"Shall we retire into the living-room or would you prefer to join your aunt and daughter in baking cookies?" He asked playfully.

"Do you really want to eat cookies that I had a hand in?" she responded in kind.

"No," he said. "I think I'd prefer my cookies to be edible this evening," he said mimicking Elizabeth's words. "Shall I open a bottle of port?"

"I'll get the glasses," she said and smiled.

They devoted about ten minutes of their time to incidental chatter as they sipped the port on the living-room sofa before he opened the gate. "Tell me, why have you come here this evening?"

"Am I that horrible a daughter that I need a reason to come?" she asked

"You were only just here and it is a little out of the ordinary for you. You are a very busy woman, my darling daughter and I am very proud of you. I would love it if you were here every day, but if there is something on your mind I want you to know that I'm here and that I'm listening."

She looked up at her father and began to cry. He took her glass and put both his and hers down and held his little girl. 'I would be there if ever she should fall,' he thought. "What is it?" he asked. The fear was welling up inside him. "It's not your health?"

"No," she promised. "No, I am not ill and Shannon is fine. I've started therapy a few weeks back," she confided.

"A psychologist?" he asked.

"He's a psychiatrist as well, but I'm not seeking medication just yet," she said. "I was hoping to wait for middle age to get the really good stuff."

Robert frowned at that last remark. "They've come a long way with medications," he said. "I continue to read up on them."

"I didn't mean to be so flippant, daddy."

He took a handkerchief from his left pocket. He always kept a clean handkerchief in his left pocket and the one he used in his right. Emily took it and dabbed at her eyes and clamped it beneath her nose. "Are you suffering from depression?" he asked gently.

"Not so much depression as anxiousness," she said. "I get a little scared sometimes, daddy."

"Welcome to the human race," he said with a smile that was both warm and sympathetic.

"I stress a lot."

"You work too hard."

"I think I work too hard because I stress a lot," she said. "I think I'm trying to get lost in my work."

He nodded. He understood. "At least you're productive. Did your doctor explain this to you or was it you who explained this to him?"

She smiled. "I suppose I knew this going in."

"You needed to have it confirmed by a professional?"

"I guess," she said. She was a little girl again and talking to her daddy. "Do you disapprove?" she asked.

"Disapprove?"

"About the shrink, I mean?"

"No," he said and then he put his hand on her knee. "I'm proud of you, Emily. I had always actually feared that you wouldn't get therapy."

"You thought I was nuts?"

"Put the jokes aside," he said quietly. "Talking is good," he said with resolve. He averted his eyes from hers and stared down at his shoes. "I was not much of a talker on things that mattered."

"That's not true," she said, but even to her the words did not ring true.

"I kept things inside, Emily." He looked up at her. "You've kept things inside. I wanted you to talk then, but you did not. You seemed so well and well adjusted and I wanted to believe that you'd always be all right. I should have forced the issue back then, but I was afraid I'd push you away from me. I wanted us to be on the same side," he said.

"We are on the same side," she said and took his hand.

"Are you talking to your therapist?"

"I'm trying."

"Just open up and trust him, Emily. You need to speak of it."

"It was so long ago," she said. "It's ancient history."

"It'll never be ancient history, Emily. I can promise you that it will always be right beside you. You need to talk and you need to deal with it and cope. I'm afraid that I haven't been much of a role model in that respect. We all tend to hide from our ails in one form or another. Maybe I'm to blame for what ails you now."

"It was never you," she said.

"I should have dealt with things differently. I could have saved you from that back then. Perhaps I could have saved..."

"No," she interrupted. "You did all that you could have done. You tried. I saw that then. I was there."

"You were a child."

"I was never a child."

"No," he said. "No, you never had the chance to be a child. You had to grow up much too soon."

"I like to think that I was born that way. You were too," she said. "We are two old souls."

"You may be right," he concurred. "Circumstance may have precipitated it, though."

"Was it very bad for you as a child?" she asked

"No, not really," he said.

She looked at him hopefully. Talk to me, she said without using words.

"Yes," he said. His face changed and visions of the past were fading in and out on him. "It was rather bad for me," he said after a time. "It was bad for your aunt as well." He looked at his daughter. His heart was broken. "It was worse for you."

Emily broke down then and he held her with all that he had. He too wept, but he was silent and steady. He was as strong as he could be for his little girl and if it were possible, he would never again let her out of his grasp. How I've messed everything up, he thought. "I love you," she said.

"I know you do," he told her. "I am so sorry for not being strong enough. I should've taken you away from here."

"Where to?" she asked. "Where could you have taken me? We didn't have the support then. We really don't have it now," she said reflecting on her life with her daughter. "I come from a tiny family and brought a child into the world with a man who had no family of his own to speak of. Then he left us," she said sardonically. "What a fool I was to do that. Family is so important."

"I had a sizeable family," he said. "I was still pretty much on my own. I suppose it's true," he continued. "Size doesn't matter."

Emily, surprised by her father's uncharacteristic quip, put her hand to her mouth and muffled the laugh. She attempted a look of disapproval, but failed miserably and began to laugh all the more.

"I got you on that one," he said with a mischievous grin. "I'd been waiting to shock you for years." He picked their glasses up from the coffee table and handed Emily's to her. "A toast," he said. "To open, honest and straightforward; three friends who've evaded us for some time; that they should show their faces and be seen," he said and then lifted his glass and waited until she lifted hers. Emily was hesitant at first. Finally she relented and drank to the toast and deeply enough to drain the port in a single gulp.

He took the glass and stood up to fill it. "Don't' be too difficult with that doctor of yours. Speak to him and not at him."

"What do you mean?" she said.

"You know what I mean. Tell him. Tell him everything," he said staring into her eyes.

"How do you know that I haven't told him already?" she said almost defiantly.

"Because I know you," he said. "You get that from me."

"He suggested that I bring you into a session," she said. She watched his eyes carefully and saw the flicker of what? Was it pain? Was it fear? Was it regret? "I told him that it was out of the question," she said mercifully. She felt that she had hurt him and for a moment she believed that it was deliberate. Why did she want to hurt him? Was it to share the pain? Perhaps she should ask Dr. Freud, she thought.

"Would it help?" he asked.

"What?" she asked.

"Would it be helpful for me to come? Do you want me there?" he asked. "I'll come if you want me to be there."

"Do you want to come?"

"Of course not," he said. "I'm a coward. But I will come if it would be of help to you. If it helps you, I would want to come."

"No," she said. "I wouldn't do that to you. Seeing a shrink was a tough decision for me."

"Talking to the shrink may be tougher." He carried the glasses back to the sofa and sat down. He looked at his daughter imploringly. "Talk to him," he said. "You need to open up."

"Maybe I have," she said softly.

"Have you?"

"No," she said. "I don't know that I can, daddy." Her eyes filled again, but she managed to hold her composure.

"Yes you can," he said. "Let go, Emily. Don't carry it around with you any longer."

* * *

The breeze is dying down a bit and Robert takes his hands from his pockets. The old man next to him seems indifferent to the weather. A tough old bird, he thinks as he watches the man extract another nut from the bag. The bag, he thinks is bottomless, as the old fellow never seems to be at a loss. "Emily is a term in contradiction," he says. "She is at once as delicate as a flower and the pillar of strength. At times she seems to encompass the properties of steel and at other times I fear that she may break like glass yielding to a stone. I was glad when she had told me that she had sought professional help. I know that it was neither easy for her to seek it nor was it easy for her to share that knowledge with me. Emily, you see, had always put on airs of strength and independence. Of course she possessed these traits and I submit that she had a greater command of them then I myself had ever dared dream, but she is human and that I think she had tried to stave off the truth of how utterly human she truly is. I think, too, that she feared my response to her seeking help. I am a private person to a fault, Toby. I've never truly opened up to another being other than you and one other. Perhaps she, she being Emily," he explains, "felt that I expected as much from her. Of course that is not the case, but how could she possibly know. I told her to talk. Do as I say and not as I do. I'm great for telling others," he says quietly. He shifts uncomfortably on the bench and retrieves his handkerchief to wipe away the beads of perspiration that does not exist from a face flush with grief.

"I sought help for Kathleen, but that did not work out so well. She needed to seek it of her own volition, but she would not. I forced it upon her. Eventually she tired of me and my bullying and relented." Robert bites down on his tongue and ceases to speak aloud for the time.

* * *

Emily continued to be uncharacteristic by spending the night and taking the following day off from work and allowing Shannon an unscheduled holiday from school. She, of course, made the proper phone calls to make the appropriate arrangements. She kept Shannon and Elizabeth up late into the night and her father even beyond those hours. She asked him if he had begun to write which brought great discomfort to him. She continued to press and grill him, despite his discomfiture, until he had made a promise before her that he would take up the pen to paper and be the creative genius that she believed him to be.

Robert slept poorly that night. Visions of Maria had stirred him to exhaustion with both pleasant and unpleasant emotions. Emily crept in and out of his dreams as well and from beyond the grave, Kathleen appeared before him for the first time in many years. She looked good, he thought. She looked better to him on this night than she would have appeared on even one of her better days. She was not the Kathleen of their youth, but the Kathleen of middle age and possibly, he thought, the Kathleen of her last days. Her eyes were bright and she smiled gaily at him. Was she trying to tell him something, he wondered? Was she smiling at his misfortune and his turmoil? No, he thought, she was not. Her smile was one of affection and kindness. He had not seen that smile from her in so many years. He had not seen that smile from her in the last several years of her life.

He wanted to speak to her. He wished to ask if she were happy, but he could not speak. His tongue had been held, but by what he did not know. It wasn't fear that had held him back. He felt very much at peace during his brief moment with Kathleen. He was so utterly calm for the first time in quite a while. She put her hand out to him and he very badly wished to take it, but he could not. He felt as though his hands were tied at his sides. Kathleen put down her hand, but continued to smile and he returned the smile, but did so ruefully. Kathleen, as though on a conveyor, moved away from him and slowly began to fade away and with her went the calm.

John McEntyre replaced Kathleen. McEntyre was also smiling, but his smile was grim and sympathetic. I don't want your sympathy, Robert thought, but again could not say so. Maria also appeared again. She was standing just behind McEntyre. Maria did not smile at him. She stared at him contemptuously and then turned away. I'm sorry, he wanted to say, but before he could speak he found himself standing beyond the gates of the school and he could not get in. Others passed him by and went through the gate, but he could not do so. He tossed and turned for what little time he had had before his alarm so mercifully interrupted his suspended consciousness.

The blaring of the alarm buzzer penetrated his nightmare and he awoke trembling and soaked with perspiration. He turned off the alarm and sat up in his bed. He buried his face in his hands and struggled to compose himself. His future was so very uncertain at this moment and he was unable to share his consternations with anyone, but himself. He, after all, had always been his greatest ally and confidant. He was at home and his house was filled with all of his family, but he felt so very alone. Why could he not talk as he had encouraged his daughter to do?

He was so thoroughly exhausted now, but he did not wish to sleep for fear of his subconscious. He forced himself to wake and dragged himself in to shower and shave and make himself presentable. He was still in a fight for his life and he wished not to show weakness. He had to right himself before Maria and impress himself before the school board if they would afford him the opportunity to do so.

He looked closely into the mirror. He had the clarity to see that his face reflected his mental disquiet. It would not be a good day, he thought, but again he could not bring himself to cower in the comfort of his home even with the formidable excuse of the unexpected visit of his daughter and granddaughter. No, he would again have to face the day and hope to make things better. He took a deep breath and went on down the stairs.

Elizabeth was not yet up. Robert hadn't considered that she would have slept in although it had been rather late before she had retired the night before. Elizabeth was usually up at the same time every morning no matter how early or late she had turned in the previous evening, but he, instead of questioning her absence, welcomed it. Refusing the chance of waking her, he did not prepare a meal for himself. Instead he left quietly like a thief in the night.

Up in her bed, Elizabeth listened as Robert struggled to leave quietly. As much as he did not realize it, he could be rather clumsy while attempting to be stealth-like. If she were not so upset, she would have laughed. If only things could go back to the way they were, she thought. There had been a great change in her brother over the past year. She had not imagined it to be a desire for companionship. It had never occurred to her that after all of these years, he would again awaken the sensibilities of a younger man. For a moment she thought of getting out of bed, but the desire was not so fierce. She laid her head back onto the pillow and pulled the covers over her head.

On his way to work, with the pangs of hunger penetrating his line of thought, he stopped in a little corner delicatessen where he picked up a newspaper, a cup of black tea and an egg and sausage sandwich. He had frequented this particular place for years, but never for breakfast. He asked Max, the crusty old man behind the counter, to add a little mushroom, but no onion to his sandwich. As he waited he noticed a woman watching him carefully. She was an attractive woman with rather large and expressive eyes. There was something very familiar about the woman, but Robert could not place her. She smiled at him and he did likewise and tilted his head as a gesture to confirm that he had in fact acknowledged her smile. He believed that he did not have the ability to smile sufficiently on command. For one reason or another he did not wish to leave this woman in doubt. He began to say good morning, but Max was tapping him on the shoulder in order to get his attention. Robert apologized to the man, not knowing how long he'd been lost in distraction, and paid him. Upon turning, he was disappointed to see that the woman had left. She was really rather pretty, he thought to himself.

He walked out of the store with the newspaper under his arm and his breakfast in a little brown bag and searched the avenue to his left and right, but to no avail. The woman with the beautiful eyes had evaded him. He shrugged with a hope of indifference and walked on to the school in a perfunctory manner.

"Good morning Mr. M," he heard many times from many different faces as he walked through the school corridors. He nodded and smiled and waved to the students with his newspaper and walked on to his office. For the moment he was so famished that he could think of nothing but the contents of the little brown bag. He had not thought of Maria at all since the rumbling of his stomach had begun. He removed his jacket, sat down and began to retrieve the little foil wrapped package from the bag. He opened it with considerable delight and took on a rather large and messy bite when Maria walked into the little room.

"Good morning, Robert," she said stoically.

With his mouth full he looked up at her with wide-open eyes. For a moment he did not know what to do. The sausage was in tact and if he should choose to swallow he would have most certainly choked. Chewing the food, he thought would make him look foolish, but to spit it out into the wrapper would no doubt leave her repulsed. Quickly, he put a napkin to his mouth and chewed furiously and swallowed hard.

"Maria," he said getting to his feet. "I was going to call you last night," he lied, "but I was taken by surprise and received a visit from Emily and Shannon."

"It really doesn't matter," she said coldly. "I'm just here to apologize for the other night."

"Apologize?" he said. "You've no need to apologize. It was me who acted the fool," he said.

"No," she said. "I made a fool of myself and if possible I would like to put it behind us." She searched his eyes, but could not read them. Clearly there was confusion and embarrassment, but what else, she did not know. "I hope you were discreet about my actions."

"Discreet?" he asked. "Oh," he said as the light came on in his head. "Yes, of course. I said nothing of this to anyone. I'd like to explain myself," he began, but then remembered he had no explanation worked out. Maria waited as he stood there with that lost look upon his face; she quickly grew impatient with him.

"When you have something to say to me," she said, "put it writing."

He stood there looking and feeling like a fool. "Yes," he said. "I most certainly will."

Maria put her hand on the doorknob and began to pull it shut. She hesitated for a moment and then she could not resist one last remark. "Incidentally," she said with just a hint of a smile breaking her guise.

"Yes?" he said hopefully.

"You have egg on your face." And with a look of satisfaction, she slowly pulled the door shut.

With the door closed and the blinds still drawn, the room went dark. Robert reached up to his face and retrieved a piece of scrambled egg and popped it into his mouth. That went well enough, he thought sardonically.

At home, Elizabeth hurriedly prepared breakfast for Emily and Shannon and disappeared as they were going up to wash and dress. She had gotten herself ready shortly after Robert had departed and wished to be well on her way to a new life before long. She picked up several papers promising employment and brought them back to her rooms. She had intended to scour them thoroughly, but found herself relentlessly interrupted by unwanted telephone solicitors to the point of her disconnecting the phone altogether. Perhaps, she thought, I am fated to be amongst those callers.

As much as she would have normally esteemed their company, Elizabeth was greatly pleased upon the departure of her niece and grandniece. It was nearly ten o'clock and there were yet several hours in front of her to achieve her objective. She carried a tray, containing a pot of Earl Grey tea and a slice of lightly buttered toast cut up into triangular quarters, back to her sitting room and splayed the papers out onto the table before her. She was at it but a moment when the sounds of halting trucks, clanging ladders and the overtures of churlish workmen had overtaken her concentration. Annoyed by this disruption, she immediately advanced towards the widow to investigate. She watched with confusion until it became apparent to her what their intentions had been. She watched with increasing horror as their objective became more evident to her. The papers upon her little table had suddenly lost their urgency. "Dear God," she said aloud. "This will kill him."

Chapter Ten

The day had crept along much too slowly for Robert's taste and this was somewhat of an anomaly to him. Throughout the morning he found himself incessantly glancing at the clock in the rear of his classroom. His distractions had been playing upon the minds of some of his more perceptive students. These students had been watching him all the more closely throughout the year, but had not commented on their observations to anyone at all. It was their love of him that had held their interest in the first place. But his exceptional distraction of today was more disconcerting to them. On this day he appeared to wish as though he were elsewhere. Robert Montgomery had never given them that impression before. This behavior was typical of most, if not all, of the students and perhaps even for most of the faculty at one time or another, but not for Mr. M.

Just before the last bell rang, John McEntyre entered his class. "Robert?" he said from the back door of the room.

"Yes, John," he said with a false air of confidence.

"Could you please stop in and see me before leaving today?" he asked with equal warmth and firmness.

"Yes," Robert replied. "I'll be along shortly." He watched as the door closed and then turned to his class. "Well," he began, but just as he did the final bell had rung. "All right," he shouted over the noise of books being slammed shut, chairs dragging along the floor and voices that had been reprieved from a muted state, "tomorrow we shall finish up our discussion of…" he started, but was unable to finish the thought.

He always started with words of such, but he could not remember what works they were in the process of discussing. His students, mercifully, did not wait for him. They slowly trickled from the room as sand through an hourglass. He watched and listened as the room filled with silence.

Before going into McEntyre's office, he walked into his own. He looked around for his briefcase, but it was not to be seen. He tried to think where it was that he had had it last. He retraced his steps of the day and thought back to the woman he had seen in Max's deli that morning. Perhaps, he thought, I've left it with the grocer. I don't know that I carried it back from there. He shrugged it off and decided he would stop in to see on his way home. It must be somewhere, he reasoned with an almost childlike attitude.

"Come in Robert," McEntyre said from behind his rather large mahogany desk. The desk was his own possession; his father-in-law, as a gift, had purchased it for him on the day he became the schools principal.

Robert walked through the doorframe feeling somewhat small. Thoughts of his childhood flooded his mind. He had been summoned to see the headmaster. It would not be good, he believed. "Hello, John," he said and took the proffered hand that had extended across the desk. This was rather formal, he thought. Had John ruminated over his actions prior to this meeting, he wondered?

"Sit down, Robert," the man said gesturing to the chair before him. He did not offer a beverage.

Robert rarely came into McEntyre's office, but on those few occasions when he had he had never felt the least bit intimidated. Today he had such feelings and tried desperately to counter them with indifference. At the very least he would keep hold of his dignity. "So?" he said with little hope.

"It's not what you were looking for," he said grimly. "I did all that I could do on your behalf," he said truthfully. "This is," he said with his hands positioned palms up hovering above his desk, "out of my hands."

"I see," he replied easily. "I appreciate your time, John. I know that this wasn't easy for you."

"The package, Robert..."

"Yes," he said with a faltering smile. "I'm sure it is quite reasonable."

"We can go over it at length," McEntyre said with all the enthusiasm he could muster.

"Not now," said Robert wearily. "I need a little time to digest my future."

"Of course," he replied. With no hope of sending Robert Montgomery off in good cheer, McEntyre lowered his head in consolation. The wind had been knocked out of his sails as well. "I'm sorry," he said. "You're the best teacher I have ever known."

With that, Robert stood up and smiled. "Thank you, John. I'm glad that it was you who'd given me my walking papers. I should hate to think that it had been done by someone who would have received pleasure from it." He extended his hand to McEntyre and shook it firmly. "I assume that I can finish out my last few days of the semester?"

"Of course Robert," McEntyre looked bewildered by the question. "You're not being fired," he said.

"No," said Robert. "I'm being put out to pasture. You know," he said from the door. "Some Eskimo tribes used to put their elderly on a raft or perhaps a block of ice and push them out to sea. I used to think that was barbaric. I wonder now if that was not a kindness." He left the room and left McEntyre to ponder his closing words.

* * *

"I was devastated, Toby. That was a crushing blow to me. It wasn't about pride or vanity, but purpose. I know you think that I probably should have been expecting it to come to pass and I suppose I did, but the reality of it was more painful to me than I had believed it could be and I had expected it to be quite a jolt. It was," he says with darkening eyes, "the first time in my life that I had ever truly wished to be dead. Of course," he continues, "suicide was quite out of the question. I could never have done that to Emily. It would," he resumes after a moment of reflection, "have been bad for Elizabeth and Shannon as well, but Emily, I fear, would have been damaged beyond all repair. Truthfully," he goes on, "I am too much of a coward to take my own life. It always makes me wonder what it is that can bring someone to go beyond the contemplation.

"I knew that I had to go home and tell my tales of woe, but as I explained to John, I needed time to digest my situation and I couldn't bring myself to discuss it with Elizabeth. Elizabeth was never so good with things as such. She's not particularly delicate with such matters," he explains. "She would say things that would give me more reason to distress. Sometimes you need to talk and you need someone to just listen and prompt you in the right places. You need someone who can relate and identify with you. Do you follow me, Toby?"

Toby sits there staring straight ahead. Robert wonders what, if anything, the man is thinking. "It's getting a little chilly out here. You ought to bundle up a bit." He steps in front of the old man and buttons the top button of his pea coat. He pulls a scarf from his pocket and drapes it around Toby's neck. He steps back to survey the old man and decides that he's been indifferent to the climate. "You must have been a fierce young man in your prime," he says. "You were probably of great value."

Robert turns away and looks again towards the river. There are tears welling up in his eyes, but he pays them no attention. "It's rather cold out there," he says.

* * *

Robert went directly to Farrell's and ordered a pint. He discussed matters of inconsequential interests with casual acquaintances until Henry Grifhorst arrived about an hour later. "How far behind am I, Monty?" he asks.

"Just about three pints," he replied.

Henry stepped up to the barstool and sat beside Robert and ordered two pints. "I've got good seats for the Mets on Friday night," he said. "Think you can drag yourself away from your lilies?"

"I think I can find the time, but only if you promise to buy me one of those giant frankfurters."

"Done," he said. "You wanna talk?"

"About?"

Henry gestured towards the beer in front of Robert. "Three pints before I walk in the door? That isn't like you. It's only four-thirty."

"This is a special occasion, Henry. I'm celebrating," Robert said.

Henry studied Robert's face and knew that there was no celebration in his eyes. "Okay," he said. "What are we celebrating?"

"My retirement," he said and drew heavily from his glass.

Henry lifted his in a mock toast and clanked Robert's glass and then drew heavily on his own beer. "Retirement doesn't mean death, Monty."

"It does for me," he said staring into his beer. "You left something you'd grown weary of to do something you'd prefer to do. I'm leaving what I love most to do with no prospects."

"That's today," Henry said gruffly. "Cry into your beer all night and tomorrow wake up to a new life filled with promise. Stop seeing the glass half empty," he said lamely.

Robert picked up his beer mug. "It is half empty," he said.

Henry picked up his mug and poured its contents into Robert's, filling it to the brim. "Now it's full," he said grinning.

"So it is," he said with a hint of smile. "You're a genius."

Henry took notice of that hint of a smile and for a moment was filled with encouragement, but the hint receded and the face darkened and he could see that his friend was dying on the inside and that it bled to the surface. "There are so many great things that you can do. I can get you involved."

"I appreciate that, Henry. For a while, though, I think that I need to be alone. I need to make things right in my head again before I'm of any use to anyone. I'll be a little withdrawn for a few days. I'll putter about in my garden and I'll get lost in my books. That will help me to maintain my sanity. After that we shall see."

"I'll give you some time, but don't take too long. Life's too short to be frittering it away on self-pity."

"Agreed. Henry," he said and gripped his forearm. "Don't speak of this to anyone just yet. I don't wish to discuss this for the moment."

"Including Lizzie?"

"Especially Elizabeth," he said.

"Okay, but don't let on later that I knew anything about this. I may be a big tough guy, but I'm afraid of her."

"I made telephone calls all afternoon," Elizabeth cried out as Robert walked through the door. It was seven o'clock and he'd had six pints of ale swimming through his system. "They had approval from the city, Robert. They had all the papers and they said that there was nothing that we could do to stop it." Elizabeth had tears and fury in her eyes.

"What are you saying, Elizabeth? Calm down and start from the beginning," he said in a soothing manner.

"They put up a second story," she said and the tears came streaming out of her eyes. "I'm sorry, dear. I tried to stop them, but they wouldn't listen. They said it was their right and that we had no recourse."

"What second story?" he asked. Her words, his grief, and the alcohol were all jumbled up in his head and he was so very confused. "What are you saying, Elizabeth?" he implored. He put his hands on her shoulders and gave her a slight shake to awaken her from the hysterics.

"The wall behind us is twice the size now," she said. "They built a second story above that old garage."

He understood her now and his heart sank. "No," he said still holding her, but his grip lessened. "There must be some mistake." He would not believe her. He must see this for himself. This could not have happened. "We'll fight this," he said. "We'll not let them do it."

"It's done, Robert," she said. She grieved more for him than for herself. "They did it all this afternoon. The men came with the trucks and the bricks and just like that it went up."

There was a look of horror in his eyes and he felt his chest tightening up. "No," he said. "No." He shook his head and repeated himself over and over. "No." He lifted his feet heavily from the floor and made his way to the kitchen door and walked out into his yard. It was true. A big ugly brick wall was facing him now. It was twice its original size. No longer could he see the treetops in the distance. The climbing vines on the wall had been cut or perhaps torn away without care. Cement hand run down the wall onto his flowerbeds. "Mother of God," he whispered as if to the Virgin Mother herself. He fell to his knees on his little patio and began to cry. Elizabeth ran to his side, but there was no consoling him. He wept quietly for quite some time and all she could do was stay by his side.

Emily came to the house the following day. Elizabeth had summoned her first thing that morning and Emily immediately understood the gravity of her fathers' loss. She took Shannon to school and contacted the office and traveled immediately by a hired cab. "Where is he?" she asked her aunt without as much as a hello.

If this had put off Elizabeth, she did not show it. "He's in his room, dear. He won't get up. I knew it would be bad, but he's taken it much worse than I'd expected." Elizabeth put her handkerchief to her mouth and began to cry again as she had much of the night.

Emily put her arms around her and hugged her tightly. "It's going to be all right," she said and then kissed her aunt on the cheek.

Without going to look at the new construction, Emily charged up the stairs taking the steps two at a time. She hesitated at her father's door to catch her breath and think a moment what she might say. It was not like her father to break down this way. At the worst of times he had always managed to maintain his composure, she thought. He would get a little more quiet and a take on a little added reserve, but never had he broken down as her aunt had described. The very fact that he had not gotten out of his bed to make his way to the school proved some validity to her aunts' description.

She tugged at the ends of her white hooded jacket and with some trepidation raised her hand and gently knocked at the door. She waited a moment and then reached for the doorknob and opened it slowly. "Daddy," she called. Her heart began to pound in her chest and her hand trembled on the knob. "Daddy," she called again. She was crying now. She was a child again and frightened for her father. "Daddy," she called once again, but her voice was louder. She would not open the door any further.

From beneath his pillow, Robert heard his daughter calling. He could hear the fear in her voice and his heart skipped a beat. "Emily," he called. He tried to scramble out from under the covers. He forced them away from himself furiously as a man fighting for his life under an avalanche. Elizabeth had tucked in the blankets to hold him securely the night before as one might do for a child. "I'm coming, Emily." He ran to the door and pulled it open and there she stood. Both father and daughter stood there with hearts racing. They stood there staring at one another until the relief set in.

"What is it?" he said. Are you all right?"

"I was worried for you," she said, the terror still in her eyes.

"You needn't have worried before," he said, "but perhaps you might start to worry now." He grabbed at his chest and ambled over to a chair. "You scared the hell out of me."

"Well you scared the hell out of me first," she rebuked. "Why are you still in bed?"

He looked at the clock on his nightstand. "It's nine-fifteen," he blurted out. "I'm tired."

"It's a school day," she said.

"I've only missed about a half dozen in over thirty years. I think I'm entitled to one more."

"I heard about the wall," she said gingerly. "Aunt Elizabeth said you took it pretty badly."

"Yes," he said. "I did at that."

"She said you cried."

"Your aunt is a bit of a gossip," he said angrily.

"She was worried about you."

"Yes," he said and softened. "I was a bit melodramatic last night. Have you seen the wall?"

"No," she said.

"Go into my study. You'll get the full effect in there." He got up from the chair and went into the bathroom.

Emily walked down the hall and opened the door to his study. The laptop computer she had gotten for him was as it was the night she had set it up for him. The manuals had not been opened and the wireless card had not been inserted. She turned towards the window and reached for the cord. She pulled at it and saw what would face her father for the rest of his days should he remain in this home. "Christ," she said.

"Yes," he said from the door. "You know that it took me over a week to put the tile floor down in my bathroom? It's not a very large room and more than half of it is taken up by a tub and toilet. Still, it took me more than a week to cover a little flooring with tile. The men who did that must have been gods of some sort."

"You've lost your view entirely," she said.

"You noticed that too?"

"I'm sorry if I sound like a fool, but you don't have to hurt me with sarcasm."

"I'm sorry, Emily," he said as he came by her side. He took her hand with his right and placed it into his left and cupped it. He patted her hand and brought it up to his cheek and together they looked out at the monstrosity before them. "I'm not handling things very well of late. I fear that I've been failing everyone these past few days. I'm failing myself, assuredly. I'd probably be better off left alone for a while," he said solemnly. "Just to work things out for a bit, you understand."

"You don't have to do that alone," she said. She turned to face him, but he would not allow her to capture his eyes. "If you can't talk to me, perhaps you might do better with a complete stranger."

"Perhaps," he agreed. "You suggest professional help." It was not a question that he was asking.

"Yes," she said; "maybe not the same therapist that I see, but another."

"That would make you uncomfortable," he said. Emily did not answer, but of course they both knew that it was the truth. "I'm just not ready for that yet," he said. "You understand that, don't you?"

"I do," she said. "Still, I think it might help."

"It's only a wall," he said with a grim smile. "I'll get over it." They both knew that it was more than just a wall, but she would not press the issue any further. He had never pressed her and she would offer him the same unsound consideration.

"I love you, daddy."

"It's so dark in here," he said not hearing her at all. He looked out at the wall and down at the ruins of his haven. "What's left for me?" he said aloud not thinking that Emily would hear.

"Everything is left," she said. "You have a family and friends and your work. You don't have to stay here. You can move someplace else with a view all of your choosing."

He thought about losing his friendship with Maria and the loss of his work. Now he had to think about leaving his home and that was too much. "No," he said at last. "I will adapt to this. In time it will be as though it had always been there. "I'll make it acceptable to me again. Perhaps I'll have a mural done with the old view," he said, but of course that would never be done. "I'll adapt," he promised. "Now, why aren't you at work?"

"I can take another day off," she said.

"Go to work, Emily. Losing two days in the same week will be too much for you to bear."

She smiled up at him knowing that it was true. "Will you be all right?" she asked him.

"I'll be fine."

"You could write."

He looked over at the little computer on his desk and then glanced back at her. "I could," he said. She tilted her head and pursed her lips and Robert could see the hint of admonishment in her eyes. "I'm obligated to do so?" he asked.

"Yes," she said. "You're obligated."

"I'll try, Emily. I really will. I need a little time to get things worked out in my head and then I'll get to it. I just need to talk to myself for a while and then I'll be okay again; right as rain as they say."

"Nobody says that any more. Write a story, daddy. It will do you good." She kissed him on the cheek and left him alone in his study. At the top of the stairs she had to steady herself. Her hands were trembling and she gripped the banister until her knuckles whitened. She looked down the hallway and up to the trap to the attic and then looked away. She wanted to go back to her father, but instead she walked down the steps and kissed her aunt goodbye after giving assurance of his well-being.

"It was in mid-February," she said. Her breathing was shallow and deliberately controlled. She was not facing him, but he faced her on her left side. She was seeing that day in mid-February as she had seen it on so many days and nights before. The eye that he could see was cold as was the side of her face. There were no lines to suggest any emotions and the tone of her voice was singular. She spoke as though outside of her own self and it was chilling even to him. He waited.

"There'd been a heavy snowfall that morning and I didn't have to go to school, although the schools were open. My father left home earlier than usual that day so that he could get to work on time. I argued that there wouldn't be any work done in school that day and he was happy to let me have the day off. All of my friends were staying at home," she said. "Or at least they weren't going into school. My mother had been indifferent"

Dr. Hiller noted a flicker in her eye, but nothing else in her manner had shifted. It was a minute or two before she resumed. "My mother was quiet that morning, but it didn't strike me as being out of the norm. Perhaps she was quieter than what was typical, but I was looking out of the window and at the snow and not taking so much notice of her." The doctor wanted more information on this, but dared not to interrupt her. "I just wanted to play in the snow. I wanted nothing more than to get out of the house. Away from her," she said and then the ice began to melt in the form of tears that collected slowly in her eye and took a very long time before trickling down her cheek. The doctor did not offer her the box of tissues. He sat and he waited.

"My mother helped me to dress. She lay out my clothes on the bed as if I were still a little child. There were so many clothes. She wanted me to be kept warm and dry, but she said very little and I didn't wish to argue with her over the clothes. I was afraid to get her angry and then lose my chance to go out. I put on the clothes and then the heavy coat and hat and a scarf that was much too long for my size and not my style at all. I didn't care so much, though. So long as I got out into that snow, I didn't care.

"We lived near Prospect Park and there they have great hills for sledding. I had a little wooden sled that my father," she stopped and paused a moment. "A sled that my father and mother had gotten me for Christmas and this was the first real snowfall to get to use it. I went to the park with my friend Amy and her two brothers, Ronald and Brian. I had a crush on Ronald and promised him the first ride with me on my new sled. I had told my mother that I would be home for lunch, but I lost track of the time." She stopped talking and wiped the tears from her eyes.

"No," she said. "That's what I've always told myself, but it isn't true. I didn't lose track of the time. I thought about the time all of that day, but I pushed it aside. I didn't want to go back home. I wasn't hungry for lunch. I wanted to play and I didn't want to go home. I wanted to be happy and stay out all day long and ride those hills. The snow was so deep and the hills, after a while, were packed down and the sled moved so easily and so quickly. Ronald was two years older than I. He had thick black hair and his eyes were blue like my fathers'. He was tall, or at least I remember him being so. His shoulders were broad. I remember thinking that he had the body of a man now. He'd grown so much in such a short time. He was in high school," she said and a small flicker of a smile passed her lips. "He lay on the sled and I lay on his back and we drove so quickly down those hills. My heart leapt as we did. I wanted to stay there with him forever.

"It was Amy that insisted we go home. It was nearly four and I felt that I'd be in trouble, but I didn't care. I had that day, I thought. Nothing could take that time away from me. Ronald carried my sled with one hand and then held my hand with the other. Even through my ridiculous pink gloves and his black ones, I could feel his hand and imagine its warmth. He carried the sled up my stoop and leant it against the wall by the door. I wanted him to kiss me and I think that he wanted to as well, but we were so young and awkward and just knowing it made my heart skip a beat.

"I ran into the house wishing to tell someone about my day, but I didn't want that person to be my mother. I didn't think she would approve. I was twelve," she said. "I took off my gloves, scarf and hat and then wrestled out of my coat and boots for what seemed like an eternity and began to wonder about my mother. She wouldn't have gone out, I thought. She detested the snow. I looked around downstairs for a bit and called for her, but she didn't come. I went up the stairs and searched the rooms on the second floor, but again nothing. I prayed silently to myself that I would not find her crying on the third floor. I didn't even want to climb the stairs to see, but I did. I lumbered up the steps very slowly. The joy of my day was passing away in waves and my thoughts were filled with dread.

"I began to hate her," she said. I felt that she'd been nothing but a burden to me and to my father. She was sucking the very life from our souls. I first looked into the room that is now my fathers' study and then as I turned I saw her hanging through the attic door. She had tied a rope around a beam in the attic and made a knot around her neck and jumped through the trap. They said her neck was broken and that she must have died immediately. I couldn't see her face from where I was. Her head and shoulders were still in the attic. Only her legs and torso hung through the door. I didn't get any closer to her and so I couldn't see her face. I suppose I was frozen, but I really don't know. I can still see her hands dangling at her sides and her feet… She only had on one shoe. The other must have been on the floor in the hall, but I don't know. Her hands were so white. I see those hands all the time. I see her hands when people offer to shake mine. I don't like to shake hands, doctor.

"They said that I was screaming and screaming, but I don't recall that. The man next-door was a truck driver and had stayed home due to the snow. He had to break the door down to get in. He came up and saw what had happened and carried me down the stairs. I don't remember any of that. I only remember my father being with me in the hospital. I was being treated for shock. I didn't stay there long. They wanted me to talk with people like you, but I refused. I had calmed down that evening. It was like I'd been sleeping and when I woke my father was sitting on the bed holding my hand. I hugged him and that was all."

Dr. Hiller gave her some time and then when it was apparent to him that she had concluded he spoke to her. "What do mean when you say that is all?"

"I told my father that I was all right now and that I wanted to leave the hospital," she said without emotion.

"Did you leave the hospital very quickly?"

"Yes."

"Did he take you home?"

"No. We stayed with friends of my father for a while at first. It was I who had asked to go home."

"Were you frightened? Going home I mean."

"Yes," she said flatly. "I tried not to show it though. I wanted to get on with life again."

"What were your feelings towards your mother at that point?"

"I hated her more in death than I had in life," she said. Dr. Hiller had surmised that by the celerity of her words the response had been well considered and not at all spontaneous. "I don't hate her so much any more," she said and faced the doctor full on for the first time. Her cold eyes had warmed over, but he knew that she was fighting to maintain the chill.

"But," he said, "You still hate her?"

She averted her eyes from him and then turned away altogether and looked out of the window. She despised the doctor for the moment. She knew that it was irrational on her part to despise him, but she did. She was being weak and he was analyzing her and she hated herself and him and yet it was she who had sought help from him. "I hate you more," she said.

"I know that, but I don't care. Do you still feel hatred towards your mother?"

"For killing herself?" she asked.

"You tell me."

"I pity her now," she said. "There is some anger and maybe not so much hatred any more. I don't really know. I struggle not to think about it. I work so that I don't have to think about it."

"But you do think about it," he said. It was not a question.

"Yes, of course I do. I see my mother hanging through the ceiling for a moment or two most every day. I want to erase that memory. You have a pill for that?"

"No," he said. "I do not."

"I guess I've wasted my time."

"You'll never erase the memory, Emily. But you can cope with it a little better. You can accept it and try, hard as that may be, to understand it."

"How am I to understand it?" she asked angrily. She was crying now and her hands were balled up into fists. Dr. Hiller put his hands gently over her fists and patted them to tranquility.

"Your mother was suffering. It was not about you and most probably not even about your father."

"I think you're wrong," she said almost pleading. "I think she hated me immensely."

The doctor wanted to tell Emily that her mother had loved her, but of course he had no foundation to base that on and knew that it would be unprofessional to say such things. He needed to know more about her mother, but that could only come with more time and time was running out on their session. This particular session had been unscheduled. Emily had called and he was able to just fit her in, but now, as he glanced at the clock behind her, he could see that they only had a few minutes left. He was very much distressed that they had just opened a door of such importance when he hadn't the time to delve deeper into its chamber. If the door had closed on him, he wondered if he could ever get through it again.

"She knew," Emily began, "that I would be the one to find her. How could she do that to me? I'm a mother. I could never do such a thing to my child. A mother protects her child," she said. She was sobbing heavily. She no longer despised him and was able to fall completely apart before him. Suddenly there was trust and he knew it and yet there was the clock on the little table just behind her.

"People in such a state aren't always conscious of the consequences to others," he said hurriedly. "I'm sure that she was thinking only of her own pain. Perhaps she thought it in the best interests of her family to end that pain." He grimaced at his words. They were out there and he could not take them back. He'd been unprofessional and if he attempted to backtrack he would surely display the infirmity of his words. Emily, he knew, was far too clever to not pick up on a retreat of what should be his convictions. He stressed over this, but all to no good reason. Emily had not heard a word that he had spoken. Her mind was in her past and on her own failings.

"I didn't come home," she cried. "I promised that I'd be home for lunch and I wasn't."

Her words came as a relief to him. He was the doctor again and in control. He could soothe and explain and offer her food for thought. "It's not your fault," he said. "Your mothers' actions were not a direct correlation to yours."

She turned and stared at him with eyes so cold that he had to sit back a little. "How can you know that?" she nearly spat. Her mouth, too, was cold and cruel and he thought it almost like a mask.

"I ca… I don't…" he stammered. "What is it that you want?" he blurted with some semblance of authority. "Do you wish to take the responsibility for your mothers' death?" He increased the strength of his voice dramatically.

"Perhaps," she said weakly.

"You were a child," he said. His voice was firm yet soothing. "Go home, Emily," he said after looking at the clock. "Be with your daughter and know that you are a good mother to her and call me tomorrow. We'll try to fit you in for another session."

"No," she said. "I don't think so. I'll come back next week as scheduled unless I decide to cancel. She turned and glanced at the little clock behind her. "I better get out of here. You'll only just make your next appointment."

* * *

"Emily has always been a wonder to me, Toby. She'd always run hot and cold with her emotions. I never should have let her leave the hospital, but it was what she had wanted. She seemed well enough to me, but I should have given it more consideration. After all she'd only been a child no matter how mature I thought her to be. I'd gotten a phone call and went directly to hospital." He stopped and smiled. "To 'the' hospital," he said correcting himself to the American English that he'd lived with for most of his life. "Emily was lying in a bed, still wearing her street clothes. She was quiet, but I'd been told that she'd been screaming hysterically from the time she had seen Kathleen until just about five minutes before I'd arrived.

"My head was swimming with thoughts of I don't know what. My wife was dead and my daughter in shock and can you come and help make sense of this? Mother of God," he whispers. There is a light mist falling on them and soon they would have to take cover, but Robert and Toby can wait to be summoned. Robert paces before the bench. The sodden leaves are being crushed beneath his feet, but are muted by the moisture that has been dancing through the air and settling on the ground. "My concern had been for Emily. There was no longer anything that I could do for Kathleen. Grieving for her and taking guilt upon myself for her death would have to wait for another time. My little girl was in shock.

"They'd medicated her with something or other and I wondered, but did not ask if she seemed better before or after the medication. I asked very little about her condition, actually. I couldn't bring myself to ask for fear that there might be an answer that I couldn't bear. I just sat there on the bed and held her little white hand. I would kiss her every now and again and then rub her hands to warm them. Her poor little hands were like ice, but her face was warm. Her eyes were open all the while, but she seemed oblivious to everything." He looks at the old man and nods an almost imperceptible nod. "Her eyes were not dead, though," he says gratefully. "I was comforted to see her eyes move as though she were in thought. She would not look up at me, but she did not pull away either. This I took to be a good sign under the circumstances.

"I was told to let her know that I was there. I understood without listening further. I needed to reach her. I wanted to speak, but I could say nothing. I was choking on air. I could only hold her hand to let her know that I was with her. In the end, I suppose it was enough. She came around eventually." Robert can see his little girl lying there on the bed. Her face is as white as a sheet. Her hair is a long and tangled mess with a pink clip that had once been carefully put into place and now appears to be trapped within the knots. He can see the little freckles that pepper her nose and the few strays that spill high up on her cheeks. He can still see the terror that reflected from her eyes and even now that terror mirrors out of his own.

"Perhaps I should have forced her to speak with the doctors, but my faith in them was weak and the desire to force her was not a task that I could have performed. When she began to speak later that night she asked to leave and I wanted to do what was most pleasing to her. She was scared and truthfully not very trusting of doctors. We stayed with friends of mine for just a bit, but Emily insisted on going back home shortly after the funeral. She has always cherished her privacy as much as I," he says thoughtfully.

"I suggested that we might move from our home. I thought it might be good for her to make a fresh start of things, but she resisted and I, not truly desirous of leaving my home, failed to press the matter. As it turned out, I suppose that it was right not to move away," he says without conviction. "I liked my home and there was plenty of room for us and later, for Elizabeth to come and join us."

* * *

"I'm sorry that I couldn't be there to pay my respects. I really wish that I had gotten the chance to meet with Kathleen. I was so very fond of our telephone conversations," Elizabeth said speaking into the telephone. They were an ocean apart and had not seen each other since he had first gone away, but the sound of their voices was so clear.

Elizabeth felt as though they were speaking to each other from different rooms in the same house.

"Don't give it another thought," he said. It was a week that had passed since Kathleen's funeral. There had been some question as to whether or not she would be permitted burial in consecrated ground. After some debate and long discussions on prescribed medications, Kathleen's body was finally accepted. There had been no need for Elizabeth to be privy to this information, nor was there need for her to know the true circumstance of Kathleen's death. She had fallen from the attic and had broken her neck. No more information was necessary to be given to Elizabeth or to his mother for that matter.

Robert wrote a letter at the end of each month addressed to Elizabeth with sections to be passed along to his mother and words of kindness to be passed on to Bernard. Elizabeth always answered his letters and with the letters there were paragraphs that were supposedly dictated by his mother and Bernard, but Robert knew them to be fabrications from his sister. The wording was never quite right and the sentiments could not pass as those of neither his mother nor Bernard.

He would telephone England on special occasions, but the calls were generally brief to keep down the costs and the telephone conversations that Elizabeth remembered fondly with Kathleen never amounted to more than that of "happy Christmas" or "birthday" and "I'm thinking of you" or "you're remembered in my prayers".

"I want you to know that I would have come to the funeral, but…"

"It's all right," he said not knowing if that were true.

"No," she said. "You don't understand." She had planned to put it all down in a letter, but that, she thought, would be most unkind and an act of cowardice on her part. It had not been so very easy for her to speak with him. It was not like it was way back when. Robert had changed in her mind. He was a man who had a career and a family and traveled to America, while she had merely gotten older. He'd been moving with the world and she'd been letting it pass her by.

"Father died," she said.

He was stunned to silence for awhile and then just to let her know that he was still on the line, he said "what?"

"Father died," she repeated.

"I don't understand," he said. "When did this happen?"

"The very night that you had called to tell me about Kathleen," she said. "It was not expected. He'd had a heart attack while watching the telly. He didn't suffer," she said firmly. "I was with him when it came. He dropped his glass and fell over. There was nothing to be done. I screamed for Mr. Firth next door. He was a medic during the war. He came immediately and tried to bring father around, but he could do nothing."

"Why didn't you tell me?"

"There was nothing you could do. You couldn't be here and mother and I felt the grief you were carrying would be all that you could bear. We decided that you would only put guilt upon yourself for not being here as well as there."

"Are you all right, Elizabeth?"

"Yes," she said.

"Is mother all right?"

"No," she said. "But it has nothing to do with father's passing, though. Mothers' health has been in a decline."

"What is it?"

"Her mind is a bit unclear. Even without the drink she seems a bit unstable. She won't see a doctor. She won't leave the house. She sits in front of the mirror adjusting and readjusting her make-up and hair and cries when she sees that it doesn't come as it used to. She can't handle the aging, Robert. She wishes to be young and beautiful, but with her it is not just a wish so much as it is an obsession that can never come to be." She went silent for a time and he let the silence linger, as he had nothing to say. "I'm frightened," she finally admitted. "I don't know what I am going to do. With father gone I've had time to look more closely at mother and I'm just realizing that I live with a crazy woman."

"There's a spring break coming at Easter next month," he said. "I'll come home to see you then."

"Will you? Will you truly come and see me?"

"Yes, dear," he said. His eyes filled with tears for her and for his mother. He shed no tears for Bernard. He felt only pity for a life that had passed the man by.

Elizabeth was unable to greet them at the airport. Mrs. Reardon, a good friend and neighbor, had to work that Saturday morning and was unable to look after Margaret. Robert and Emily came directly from Birmingham International, but would not be staying at the little house on the canal. Instead, Robert thought it best to make arrangements in a hotel in town so that Emily could have a more comfortable trip with the activities of a city.

"My God, Robert," Elizabeth said as she greeted them at the door. "You look so old."

"Thank you," he said grinning at her honesty. "I feel older than I look, though."

"Poor dear," she said. "Of course you must." She turned to Emily and smiled. "You are a beautiful young woman," she said. There was a moment of awkward hesitancy until Emily reached in and hugged her aunt. Elizabeth embraced her mechanically. It would be some time before a hug and a kiss would become a gesture made in comfort for her. "You must both be exhausted after such a long journey."

"Not at all," he lied. "We were able to sleep on the plane last night. You look wonderful, Elizabeth." He looked her over closely and silently grieved for her. She did not look at all well, he thought. She was but a young woman and yet seemed determined to fill the role of a spinster. "I'm so sorry about Bernard," he said with as much empathy as he could muster. "He was a good man."

"He wasn't as bad as you might think him to be," she said behind her fading smile. "You had to look at the world from his point of view. You had to grow up the way he did and live the way he lived and be judged the way he'd been judged. People are cruel, Robert. The cruelty can shape a weak person."

"Of course," he agreed stupidly. He looked at Elizabeth more closely and saw that she had resembled Bernard more now than he had remembered. There was something in the eyes that shook him a bit. Her eyes, though, were not yet dead as Bernard's had been. She was not as hopeless as her father. Had Bernard been more like her at her age? Would the trace of light flicker and go out as well? He looked around the small room and saw that very little had changed in his absence. "I've lived in the world for a bit now," he said. "I don't wish to judge another being for as long as I shall live."

She stared at him for a moment, but could think of nothing relevant to say. "Would you like to see mother?"

"Yes," he said, but truthfully he would have rather had their meeting put off for a bit. He turned to Emily and put his hand on her shoulder. "Give me a moment," he said gently.

"Okay daddy," she said carefully. She did not want him to pick up on her relief. "I'll just walk along the canal for a bit."

"Don't wander off too far," he said knowing that his words would not be followed. He turned to Elizabeth and waited.

"You go along," she said. "I'll just put on the tea."

He nodded, meaning to say 'yes', but the word did not come out. He walked slowly to his mother's room and knocked on the door.

"Just go on in," Elizabeth called from the kitchen. "Mother never answers to calls or knocks."

Robert opened the door a few inches and knocked again before entering to give her a final warning. Margaret was sitting in a chair by the window. She was wearing an old dress that he remembered from his childhood. The dress was worn and faded and she wore it the way sand wears a bag. Her body was lumpy and her hair, that once gave her such pride, was now like straw. She wore a ribbon at her throat. The ribbon was tattered and frayed and it too had faded. Her face was wrinkled badly. She was staring out of the window and he could only see her in profile. If he had come across her on the street, he would not have recognized her. He did not recognize her now.

"Mother," he said. "It's Robert."

She turned to face him and smiled with teeth blackened with nicotine and rot. Her make-up had been applied poorly and much too heavily. The rouge on her cheeks was streaked on like rust against a white sheet and her blood red lipstick was smeared on and made her mouth looked lopsided. Her eyes were still bright, though. They were the eyes he remembered from his childhood. "Robert?" she said. It was a question.

"Yes, mother. I've come to see you."

"All the way from America?" she said.

"Yes," he said. "I'm sorry about Bernard."

"No," she said. Her eyes looked away from his. "We are not sorry about Bernard. Bernard was a mistake; a mistake that I made for you."

"What are you saying?"

"You know what I'm saying, dear. Lizzie will miss him, though." She lifted her hand to her head and ran her fingers through her lifeless hair as she had always done as a young woman. The flesh on her arms fell back and forth as she moved and the sight of it disgusted Robert and his disgust embarrassed him. She looked to be a woman of eighty or more and yet she was only in her sixties. The fast life was carrying her quickly to the finish line.

"I am sorry about Bernard."

"Please don't do that," she said and put up her hand to halt his protests. "My mind is clear," she said. "It's not always so. Just for a little while be a Robbie or a Bob and give Robert a rest, love. Say what you think and feel and let's not be proper. We did not care for Bernard and Bernard did not care for us. We married to make a family. I was trying to be what you wanted and Bernard was trying to be what others expected. I tired of the charade first and he stopped caring immediately thereafter. Bernard was useless as a man. If not for Lizzie, he would have left and I would have been grateful."

"Bernard was not a saint, but you were closer to a demon, mother."

"That was cold, love," she said and looked directly into his eyes. "Perhaps we should ask Robert to come back to us."

"I'm sorry mother, but I was there. Bernard had given more of an effort than you had."

"Bernard was a dullard," she said flatly. "He gave no effort at being anything but what he was. I had to be completely different."

"You didn't have to be completely different," he said making an attempt to keep his voice controlled. Margaret could see the tension in his body and hear it in his voice. "You needn't have married Bernard or anyone else. You could have sung and danced and remained the carefree soul that you wished to be. All I needed from you was to be a mother to me and to stay around."

"And not carry on with so many men?" she said coldly.

"Yes," he agreed. "And not carry on with so many men."

"That is who I am," she said. "I suspected that that was also the way of your father."

Robert looked at her quizzically. "Suspected?" he asked. "Didn't you know the man you first married?"

"Of course I knew him," she said. "Robert Montgomery was a decent sort of fellow and I do believe that I loved him, but that would never have worked. No," she continued. "I wasn't talking about him at all." She looked up at Robert stoically. "I was speaking of your father. Of course I only knew him for a few hours and he was tight at the time. We were both quite tight actually. He was an American soldier and here on leave. Bigger than you, but I could always see a lot of him in you."

Robert went a little weak at the knees and sat down on the edge of his mother's bed. "My father was not Robert Montgomery?" His voice was almost a whisper. "Are you in your right mind, mother?"

"Yes," she said. "Quite so, actually; are you really so surprised?"

"An American?" he asked.

"Yes. I suppose that you were called home. Do you fit in well in America, Robert?"

"Why are you being so cruel?"

"I left you at times Robert, but I always came back."

"You hate me for leaving?" he asked. His eyes looked at her dully as he waited for her to answer him.

"No," she said. "I envied you a bit, but I cheered when you left. You had more courage than I had. You just picked up and went."

"I didn't leave a family behind."

"Of course you did, love." She smiled at him with those hideous teeth surrounded by the lips of a clown. "We were a family. Perhaps we weren't the family of one of your silly little storybooks, but we were a family. We were flesh and blood people and not just the words on the pages of your silly little stories. Your sister and I were your blood, Robert," she said with cold spiteful eyes. "You left a family behind and you never came back."

Robert stood up and paced the room quietly, methodically. "You cheered my leaving?"

"Yes, love. Of course I did."

"Because you had wished to do the same, mother?"

"It's not so easy for a mother to leave a child behind."

"You seemed quite capable. Truthfully, I thought that you only returned after others tired of you."

Her eyes cast downward. Robert could see that there was truth in his words and he regretted saying them to her, but did not attempt a retraction. She was hurt and he would let her be so. "Perhaps there is a little of me in you after all," she said without looking up."

"Who was this man?" he asked. "My father, I mean."

"His name was Jack," she said. "Or at least that's what he called himself. A lot of American military men called themselves John or Jack in those days."

"How do you know which of them was my father?"

"There weren't as many men in my life in those days as you may think, love. I was never unfaithful to Robert Montgomery," she said with conviction.

"I was born ten months after he died."

"So you knew."

"I suspected for a time, but I never questioned."

"You shoved your nose in a book, I suppose."

Her words stung him more at this moment than any other. "A boy needed an escape from the treachery of his mother," he said. "Did Jack have a last name?"

"Not one that I remember. Did you wish to look him up and go fishing or something?"

"It would be nice to know where I came from. I would have liked to know whose blood ran through my veins."

"I'm sure your father grew up to be quite proper," she said. He couldn't have been any more than twenty when we… He was kind and spoke respectfully to me. He was not at all vulgar. You would have approved of him."

"I'm sure."

"I do believe, however, that he was of Irish descent. Is that a problem?"

"No," he said. "I suppose very little matters now."

"What about you, Robert? Were you at all like him?"

"How could I know?" he asked with a sarcastic laugh.

"Were you adventurous with women? Did you break many hearts in America? I should think that American girls would go wild for English boys."

"I'm sure you'd have been quite disappointed with me. I stayed faithful to my wife."

"Did you find love, Robert?"

"Yes."

"Did you ever fall out of love?"

"No," he said and turned away.

"I'm sorry for your loss," she said. She no longer wished to hurt him. "I shouldn't have told you."

"You were right to tell me, mother. Please don't speak of it to my daughter, though."

"No," she agreed. "I'll not be the woman who raised you."

"Let's stop this," he said. "I'm tired of it, mother.

"We'll start another chapter, then."

He looked at her and smiled. "You speak so differently now. I don't remember words being so cold and biting. It was only your actions that hurt me then."

"You're a man now, Robert. Besides I can no longer act as I wish. I'd be better off with Bernard," she said with a vague detachment. "Shovel the earth over me."

Robert thought of Kathleen. "No," he said quickly and fought the urge to shake his head vigorously. His neck muscles strained against his countered protest. "Don't ever talk like that."

"I'm just being practical, love. While I live in this world I only cripple your sister."

"Perhaps you'd consider living in America."

Margaret's face brightened. "America," she said. "I should live with you, Robert?"

"Yes," he said. "Live with me and Emily and Elizabeth, if she'd like to come with us."

"Of course she would like to go." Margaret turned her face to the window. "America," she said dreamily. "Are the streets paved with gold in America, Robert?"

"There's opportunity in America."

"There's opportunity everywhere, Robert. You just have to have the courage to take it."

"You're welcome to come with us," he said.

"I don't need your charity."

"I'm not being charitable, mother."

She turned to face him again. "It's not what you want, though. You're being the good son, I suppose."

"I wish I felt that I owed you something, but I do not. Come to America if you like. I have a big house with plenty of rooms."

"Are you a millionaire, love?"

"No. I struggle in America, but I do it with more comfort and freedoms than others that struggle in this world."

She turned away from him again. "I'll not go, but take Elizabeth with you. Let her see something of the world before it is too late for her."

"She won't leave without you."

"No," she said. "She will not leave until after I've gone. When I am gone she must go to live with you."

"You're a young woman, mother."

"Am I? The glass tells me otherwise," she said with a bitter smile crossing her ridiculous mouth. "Leave me be for a bit, will you?"

"Can I get you something?"

She looked out of the window, but said nothing further. He waited several minutes and then got up and left the room closing the door behind him. He stood motionless for a time at the closed door reflecting on the words exchanged and the revelations made. There was less clarity now than there had been previously. He snapped to attention when Elizabeth entered the living room carrying a tray with a teapot and little cucumber sandwiches.

"Was it all gibberish?" Elizabeth asked as she settled the tray upon the little table before the sofa.

"What's that?" he asked not understanding her.

"Her mind, Robert, it's not altogether there much these days. I should have warned you, but ..." her voice trailed off and she concerned herself with filling the cups and moving the sandwiches from the tray. "Emily is such a pretty young thing. Her photographs do her little justice. I see a little bit of mother in her. Do you see that as well?"

"I suppose the mother I remembered is in Emily a bit, but Kathleen is there very much as well. Mother's mind seemed quite well to me Elizabeth," he said returning back to her original question. "She looks dreadfully old, though."

"Yes," she said flatly. "How do you take your tea?"

"I'll take care of it," he said as he sat beside her on the sofa. "Is mother getting forgetful or something?"

"Mother rarely knows who I am. She has moments, but usually there is no coherence at all. Was she clear for you?"

"Very much so, I should think. Is she not well?"

"She's dying, dear. I am glad that she had her wits about her for you. Perhaps she willed that upon herself. Perhaps she saved that just for you."

"Yes," he said. "Perhaps she had.

* * *

"She did not know me after that, Toby. I came in to see her each day for the rest of that week, but no hint of recognition registered in her now vacant and sometimes childlike eyes. When she spoke she asked me if I liked her hair or what I thought of her dress. I conversed with her as I would with a child of an acquaintance. I smiled and soothed her with praises that were ridiculous to me. She left me horrible new revelations without answers to questions that haunt me still and will so long as I maintain my faculties.

"I thought it best not to expose Emily to my mother's condition. I told her that I did not wish her to remember my mother as the person she'd become. Truthfully I did not wish to expose Emily to who my mother had been. Either way it made very little difference. Emily did not insist. Actually I think she'd been a little frightened, for some reason, at the prospect at meeting mother. Possibly I'd made comments that had put her off on mother, but I can't remember ever doing so.

"Elizabeth was great with Emily. It was good to let them go off into the city while I watched mother. They saw some films and did a little shopping. They walked through the parks and along the canal. Elizabeth explained what little there was to explain about Birmingham. I saw Elizabeth being somewhat of a mother to her. It was very good for Emily as she had quite a void in her life, but I think it did more for Elizabeth than anyone. She'd had a dreadful time as caretaker and it alleviated my guilt but a modicum. My last trip home helped me to justify my ever leaving there in the first place, save for my sister. When mother passed three months later I was relieved for Elizabeth's sake. She had managed to put everything in order and then come to live with Emily and me just two months after mother's burial.

"I did not return to England for the funeral. I feared leaving Emily home with friends and Elizabeth encouraged me not to come. I am not afraid to fly, but I did fear making my daughter an orphan. My life became more important to me for her sake. Sadly, I don't regret not attending her funeral now and I did not then." Robert puts his hand to his mouth and looks down at the man sitting on the bench. He looks up into the sky and then again he turns back to the man. "Does the mind let go of the people?" he asks, "or do people let go of the mind?"

Chapter Eleven

It was just after seven in the morning in early July. It was Tuesday or Wednesday, but really it did not matter much to Robert Montgomery. One day would merely cascade into the next and the days would do so without intention. Would he come to accept this new life or would he eventually rise to challenge it? This question had hovered about him, but he would not mete out any time to ponder it. He sat idly by in his wrought iron chair watching his flowers bloom despite the wall that blocked much of the day's sunshine. He thought that he might eventually come to like the wall and the blanket of protection that it provided. The vines had been tended to and soon they would climb again to camouflage the hastily laid bricks.

As was his usual routine, he came out each morning and plucked any undesirable or unattractive plant life that threatened the beauty of his sanctuary and dropped them in a little pail to be discarded. With reflection he would look down into the pail and then look around at the walls that surrounded him and then up into the sky. Once he smiled at the irony and then he dismissed the image that could have swept him away and carried on with his necessary work.

He had not left his home since the night of the party that had been given him. The party, arranged by the school board, should have been a surprise to him, but it was not. Emily and Elizabeth held out as long as they could, but eventually he needed to be told, as he had no desire to leave his home on that night. Hastily, he had explained his desire for early retirement; the occasion of his party left little time for his daughter and sister to pursue a lengthy question and answer session. The questions sought for, would have to wait. He drank down two glasses of scotch before leaving his home with hopes of it carrying him through the early hours of the evening. He thought it a masterful performance, but others saw through his half-hearted act, but chose not to burden him or themselves with awkward and disquieting questions.

It should have been a grand night for him. There were so many kind words and high praise that had brought tears to the eyes of his family and friends. Maria was there and sat at his table. She too cried, but her tears left her lost and confused. He watched her from across the table. She was so beautiful, he thought. Elizabeth glanced back and forth from Maria to Robert. She had wondered why they had not danced all of that evening. She wondered why they had barely talked with one another. She could not ask about this and her feelings about their awkward silences were mixed. Quite rationally, she decided that it would be in her best interests not to interfere. Henry Grifhorst sensed the unease that worked its way through the evening and managed to keep the atmosphere light.

When asked to make a speech, Robert was able to offer only a few words of thanks and gratitude and apologized for being left speechless and utterly unprepared. His throat closed up on him rather quickly and he could only blow kisses and wave across the filled auditorium. He got home at midnight on that last day of June and went to his den and immediately tore off the month on his calendar before settling down in his chair. His mind began to wander towards the dark and so he picked up a book and began to read. He read until he could no longer do so and Elizabeth found him the following morning sleeping in his chair. She had taken the glasses from his nose and the book from his lap and had turned off the light.

Elizabeth carried a tray out to the yard and placed it down on the table before her brother. "I'd like you to eat this morning Robert," she said sternly. "Much of my food has gone wasted on you of late."

"It's quiet here," he said.

She looked around not knowing what to say. "Yes," she said. "It is quiet this morning."

"No," he said. "The wall makes it quieter. It muffles the sounds that used to come from the park."

"That's good," she said.

"No," he said.

She poured him a cup of tea and set out a plate of eggs and sausage for him. She took the newspaper from a little slot on the bottom of the tray and put it down in the center of the table. "When I went out to pick up the paper this morning I found your briefcase on the porch."

"Really?" he said. "Was there a note?"

"Perhaps inside the case, but I wouldn't know. There wasn't any note visible to me," she said. "I suppose you'd left it in your office at the school after you'd packed up your things."

"No," he said. "I'd searched there. It had gone missing a few days before I had left. I'd meant to inquire, but…"

"Eat your breakfast 'fore it goes cold, dear." She sat opposite him at the little patio table to see to it that he did, in fact, eat this morning. As of late he needed to be reminded of such things and prompted to eat as you might prompt a careless child.

"I must go see if there is a note," he said and got up from the table. "Where did you leave the bag, Elizabeth?"

"Just in the kitchen, Robert; do come back and eat, though." She too had wondered about the case and had already ascertained that there was no note to be found within it. Of course she could not tell him this. She watched as her brother made his way into the house. She did not know what to make of his sudden withdrawal from life. In her estimation it was all due to the wall before her. She shook her head menacingly at the wall as though it would be intimidated by her scornful look and shrink away in retreat.

Robert's sudden decision to take early retirement had astonished her. If anything, his work, she believed, had always taken precedence over his little garden. Also, he had stopped going out. Henry had called upon him often, but he shied away from his dear friend. Elizabeth suggested that Henry give him some space. He would eventually come around, she'd said, but was that the truth? She had grown circumspect about her brother and how this new development had affected her. If she were to benefit from his despondency would that make it all right?

And, she thought, what of Maria? Why had he ceased to sneak around with her? Why had she not called on him? Elizabeth pondered this over her black tea. How long, she wondered, would he spend searching for something he would not find? "Robert," she called. "Come back and eat."

Robert spent a good portion of the day wondering about who might have returned the case. He was most certain that he had not left it with Maria and surely she had had many opportunities to return it prior to now. He knew that there was little use dwelling over such matters, but he also knew that much of his time these days was doing just that. He was wasting his time and that was a crime against nature. It was a crime against his nature.

For the past two weeks he'd spent the mornings working in his garden and the balance of the day in his rooms. He read his books with little comprehension and stared blankly at his television screen. Emily had phoned him a few times, but she had been preoccupied with her work. He sensed that she was not hearing him much at all, but it mattered very little as he had very little to say. She too had been surprised about his sudden decision for early retirement and had attempted to grill him as to why, but he had easily thwarted her attempts as her workload had escalated dramatically in the last two weeks. He needed a break from his usual routine, he had insisted.

Emily briefly recounted the details of a rival firm that had suddenly declared bankruptcy on the heels of an investigation on the accounting practices of said firm. Suddenly there were several big name authors with projects left hanging about and all of her competition scrambling to pick up the pieces. Robert nodded as she spoke and gave her his best face depicting his utmost attention, but truthfully most of what she had said was lost on him. If she understood this, she had not shown as much.

In his den, later that night, he peered across the room and to the little laptop computer that sat upon his desk. There was a light layer of dust covering the whole of the desk and all of its contents. This in itself was a unique state of affair as he had always gotten much use of his desk and had always taken great pains in keeping it forever tidy. He closed the book that had been resting on his lap and put it aside as he got up and crossed the room. With much trepidation, he sat down at the desk and wiped away the dust with the edge of his hand and uncharacteristically, brushed the soiled hand against his trousers.

He pushed the glasses that had come to rest upon the tip of his nose up to the bridge and then opened the little black shell and gave it some much-needed power. Within seconds the screen came to life telling its user, much too quickly to comprehend, the power that it contained and the promise of the superiority that it held over him. he looked for the little icon that would allow him to create a new document and gave it a quick double click. Once inside this program he eased into a sudden and incomprehensible comfort.

At the top of the page he wrote "CHAPTER ONE". He looked at his little heading and at the vacancy beneath it and pondered it for several minutes. Suddenly his fingers began to peck down heavily on the keys and the vacancy on the screen became less and less. Within minutes he began to settle into a rhythm that he had not connected with in many years. He had a surreal sensation of being outside of himself. He watched as this man who looked very much like him typed away before him. The words were filling the page and then after a while another page began to fill and then another.

He continued on like this for nearly an hour before the sharp ring of the old rotary phone interrupted his rhythm and startled him into near shock. He stared wildly at the phone as if it were foreign to him and wished it to stop its threatening shrill, but the sharp ring persisted until he could no longer refrain. He clutched it from its cradle and hesitantly held it to his ear. "Yes," he said softly.

"Mr. Montgomery?"

"Yes," he said again. He was at a near whisper and his chest pounded as the voice on the other end of the line continued.

"I don't know if you remember me, but this is Madeline Marceau."

His eyes grew wide as his mind did a search. "Madeline Marceau?" he said cautiously.

"Yes," she said. "I was a student of yours many years ago; a little more than thirty years ago, in fact."

"Yes, I remember you," he said tentatively. "I'm sorry, but you've caught me a little off guard."

"I apologize for calling so late."

"No, no," he said. "It's not at all too late." He wished to continue speaking, but was at a loss for words.

"Did you get your briefcase?"

"Was it you who returned it?"

"Yes. It was early so I'd left it on your porch. I would have left a note, but I'd preferred speaking with you."

"How did you happen to come upon it?" he asked.

"You'd left it in the little delicatessen. I saw you there that morning and immediately knew that it was you."

"Was that you I saw that morning?"

"Yes," she said. "I hoped you might recognize me and then I thought myself such a fool. You'd had a million students over the years and I only a handful of teachers. When I saw you I felt all of those years rolling back on me. I left not knowing what to say and then I returned, but you had gone by then. I saw your bag by the counter and took it thinking it a good excuse to find you.

"I'm sorry," she said. "I must sound like such a fool. My mind is all a jumble and I'm expressing myself rather poorly."

"No," he said. "That's not true at all."

"I tried to return your bag to the school. They said you've retired."

"Yes," he said. "I've taken an early retirement." He put his hand up to his forehead and closed his eyes. "That's not entirely true," he confessed. "Actually it was they who had opted to give me an early retirement. I've been put out to pasture, so to speak."

"You had wished to remain?" she asked.

"If it were my decision, I'd have taught 'til my last breath."

"I am sorry for you. You look well and much too young to be out to pasture. What's next for you?"

"Actually I've taken up writing. I've only just begun this endeavor this very evening and truthfully I was quite frightened of the very thought of it, but my first hour has gone well and then you called."

"I'm sorry if I've interrupted."

"Not at all," he said with a light heart. "The sound of your voice has given me inspiration to continue on."

"I don't understand."

"I can't really explain it myself, but I believe that it was the sight of you in that Max's delicatessen that has inspired me to begin."

"You're lying to me," she said, but he could hear the smile in her voice and see it clearly in his mind.

"I'm telling you the truth, Madeline. May I call you Madeline?"

"Yes, of course."

"And you must call me Robert."

"Robert," she said.

"I must confess that it has been a rather rough month that has crossed me up and that I was beginning to let myself slip a bit, but sometimes when I look about and see that life does in fact go on, I have to stop and remind myself that there are always new beginnings and that the past is better left just there."

"That's a healthy attitude."

"Yes," he said. "I've been rather unhealthy as of late and I'm just coming alive again. It was you who I had thought of as I began to write this evening."

"You didn't recognize me, Robert."

"No," he conceded. "I did not recognize who you were, but I did see a smile on your face and that smile lifted my spirits. I only just recalled your smile this evening as I set out to write. The recollection of your smile was to me in many ways like that of the early signs of spring. It was like the feeling of the sun on my face after a rather long and hard winter. It was like the bloom of a rose after the thaw of the frozen ground that had held it back. Your smile was a great gift to me, Madeline."

"That's very kind of you to say."

"I had taken your smile as a great kindness to me."

"Would it be all right for me to call you again, Robert?"

He gripped the receiver firmly and closed his eyes tightly. He did not know that it was all right. He also did not wish to send her away. "Yes," he said finally. "I should welcome another call from you."

"Write your story and I will call on you again," she said.

The line went dead and Robert listened to the silence for a time before resting the receiver into the cradle. A chill went through him and he shuddered and then there was a knock at the door. He looked up fearfully. "Yes," he said.

Elizabeth opened the door and carried a tray of tea and sugar cookies over to his desk. "I have a pot of decaf," she said.

"Thank you."

At first she could only see the morose look on his face that had plagued him for weeks and then a smile broke his face and he got up and kissed her on the cheek. "What is it?" she asked with some relief.

"I'm not yet dead," he said.

"Of course not," she replied somewhat bewildered. "I could have told you as much."

"No one can be told such things and be expected to hear them. Life needs to be accepted."

"All right," she said. "But don't expect me to accept that."

It rained for three days and nights and Robert remained in his rooms tapping on the keys and producing page after page of words that were dearer to him than could ever be possibly understood by another. Emily had called and had spoken with Elizabeth to find that he had immersed himself in his writing and refused to allow Elizabeth to interrupt him at work. "Let him be," she had insisted to her aunt. "This is good. This is good therapy for him."

"Yes," Elizabeth agreed at once. "I see a great change in him since the very night he'd begun. I only hope that he's not turning into that character that Jack Nicholson played in that terrifying film."

"I wouldn't worry too much about that, Aunt Elizabeth."

"I do wish that he'd at least leave the floor. He has all his meals upstairs and with this dreadful rain, he's not even been out to tend to his flowerbeds."

"Does he talk much of the wall?"

"Not a word, but he's yet to open the blind that faces it."

"He's not in darkness?" she asked with a slightness of breath.

"No, love," she said. "The other blinds are up. He has as much light as these dreary days allow and he seems happy as a clam."

"I knew the writing would be good for him," she said confidently. "I'll call again tomorrow and maybe come by this weekend if you don't mind."

"Do come," she said. "I'll put something nice together."

"Don't make a fuss," Emily nearly pleaded.

"I won't, dear."

After hanging up the telephone, Elizabeth lit a fire beneath the kettle and sat at the kitchen table. She looked down at the morning paper and her mind went again to the want ads. She did not wish to look at them as they had held little hope for her before, but could she afford not to? Her brother had been full of surprises in recent weeks and her future seemed so uncertain. In any case, she had only just come to the realization of how utterly dependent she had been on others for the entirety of her life. She had merely been a servant, but who would serve and tend to her needs if and when the time should come that she no longer was of use?

She had wanted to begrudge someone, but there was no one to blame but herself. She had always been there to look after others, but had they, her mother, father and brother, looked at her as a selfless caretaker or had they looked at her as a burden who had clung to them for support? How had she seen herself? How does she truly see herself now?

The whistle on the pot began to communicate to her and before it could scream, she mechanically got up and put out the fire and poured the water into the little teapot that she had had since childhood. Elizabeth looked down at the little pot and grimaced. She had so very little she could claim as her own. The purchases she had made for the household did not truly belong to her. She commanded these things as her own and her brother would have very little use for them, but they were, in fact, his things. If another woman were to come into her brothers' home, they would belong to her and not Elizabeth.

She sat down and opened the paper and went directly to the employment section. She had no delusions or hopes of good opportunity. She would have to begin at the bottom and had little chance of ascent. She could merely offer hard work with hopes of fair pay. She would continue living on with her brother unless or until their situation changed. She would not be a burden to him and would not feel as such for her own sake. She would be independent as her niece was and she would take comfort in that.

When the rain had ceased to fall, Robert made his way out into his little garden and set about to clean away the weeds that had flourished in his absence. He did this task with great joy and purpose. He turned the soil and fed the earth and pruned the delicate flowers for more than four hours until he was satisfied with their health and appearance. He showered and shaved and ate a hearty lunch and left his house to embark on a lengthy walk that would take him hours from his home. It was a beautiful day if not a little hot and he was feeling much at peace with himself. He had come to accept things as they were and not to fight what was to be.

He thought of Madeline as he walked. He thought of the smile that she had given him in Max's delicatessen. He thought of the broad mouth and the even teeth and of her flawless complexion. He had only seen her briefly, but he could picture her so well. Her eyes were large and oval shaped and set far apart. She had a delicate nose and not at all sharp. Her hair was of a golden brown and only shoulder length and she had had it brushed behind her left ear and had allowed it to hide the right one.

She was very pretty and she had the look of a woman who had understood that, but at the same time she was timid about such thoughts. It did not seem to be a false modesty that had plagued her, but a modesty that was genuine. She had given him a brief smile and then her eyes had cast downward. She was shy like an attractive, and perhaps, an intelligent schoolgirl.

"Hello," she said.

Robert jumped a bit at the sight of her. She was every bit as beautiful as he had remembered her from their brief encounter. "Hello," he responded breathlessly.

"I'm glad you were able to make it. I was afraid that you wouldn't come," she said.

"Of course I would come. Why would I not come, Madeline?"

"Shall we walk?"

"Yes," he said and he took her arm in his.

Chapter Twelve

Elizabeth smoothed her dress and checked her makeup in the tiny mirror of her compact. She rubbed at her teeth where a smear of lipstick had shown. She would have been mortified if this had gone unnoticed by her and detected by the interviewer. When she felt confident with her appearance, she took a deep breath and entered the office.

"I'm here to see Mr. Drake," she said as casually as she could. A very tired looking woman looked up from her magazine and without expressing much interest for Elizabeth told her to just go on in. "Thank you," she said without meaning it. If that is all the skill that is needed in the workforce, she thought, I should do quite nicely in this world.

Mr. Drake was a sloppy man in appearance. He was very much overweight and his thinning hair was plastered clumsily across his forehead. His jacket was strewn carelessly over the back of his chair and Elizabeth could see that the casters had been dragging over the hem. Mr. Drake's shirttails were untucked and there were great stains of perspiration around his armpits. He did not stand up to greet her, but offered her his hand, which she found to be limp and clammy.

"Ms. Coltrane?" he presumed.

"Yes sir, Mr. Drake. It is nice to put a face to the voice," she said.

He looked up at her with an odd expression. "Sit down," he said gesturing to the chair before him.

"Thank you, sir," she said and took the proffered seat.

"You've brought me your résumé?"

"No sir. I've no written résumé to offer you."

"You did say you had quite a bit of experience."

"I have been a caregiver since the age of eight years, Mr. Drake. I dare say that qualifies me."

Drake gave her an incredulous look. "What about references?" he asked hopefully.

"Is that really necessary?"

"Is it a problem?"

"Well the people I've looked after died."

"All of them?"

"Well I don't like to quit on people. It must count in my favor that I'm loyal and that I'm never sent away."

"What about the agencies that have placed you in your former positions, Ms. Coltrane? Surely they'll have records? They can offer references, I hope?"

"Well no, sir" she said hesitantly. "I'm afraid not."

"And why not?" he asked sighing heavily.

"Well sir," she started with visible discomfort. "I've never been employed through an agency before."

"Certainly you've needed references to give care? You didn't simply answer ads in a newspaper?"

"No sir. I've always known the people to whom I've given care."

Mr. Drake put down his pencil and folded his hands firmly upon his desk. "Do you have any formal training, Ms. Coltrane?"

"On the job training," she said sternly; almost defiantly.

He drew back and then leaned in and spoke very quietly as if in confidence. "Who did you care for, Ms. Coltrane?"

Elizabeth lowered her eyes as if a schoolgirl who'd been found out might. "I took good care of my parents," she said with firm resolve, but did not look up at him. "I've also tended to my Uncle Harold for some time. I did not live in with him, but I went to his home for an hour or two twice a day for the last three and a three quarter years of his life. After my parents passed on, I cared for my widowed brother and my niece. They no longer need looking after and now I must find those who do. I have a very strong work ethic and I take my work, no matter the task, very seriously. I am quite diligent and steadfast. I trust that reliability, honesty, and integrity are still assets in any workplace? I have only a high school diploma, but I do have the experience and the compassion." She raised her eyes to meet his. "Is there a problem?"

"Not really," he said warmly. He smiled at her manner and took an instant liking to her. "You'll need to take some classes and get some certificates, but nothing strenuous. Is that acceptable to you?"

"Yes, of course," she said subsiding demurely. "When do I begin?"

"Immediately," he said. "Mrs. Capshaw will give you a clipboard with a number of forms to fill out and I'll give you a call to come in and see me within a few days. When you come back I'll have a schedule of the classes you'll need to attend. Is your schedule flexible?"

"Yes. I will work around your schedule."

Drake stood up and shook her hand. "Very well then, Ms. Coltrane," he said. "Welcome aboard."

Robert walked into Farrell's and took the stool beside Henry and ordered a pint for himself and another for his friend. "Am I very far behind?"

"Yeah," he said gruffly. "About three weeks behind." Henry took his large hand and slapped Robert on the back. "I'm glad to see you," he said grinning ear to ear.

The bartender put a mug before Robert and smiled. "These are on the house," he said.

"Thank you Sean." Robert lifted his glass and saluted the barman. "Sorry to be away for so long."

"You missed a few Met games," Henry said as though it were a cardinal sin that had been committed.

"I'm sorry about that, too. It won't happen again, Henry."

"You all right, Monty?"

"Yes," he said with a smile all of his own. "I am well." Robert took a long draw on his beer and placed the mug on the bar. "Henry," he said and put up a hand for emphasis. "Stop me if I'm a bit impertinent, but I'd like your advice on women and relationships."

"My advice?" he said in a fit of laughter. "I'm hardly the man to answer questions about relationships."

"You've been with women. Quite a few if memory dictates and I haven't been with any since Kathleen passed. Truthfully I never thought there'd be another woman out there for me. Suddenly I find that there are some women out there who are less than repulsed by me."

"Just goes to prove that there's someone out there for everyone no matter how old and ugly you might be."

"I realize that, Henry. After all you surpass me in both age and ugly astronomically and yet you manage to attract the occasional woman. I might question her sight and sanity, but putting that aside for the moment, advise me on how to proceed with a woman."

"Well if you're looking to mess up a relationship or to ruin the chance of one, you've come to the right place. After my wife died I made the same mistakes over and over again."

"Well than tell me what not to do," he said in all seriousness. "I, too, seem quite capable of making such a mess of things. I don't wish to mess this up."

"Truthfully, Monty, my mistakes would probably go against your nature. My problem was that I typically went for young women because the older ones had always seemed to be so jaded. I was attracted to younger women because I wanted to start all over again if that makes any sense at all. I wanted to see life fresh through their eyes."

"Like seeing Christmas through the eyes of a child?" he asked.

"Exactly like that. I have plenty of money and I can afford to make every day like Christmas. Money can very quickly sweep a lady off of her feet. It takes only one flower to melt a girls' heart when the love is true, but it takes several dozen to spur, stimulate and motivate a woman's affection when there is nothing there. Money, I have always found, is a tool for a less worthy man and I've learned that it attracts a spurious love."

"I think you go too far in your estimations."

"You're right, I do, but there is some truth in it. In any case I have often ruined women. I took attractive, unspoiled, young women and spoiled them shamelessly. You start out with elegant restaurants that they could never have dreamt of. You send them designer clothes so that they'll fit in at these places. You culture them with the opera and the ballet and watch as they light up and you too light up because you think you're in love with them. You start to travel around the world and show them so many beautiful places that you have already seen and seeing it with them is like seeing it all for the first time.

"How smart and cultured and worldly you are to them. You are so immensed in your power so far as they can see, but as you are seen you are also revealed and after a while one place is much like another. They tire of it all so quickly and the gifts aren't as grand as they used to be. They tire of you after a while and they start to see how old you truly are and you can see it in their eyes if you are smart and unfortunate enough to read people well enough. Like a kid in a candy store they've consumed too much and they have wearied of it all. And then you part with them. They are a bit wealthier from the presents that they have received and cultured from the world they have seen, but they're jaded too. They are young and now life holds so many fewer surprises for them.

"As for me," said Henry. "I get to go out and do it all over again." Henry drank down his mug and gestured for another. "I lost a little bit of myself with every woman I took, Monty. After a time I felt like a devil collecting souls. I'm through with all of that," he said and looked at his face in the glass behind the bar. "My wife was my only chance at true love. We started with very little and grew together and let the world reveal itself to us over time. I should have given her more of my time instead of chasing the almighty dollar. She died much too soon and now I will always be alone."

"You've been of very little use to me, Henry. I've come to you for advice and you've managed to depress the hell out of me."

Henry laughed and slapped the bar. "I warned you, Monty. Tell me about this lady of yours and I promise to suggest nothing at all."

"I'm a little hesitant to speak of her."

"You afraid I might bid for her affections?"

"I'm afraid to speak of her at all," he said. "It's like when I was a child and happened to blow that perfect bubble that was so perfectly round and captured the sun and evoked every color in the spectrum. I feared to breathe or move in the slightest. I thought that if nothing were to interrupt, the bubble could last indefinitely."

Henry sat up a little bit and his face lost all of its humor. "Are you in love, Monty?"

"I won't say it, Henry. I can't say that."

"It's not a bubble, Monty."

"Oh, but it is Henry," he said solemnly. "It's all a bubble. Nothing can be held onto forever."

"At least enjoy the beauty of that bubble," Henry said quietly. "Appreciate it and treasure it for long as it exists."

"I'm terrified," he said and Henry could see that it was true. Robert's eyes took on a grave fear that sobered Henry like a shower of ice water.

"Fear is a waste of time. Besides what's to be afraid of?" Henry's face lightened and he put his arm on Robert's shoulder. "I've gotten something from the doctor, Monty. I'll give you a handful of them," he said conspiratorially. "Just keep this between me and you, eh."

"That's not it," he said irritably. "It's more complex than that."

"Is she nice?"

"Yes," he said. "She's perfect.

"Then just go with it and don't worry so much about it." Henry leaned back on the barstool grasping the bar rail for support. "Do you know what your biggest problem is, Monty?"

"I spend too much time on this stool next to you, I should think," he said with sarcasm.

"I'm serious, Robert. I've watched you for years and the one thing I believe to be your downfall is that you have too much imagination."

Robert stared at Henry. An enigmatical look replaced the expression of sarcasm. "Too much imagination?" he asked.

"Yes," he said and studied his friends face. "Don't look so puzzled. You know what I mean. You think too much and not only about what is, but what may come of it. You're always thinking about possible outcomes and that's not altogether bad, but you dwell on the negative possibilities."

"I do tend to think things through," he agreed. "I thought that was a good trait that I'd picked up if not inherited. Now you tell me that it's my failing?"

"A little bit, yes," he said. "In business and in life it's good to anticipate both good and bad things that may come. You do all that you can to insure the one and all that you can do to avert the other. If you anticipate bad things and let them fall that way because you strongly believe that it will fall that way Monty, it is a failing."

"I see what you mean, but I don't think that's my problem. It's not my problem where Madeline is concerned, in any case."

"Madeline?" he asked with that conspiratorial grin and an exaggerated raise of the eyebrows.

"Yes, Henry. Her name is Madeline Marceau and I'd like to keep her between you and me."

"Betw..."

"Don't even go there," he said cutting him off. "She's quite different from any woman I've ever known. I won't allow jokes that dishonor her even in the slightest bit."

"She likes you?"

"I believe so, yes."

"Well then, I guess that does make her different from any woman you've ever known, Monty."

"It does indeed you miserable old bastard. I am serious, though," he said gripping Henry at the wrist. "I don't wish anyone else to know about Madeline."

"Okay," he said. "My lips are sealed. What's the big secret? I would think Emily and Eli..." Henry paused at the thought of Elizabeth. He would have to give further consideration as to how she might feel. "I think Emily would be thrilled for you."

"It's complicated, Henry."

"All right," Henry said with his hands raised to express his intent to back off. "Who is this lady, this Madeline Marceau, who has captured your heart?"

"She was a student of mine."

"Are you out mind?" Henry shrieked in horror. "What the hell were you thinking? A little complicated," he mimicked in Robert's accent.

"Will you keep it down, you old fool?" he said, his face showing disgust. "She was a student of mine over thirty years ago. I hardly think there's anything inappropriate about that, Henry. Perhaps she's a bit young for me," he said and his face softened. "But she's a quarter century over the age of twenty-one."

"Oh," said Henry settling down. "That does make it acceptable if not a little less interesting. So why is this complicated?"

"I don't know exactly," he said. "Sometimes I think I have reasons and other times I do not. I need to be sure, Henry."

"Sure about what?"

"I need to be sure that what we have is real."

"Can't you just relax and see how it goes? You don't need to put pressure on yourself. At your age there's even less reason to be putting pressure on yourself than if you were a young fellow."

"I just need to be sure. Please understand."

"All right," Henry agreed, but he did not at all understand. "You pace yourself as you see fit. So," he said after a moment. "How did you two come together after so many years?"

'I used to think about her sometimes," he said dreamily. "But I hadn't in many years and then one day she was in Max's delicatessen looking at me from across the aisle. I knew her, but I didn't. I turned away to pay for my things and when I'd turned back she was gone. It was odd. Anyway I'd left my briefcase there when I left. She found it and returned it to me," he said groggily. "She liked me," he said with more energy. "She called me on the phone in my den and we spoke for a bit. I was a little frightened by the call."

"Frightened? Why?"

"It's hard for me to explain. It was a much-unexpected call. She's a very beautiful woman, you see. She's intelligent and likes to laugh. We have a great deal in common, Henry. I've found that we've read many of the same books," he said with unabashed pleasure. "We talk incessantly about literature." He hesitated a moment and thought about that. "I have to say that's something that gives me a great deal of joy that I am pleased to indulge in. Oddly enough I don't have all that many friends that share my passions for literature. For my preference in literature," he explained. "Even Emily, whose publishing books as we speak, has a very different taste in literature than me.

"I'm getting off track," he said wearily. "I tend to do a lot of that lately. I don't with her, though. When I'm with her I'm as sharp as ever I've been. I feel young with her, Henry. I'm a little stronger and a little taller. Food tastes better to me and the air is easier to breathe. I can't explain it, but even my sight is clearer and I can hear better than I have in years. Music, Henry, sounds like it supposed to."

"Like it supposed to?" he asked.

"Didn't music sound better to you when you were a boy? Wasn't everything a little better in youth?"

"Yes, but how does that translate to you now? Is this woman the fountain of youth?" he asked with blithe curiosity. "If so, does she have a sister?"

"I can't explain any of this," he said shaking his head. "Music sounds so much better to me these days. It lifts me up more than ever before. I am better able to focus on the words. The music speaks volumes to me. I must sound like an old fool to you."

"No Robert," Henry said patting him on the forearm. "It sounds, to me, like you're in love, old boy. I suppose it can still happen to men as old as us."

"You've been with many women, Henry. Have you ever felt like this? Am I making any sense to you? I ask because it makes absolutely no sense at all to me. Am I going crazy?"

"I've never felt the way you say," Henry said grimly while shaking his head. "I wish I had felt what you're feeling now. I have been with many women, yes and I suppose I've gone into relationships with high expectations, but they've always petered out." Henry turned on the stool to face Robert more clearly. "No, Monty, you are not going crazy. I envy you this feeling and I pray heartily to the god I do not believe in that your love endures.

"Perhaps you have too little imagination?"

"Perhaps I do, perhaps I do, but," he said with a harsh punctuation on the 'but'. "I do go into it with high expectations for success. Why are you fretting, Robert? Why are you so afraid of success?"

"Well," he said evenly. "Perhaps it is better to be pleasantly surprised." He turned around and looked at the tables against the wall.

Henry followed suit. "Are you looking for someone, Monty? Is Madeline meeting you here?"

"No," he said, but Henry could hear a little uncertainty in his voice. "No, I don't think Madeline would ever come here."

"And why not?" he asked.

"This really isn't her sort of place," he said and turned back to the bar. He raised his hand and gestured to the barman for two more.

"When are you going to see her again?"

"I really don't know. We never make plans to meet," he said casually. "We just get together somehow when the moment suits. I'm writing, Henry."

"Writing," Henry said. He was caught a little off guard with the sudden change in subject matter.

"Yes. Emily has been after me for ages to begin writing."

"Right, right," he said with recollection. "The computer she gave you for your birthday last month."

"I've always spoken of writing. I did a little writing when I was younger, but like so many other things, I've never set out to just do it in recent years. I've finally started on it," he said enthusiastically. "I'm off to a good start, I think."

"That's terrific, Monty. Good for you. What's it about?"

"Oh, I'm not ready to discuss it just yet," he said taking a draw on his beer. "It's much too early for that."

"You have it all planned out?"

"The book?" he asked. "No, I'm letting it take me where it wishes to go, Henry. I don't know that that's the best way of writing a story, but I'm just allowing this one to lead me on its journey. It seems to be more exciting that way. I'm not writing it for publication," he said. "I'm writing this for me."

"Fair enough," Henry said. "Do you allow Madeline to read it?"

"No," he said shaking his head slowly. "No," he said again. "We talk a lot, Madeline and me. She calls often."

"I'm happy for you. Have fun with this and don't think too much about it."

"I should let this go where it will?"

"Yes. Like your story Monty, let it lead you where it may. Live this for you," he said.

Chapter Thirteen

"I really don't know why Madeline had come into my life, Toby. I sometimes think that perhaps she was, in a way, a gift from God. I like to believe that God, in his infinite wisdom, had created Madeline just for me to love. She had come into my life and saved me. I was in a bad place. Everything was coming apart for me at that time and like an angel, she appeared before me."

He looks up at the clouds as they pass the sun and he feels the warmth from the sun shining down on his face. The mist that had left him damp and cold has also passed. "It looks like we've had a reprieve," he says. Toby reaches in to the bottom of his bag and pulls out another nut. He will run out them soon, Robert thinks. The bag is not bottomless. Will he go away then? He wonders. Will he leave me alone then?

He sees a woman walking along the path by the river. His heart stirs for a moment and his breath leaves him until he sees that it is not Madeline. Not even close, he thinks as she comes closer to him. This woman is not as slender as Madeline. This woman is older and her face is badly lined. Still, he thinks, she looks to be a pleasant enough woman. Why are we so quick to judge? He wonders.

"I would have loved Madeline no matter what she looked like," he suddenly declares. "I know that that's easy to say when you are in love with someone who is so beautiful, but she has beauty of all sorts. My love for Madeline was difficult for others to understand. I wish it weren't so, but I can't control everything," he says. "I don't wish to control everything, you understand, but there are things which are in my control and I feel that I should," he says and his voice trails off and his mind carries him back to another time.

* * *

It was late August and a heat wave that had melted New York for three consecutive weeks had only just dissipated two days before when the rains had come and brought back life to the grass, that had been quickly receding under the summers torment, and the people who had, for a time, deserted the streets for the comfort of artificially cooled rooms in their homes, theatres, malls and workplaces. Robert had refused to yield to the laws restricting water usage, brought upon by drought, when it came to his garden. He would accept any fine imposed upon him for the love of his flowers. He kept the water running several times a day for hours at a time to keep his precious flowers in bloom and protected from a blazing, merciless sun.

It was only eighty-one degrees today and Prospect Park had come alive with more inhabitants than was usual. The cabin fever had surely gotten to the masses and the outside world was again appreciated and not taken for granted. Robert walked side by side with Madeline who was only a little shorter than him. She wore a pretty cotton dress of white that accentuated her slender frame and underscored her sun-kissed complexion. She wore her hair tied back revealing the slightness of her neck and the not too large hoops that hung from her earlobes.

Her legs were long and lean and they too were revealed to anyone who wished to notice them, but still she seemed to be modest with her revelations. The white dress was at once sexy and conservative and her stride was demure and elegant and yet, he believed, traffic stopping. "It's a beautiful day," she said and smiled.

"Quite beautiful," he said, but he was looking at Madeline and he was seeing only her.

"I'm so glad that I've found you," she said and gave him that brilliant smile with her wide, full mouth and perfect teeth. She tilted her head further elongating her neck inviting him to kiss her and without hesitation he did so. The kiss, at first, was brief. He backed away only a bit but his eyes never left hers. He moved in again and kissed her mouth gently and took his time and as the time went on the kiss grew in intensity. He would never be able to get enough of her and he knew this with such immense certainty.

Slowly, he began to move away, but she took hold of him and pulled him towards her. She smothered him with her kiss and he would have gladly died from it. "I love you," he said and was immediately startled by his admission. She smiled and lowered her eyes and said nothing, but took his hand gently and lovingly in her own and began to walk again on the hills of the park.

"I'm alive, Madeline. For the very first time in my life I am truly alive." He looked at the children at play. He felt as though he could run out there among them and play their games. He wanted to skip and hop and jump like a child, but it was not in his normal manner or ilk to do so and so he refrained. He could not afford to be such a fool. He could not have them cast down a net on him now and ruin everything. He had to be as much of who he had always been, he reasoned. He turned his gaze again on her and gave her hand a gentle squeeze of reassurance, but it was he that he needed to reassure.

Why did you come to me? He thought, but did not dare to ask. He would not do anything to burst this bubble. He would not question his good fortune and he would not put her to any test. He loved her and that was all he needed to know. He could have these moments in time with her and he would collect these memories in an album in his mind and he would have them all the rest of his life. He would be forever with her, he thought and she with him.

They spent all of the day together not wishing to part. They sat on the swings and ate ice cream. They took off their shoes and he rolled up his trousers and they walked around the perimeter of the fountain holding hands and flexing their toes. He stomped in the water and she laughed and backed away playfully and then she kicked the water up at him and he ran at her as though he would drench her in the water. They laughed heartily for a time until he took notice of the people watching and he felt a sudden discomfort and almost shame at being seen. He ushered her away from the fountain and together they walked on for a time and sat beneath a tree.

He rested his back against the trunk and she curled into him and they spoke for hours. He talked about his childhood and of his mother and he held nothing back. He could do this with Madeline. He felt an absolute trust and faith in her. It was a trust that he had never before known. He watched her eyes as he spoke and he could see that her attention never faulted in the least. There was concern and compassion and most of all there was complete understanding to be read from her expression. He spoke of Kathleen and Elizabeth and then of Emily and Shannon. He told her everything and left out nothing at all that was deliberate. He had never done this with anyone before and he told her that as well.

He put his arm over her shoulder and drew her in and together they watched the sun go down. He gave little thought of the time and the fact that Elizabeth would have prepared a meal that would spoil. He gave no consideration that she would worry about him and where he might be. He was caught or perhaps even lost in this moment. The scope of his world was only what he could see and nothing else needed to enter it for the moment. He put his arms around Madeline and held her tightly. He put his nose to her hair and inhaled its jasmine scent and knew that he would always be able to summon the aroma at will.

"I love you," he whispered softly into her ear.

"I love you too," she said and he could feel her cheek lifting into a smile next to his.

He nuzzled her neck and caressed it with soft kisses and then he rested his cheek against the warmth of her skin. She wore no perfume and only the scent of her skin mixed with that of the soap could he detect. "I will love you for all of the rest of my life," he promised. He looked up to the immensity of the black night sky and for the first time in his life it did not make him feel at all insignificant. They stayed that way for a time and then they fell asleep under the tree and did not awake until morning.

Elizabeth was quite concerned, but was not so hasty to call attention to Robert's absence. She made the quick assumption that he was again with Maria and that again they had spent the night together. She laid waiting for the sound of his footsteps until sleep had overtaken her at three in the morning. It was after six that she awoke to creeping joints of the floorboards. She raised her head and squinted her disgust at the clock. "If I were not to have fallen asleep," she muttered under her breath, "I would have been out of my mind with worry by now."

She threw the sheet away from her angrily and climbed out of the bed. Her clock had been set for six-thirty, but she would not be able to sleep peacefully for nineteen minutes, she decided. She disarmed the clock and began to prepare herself for her meeting with Mr. Drake.

Drake seemed to have more confidence in Elizabeth than she had had in herself. He discussed the necessity for CPR and rescue breathing training as though they were mere formalities. He muttered something about automated external defibrillators for cardiac emergencies in such a passive way that Elizabeth had to fight back the urge to shudder. He went on about the care for choking and first aid for bleeding, fractures, sprains, shock, eye injuries, poisoning and burns. He said she would need to recognize a stroke or a seizure and to know with certainty the steps for care under such circumstances.

Elizabeth was quite grateful to him for not being at all put off when he recorded with ease, the horror on her face. He told her to take a deep breath and to recognize the fact that these were things she had been preparing for all of her life. She smiled at him for his acknowledgement of this fact. "Yes," she said graciously. "I suppose these are the things I've done all of my life without taking much notice of it."

"Yes," he agreed. "These classes will just give you a certification of the things that you know much about. There will be things that you will and must learn, but I know that they will be easy enough for you."

"How can you know?" she asked timidly.

"I obviously meet a lot of people who do or otherwise wish to do the work that you do, Ms. Coltrane." He leaned into her a little. "I always stop for a moment and try to ask myself would I want this person to care for someone I love?" He rubbed his hands together softly and looked down into them almost shyly. "Most often my answer is no," he said with all seriousness. "When I first met and spoke with you, I thought this person would take the time to care."

"But you know nothing of me," she said.

"It's that kind of honesty that reassures me," he said. "You're a little brash in your manner and sometimes bold in your speech," he said with a little smirk breaking his face. "But there's kindness in your eyes, Ms. Coltrane. I can see that you have compassion. You've cared for your parents and you've cared for your brother and niece. A woman has to make great sacrifices to do those things."

Elizabeth blushed at the kindness of his words and nearly cried from the recognition that he gave her. "You're very kind, Mr. Drake," she said. Her voice was a little shaky. Suddenly his appearance was not so offensive to her. He too had kind eyes, she thought. His untucked shirt and messy manner were almost tolerable if not a little endearing. "I will not let you down," she said summarily. She stood up and held her course papers firmly and shook them with a bit of determination to show that she meant what she said.

"I know," he said quite simply and jumped to his feet. "If you need any help at all, please let me know."

"I will," she promised and smiled and blushed a little as well. She turned towards the door and stopped and looked back at him. "I'm not an unintelligent woman," she said hesitantly.

"No, Ms. Coltrane. And I'm smart enough to know that."

She smiled and left his office and told the uninterested woman behind the desk to have a most wonderful day. The woman did not look up from her magazine but did manage to acknowledge her with a drawn out "okay".

"I'm glad you decided to come back," Dr. Hiller said as Emily entered his office. "We left off last time with quite a break through and then you just disappeared."

"Yes," she said icily. "My other therapist and I decided that you and I needed closure."

"Other therapist," he said visibly taken aback.

"It's a joke, Dr. Freud," she said scrunching up her face in sarcasm. "You would think that after all this time you might have picked up on that about me."

"Yes," he said. "But still it would be most unprofessional to laugh at a patient at a most inopportune time. Shall we," he said and gestured to the chair before him.

Emily sat down and placed her bag beside her. "I don't really know how we should proceed from here," she said. "I've told you that my mother killed herself. What more is there to say? You want to know how I feel about that, I suppose."

"Yes," he said.

"It's in the past. What's done is done and on the surface I know that it wasn't my fault."

"On the surface," he repeated.

"On the surface," she said. "I know that no one would put any amount of blame on me," she said shortly. "I know that if we were speaking of someone else that I might say that only a fool would blame herself for the sin of her mother. I'm sure that I'd dismiss it as such. But still," she hesitated. "If I were there I could have put her off for another day. And maybe the circumstances would have put her off for other days and maybe she would have gotten the right help before long. Why did she have to pick that day to kill herself?" she asked. She did not look away from him. She caught his eyes and waited for an answer.

"I can offer you a great deal of maybes, Emily. I can attest to so many theories that better minds than I have come up with, but I can't give you a definitive answer. I can only help you deal with the reality of it."

"I know that," she said. There was no edge to her voice now. "I know it's not my fault, but I feel somewhat responsible. I know that I can't change what has happened and that all I can do is just let it go." She shook her head, but her eyes never left his. "I've tried to let it go. I've tried to let it go for so many years, but I can't. I think about these sessions that we have," she said and got up and walked across the room to the window. "I think about our sessions and I know that all you can do is to try and help me think rationally. But if I know that coming in to this, am I half way there or am I hopeless?"

"You're probably much more than half way there."

"I don't know if I can't let it go or if I want to let it go." She turned to him again. "I don't know that I want to let it go," she repeated with the emphasis and conviction in her eyes.

"What are you afraid of?"

She thought for a moment. "I suppose that it's not so much the past that scares me any more."

"The future?" he suggested.

"Yes," she said after a time. "Yes, Dr. Freud."

"What of the future?"

"You already know that, don't you? I can see the smug look of satisfaction on your face."

"I don't know anything with certainty," he said. "If you read any smugness on my face, you misinterpret me."

"You think that I'm afraid that I'll turn into my mother."

"You're not your mother, Emily."

"No, but I'm afraid that I may go as crazy as she did."

"You don't have your mother's symptoms."

"No," she agreed. "I have my own special brand of crazy."

"You're as sane as I," he said.

"That doesn't give me much comfort."

"Am I to laugh here?" he asked.

"Not really," she said.

"Do you worry about this more for your sake or for the sake of your daughter?"

"For my daughter," she said. "I live for my daughter."

"Then you should be comforted by that," he said encouragingly. "Apparently your mother's mind was so adrift that she'd lost sight of you. She couldn't have thought the consequences through. Her troubles were all about her."

"But she must have known that I would be the one to find her."

"We don't really know that, do we?"

"I came here looking for answers."

"You came here looking for peace," he said.

"You really can't fix anything, can you?"

"I can only guide you."

"And prescribe," she said.

"You don't need to be medicated," he said. "I've seen no evidence of that and it would be against my principles. Do you want medication?"

"No," she said.

"Talk to me," he said. "Talk to a close friend. Perhaps you can discuss it with your daughter."

"No," she said with horror. "I could never talk with her about this."

"Do you really think keeping it from her will protect her? Have you been protected by the silences in your family?"

She thought about that for a moment. "But Shannon's only a child," she said. "She doesn't need this in her life."

"Perhaps it isn't the right time, but maybe later. If you show her that you can trust her it may go a long way in how she trusts you."

"Are you being my therapist or hers?"

"You're concerns are about her," he said flatly. "How you deal with all things is my concern right now. Open up to those you trust. Don't keep it all bottled up inside yourself."

"I could have gotten that advice from the lady who looks after my daughter. And she makes house calls."

"Okay, here's some other brilliant advice," he said. "The truth will set you free."

"Now you're playing with me, Dr. Freud. Where do I start?"

"Try talking with your father," he said.

"Okay," she said easily. She exhaled lightly and her body relaxed a little. "I've already opened that door a bit. I'm a little hesitant, though. His life has been in a bit of an uproar lately. He's just retired. He was a teacher and he loved teaching. I think that was a bad thing for him to do, but he said it was time. It came on the heels of a big wall going up behind his garden. It blocked out the view to the park that he cherished. My aunt found him broken down and crying. My father never cried," she said. "Oh look at you, Dr. Freud," she said turning on him almost coldly. "You're salivating over the possibilities of having a father-daughter therapy session."

"When he's ready," he said dismissing her accusation, "you talk with him. It could be a help to both of you."

"Misery loves company?" she asked.

"You might find a little solace in sharing one another's pain. Neither of you are alone in the suffering that you're mother caused."

"I'll try," she said quietly. She reached down and snatched at her purse and then stood up.

"We still have time," the doctor said.

"I know," she said. "I think my time would be better spent with him right now, Dr. Hiller."

"You are coming back?"

"Yes," she said. "I may call for an earlier appointment depending on how it goes. I don't want to hurt him."

"I thought we decided that you'd wait until you thought he was ready to discuss this with you."

"It's already been decades, Dr. I may have to force the issue."

"Like you said though, it's been a bad time for him of late. This may not be the best time for a confrontation."

"It wouldn't be like that with him," she said. "My dad and I have never tried to hurt each other. It would be a talk. It would not be a confrontation." She started for the door.

The doctor stood up. "I'm concerned, Emily. For your father, I mean."

"You don't even know my father."

"I do a little," he said sheepishly. "You've given me a little on him. It sounds like it's been a rough go for him of late."

"I'll feel him out," she said noting his concern. "Thank you, Dr. Hiller." She stood there for a moment, but could think of nothing else to say. "Good bye."

Chapter Fourteen

"Emily," Elizabeth said, a little taken aback, as she opened the door. "What a pleasant surprise, dear. Come in, come in."

"I've brought your favorite," Emily said revealing a quart of French vanilla ice cream.

"I shall apply that directly to my backside, dear." Elizabeth took the ice cream and headed off for the kitchen. "Would you like yours with the chocolate syrup?"

"Oh, why not?" she said laughing.

"Your father's not home," she called from the kitchen.

"Is he with Henry, Aunt Elizabeth?"

"I don't think so," she said returning from the kitchen. "The ice cream was easy to work with in this heat. I won't complain about it, though. It's so much cooler than what we've had to bear with. I won't miss the summer days until winter slaps us about a bit."

"I like the heat," Emily said.

"I know you do, love. I'd always feared that you run away to live in the south and I'd never see you again."

"So," Emily said. "What have you and daddy been up to these days? Is daddy getting on your nerves hanging around the house all the time?"

"No love. Actually I haven't been seeing much of your father at all these last several weeks." Elizabeth made an attempt at maintaining her composure, but Emily read her face and the thoughts that were modifying it.

"Have you had a fight?"

"Lord no, dear. Why would you suggest such a thing?"

"What keeps you and dad so busy that you don't see much of one another?" she asked without answering her question.

"Well," she said with a smile breaking across her face. "I've been taking classes."

"That's wonderful," Emily said. She put down the ice cream and put her arms around her. "I'm so happy for you. What kind of classes are you taking?"

"Well, actually I'm taking courses in home health care."

A quizzical look overcame Emily. "Home health care," she said. "Are you concerned about daddy?"

"No dear. I wish to enter the work force."

"Why? If there's concern about money, I can help. Daddy said that he had a very good package," she nearly stammered.

"There's no concern about money. I want to work. I want to be less dependent upon your father."

"Aunt Elizabeth, I think that my father is more dependent upon you then you are of him."

"I used to think as much, but now I don't think that's at all true any more."

"You're not going to leave?"

"No dear," Elizabeth said, but there was such a shift in her eyes that it frightened Emily. She couldn't imagine her aunt alone in the world and she did not wish to see her father without her. Emily hadn't realized before how comforting their union was to her.

"Has something changed, Aunt Elizabeth?"

"No," she said averting her eyes again.

"You can't hide things from me," Emily said placing her hand on her aunt's arm. I could always read you like you could read me."

Elizabeth liked hearing such things. It made her feel more a mother to Emily than an aunt. "I just think it's time for me to branch out a bit. Perhaps your father, too, would like to make changes," she said and poked about her ice cream.

"You're not telling me everything. Please don't leave me out in the cold, Aunt Elizabeth."

It was the last words that jolted her. She too felt left out in the cold and did not wish Emily to feel slighted. "Your father is in a relationship," she said not hiding her discomfort at the words all that well.

"A relationship? With who?"

"Maria Scapelli."

Emily's eyes involuntarily widened. "How long has this been going on? Daddy hasn't mentioned a word of this to me."

"Nor I dear, he's been sneaking around with her. It's been at least a month, perhaps longer. I really haven't a clue."

Secretly, Emily was delighted, but she dared not show it to her aunt. "It is a bit strange that daddy is sneaking around like a schoolboy, but why should this upset you so much?" She put her hand on Elizabeth's arm with a weak attempt at comforting her.

The narrowing of Emily's eyes did not go unnoticed by Elizabeth. "I'm not at all upset," Elizabeth said indignantly. "Your father and I have different needs and there's no need for either he or I to get in the way of the other. I'm quite happy to be moving on and it's about time that he did as well."

"Of course you're right, but you will stay here with daddy. You'd be lost without one another."

"You needn't worry about your father. He'll have Maria," she said with false pleasure.

"But what about you, Aunt Elizabeth you can't just leave."

"Of course I can," she said and wondered just how she had dug herself into this hole. It had not been settled in her mind to leave before. It had merely been a fear of hers and now she managed to make that fear a reality. She would look a fool to stay on for much longer, but in no way was she prepared to leave. How pathetic I would look to this child to cling to my brother now, she thought. "Of course I won't just run out on your father now," she said trying to recover. "When the time comes that he no longer needs me, I'll finally be free to pursue what pleases me most."

"This is all happening so fast," Emily said. "I don't know what to say. Are you certain about Maria, Aunt Elizabeth?

"Maria Scapelli has had her eye on your father for ages," she said blankly. "I suppose your father only recently took notice of her."

"I suspected Maria had feelings for daddy, but…'

"Yes dear."

"If daddy hasn't said anything, how can you know for sure?"

"They've been seen together." Elizabeth had to work hard to not show her impatience.

"But they work together and they are friends."

"They've been seen together," she said putting great emphasis on 'seen'.

"Oh," said Emily understanding that her aunt had a small network of spies offering juicy bits of gossip in exchange for an odd sort of glory. "At odd hours?" she asked with hesitation.

Elizabeth merely nodded, but her face showed her reprove. "He's a grown man, love."

"Yes, of course." Emily's face was grim, but her heart leapt with joy for her father. She would have to leave her aunt, she thought. She could not hide her delight for her father and Maria for very long. She was also pleased for Maria who she felt would be a good match for her father. She thought of them marrying and perhaps traveling the world a bit as was Maria's passion and a passion that could carry her father along with to see the world of which he so often spoke of, but never truly dared to venture out in. "I love you, Aunt Elizabeth."

"I love you too," she said and concluded that her fears were all the more realized with Emily's recognition.

"So," said Emily looking for a brighter subject. "Tell me how you like your classes."

"I'm thrilled," she said and it was true and Emily knew it to be true by the look on Elizabeth's face. "I'm doing quite well, actually. I should be certified in no time at all from what they tell me and I think I'll miss it all very much when I'm finished with it."

"You can take other classes when these are finished."

"I've already thought of that, but I'm not sure what kinds of classes would be of interest to me."

"You could discuss it with daddy," she said. "Education is his field after all."

"I'd really rather not," she said firmly. "I haven't even mentioned my classes with you father and I'd appreciate that we keep it between us, if that's alright with you."

"Of course, if that's what you want. But how do you keep it from him? He's here all day long, isn't he?"

"He's in his room all day long," she said. "He tends to his garden for an hour or two early in the morning and then he goes up to his study and writes all day long. I feed him in the morning and then I feed him late afternoon and all the while he just pecks away at that little machine of his."

"He's using the computer that I gave him?"

"Yes dear. He seems to get a lot of pleasure from that."

"He's writing?" she said and a smile broke on her face and she had no reason to hide this one.

"Yes," Elizabeth said matter of fact. "What he writes I couldn't tell you. I asked him about it, but he won't let me read a word of it." Elizabeth had a look of concern on her face and she leaned it to speak. "I wonder about it, dear."

"What do you wonder about?"

"Well," she started. "He spends so many hours writing and for so many days, but it is a rather small computer, love."

"Yes?"

"Well how many pages can such a little machine hold?"

Emily had to stifle a laugh with her hand. "It can hold quite a few pages. Why do you ask?"

"I just worry that he's pecking away for no good reason. Shouldn't he have it on paper?"

"Well I think that it would be a good idea for him to back it up. I could go up and put it on a disk for him."

"Wouldn't it be better to put it on paper, dear?"

"We could do that too," Emily said and then heard the key in the door. "That must be daddy," she said and got up to greet him.

"Emily," Robert said and threw his arms around his daughter. "Another surprise visit?" he said. "Where's Shannon?" he asked looking around the room.

"She's in camp."

"Oh," he said with disappointment in his voice. "You know, Elizabeth and I could look after her a bit during the summer if you need help."

Emily looked to her aunt. "I appreciate that, but Shannon loves her camp. She has her friends and activities, but I will take you up on that towards the end of the summer."

"I would love that.'

"So, I understand that you've been doing some writing."

"Yes," he said. "Just putting a few ideas on paper is all. Tell me, what kinds of activities is Shannon involved with?"

"Swimming and games and day trips," she said tersely. "Tell me about your ideas. What are you writing about?"

"Very little," he said.

"Can I see?'

"No, Emily. There really isn't much to see. Come out and look at my garden," he said. "I'll mix up some iced tea."

"Not that powder stuff in the can," Elizabeth said with disapproval. I'll brew some fresh tea with lemon."

"I like that stuff in the can, Elizabeth."

"It's much too sweet, Robert. It doesn't even taste like tea."

"I don't remember you ever drinking iced tea from a mix, daddy."

"Another new development," Elizabeth muttered. Robert ignored her and went out to the kitchen to mix up his tea. "I swear," Elizabeth said. "I don't know who that man is any more."

"It's only tea," Emily said, but it was like a blasphemy to Elizabeth.

"Whatever," she said. "I need to see to the laundry. You have a nice visit with your father."

They sat down at the little stone table and sipped at their tea. Despite the heat that had transpired, his garden was very lush. The vines had been steadily climbing and with any luck they would overtake the wall by summers end. "It's beautiful out here, dad. You've managed to keep everything in bloom."

"Yes," he said with pride. "Normally I try to obey the laws, but this water restriction seemed too unfair to me. Those people were given a permit to block out my sun; my view," he said. "Why should I be denied a little water to keep my flowers from death? How can one waste water, anyway?" he said. "It's the finest renewable resource in existence. The very water in our tea will rain down again one day and will continue to do so long after we are all gone."

"Why can't I see your work?"

"I'm not ready to show it to you or anyone else just yet. I don't know that it will ever be ready. For now, it's just for me."

She would have liked to argue the point, but thought her own impatience was a little too inequitable. "Can you tell me about it?"

"I've strung some letters together to make words and strung the words together to make sentences and added some punctuation to make it coherent. Other than that there is very little to say."

"Tell me what it's about."

"Oh Emily. I'd really rather not. Can't we change the subject?"

"Yes," she said. "I'm sorry to press you." She looked away from him for a moment and then cast her eyes downward. "I talked with my shrink," she said.

She had his full attention. "Oh," he said with caution.

"I told him about mother."

"Good," he said and put his hand on her forearm. "Did it help you at all?" he asked.

"I don't really know. I suppose that I had hoped it would, but I'm not altogether sure if it helped at all. I'm glad that I finally talked about it, though."

"You've never told anyone?"

"No."

"Not even Richard?"

"No," she said. Not even my husband Richard."

"That's awful." She looked up at him and he could see that she was clearly taken aback. "You should have told him at least."

"Why should I have told him?" she asked irritably.

"Because you loved him," he said.

"I've always loved you and I never said a word about it. You've never said anything about it."

"No," he agreed. "I never said a word about it. Do you think of it often? Does it hurt very much?"

"I think of it every day," she said casually. "Not a day goes by when I don't see her there," she said and stopped short of the description that had always plagued her mind.

"Why didn't you talk to me?" he said. "Why didn't you tell me how you felt, Emily?"

"Why didn't you?"

"I don't know," he said and went to turn away, but held his head in check. "I didn't know how to talk about it then. I pushed it aside and busied my mind with other matters or things that didn't matter at all."

"So did I," she said. "Or at least I tried. I tried very hard and made a little success in the mean time, but I can't not think about it. At least I made a little money for my efforts. Were you able to just push it aside, daddy?"

"For bits of time," he said. "For hours at a time and than days or perhaps a week, but it always comes back to the front of my mind and then like throwing water on a fire I put my nose in a book and try to forget. Talking about it helps, though. Talking about it takes away some of the burden, Emily."

"You know that first hand?"

"I do," he said.

"Is this recent?" she asked.

"What?" he asked.

"Who do speak of this with?"

"Nobody really," he said with some discomfort. "I've spoken with a friend of mine."

"Henry?"

"No not Henry. Nobody you know, Emily. Just a friend of mine," he said abruptly. "I think it's great that you're finally talking about this. What does you Doctor have to say?"

"He just prods me along to say more than I wish to," she said.

"He must be good if he got you to talk. I am sorry. I wish I could have helped you to talk. Sometimes it's just easier to talk with someone when they're not so close to the situation. I was always afraid that I'd break you if we spoke of it together."

"Break me?" she said. "How do you mean?"

"This is an old wound," he said. "I didn't want to open it up. You always seemed so well adjusted and I didn't want to wake anything I couldn't put to sleep. I always thought you were passed that, but I see now that I was just wishing that to be the truth. Somebody said that you were in need of help."

"Who said that?" she asked.

"A friend," he said and smiled.

"You're speaking of the friend that I don't know?"

"Yes," he said. "That's the one."

"Do I ever get to meet this friend?"

"I hope one day that you will," he said.

"When will this meeting take place?" she asked.

"Let's just put that aside," he said. "Where do you and your doctor go from here?" he asked.

"I don't know that we go anywhere from here," she said. "There's no cure for the past. I just have to deal with it, I suppose."

"What does he say, other than prodding?"

"He tells me that it wasn't my fault."

"Of course it wasn't your fault," he said. "Why would he even put such a thought in your head?" he asked. He looked at Emily, but she said nothing. "You never thought that Emily did you?"

Emily tried to nod, but sat there frozen in her chair. The tears welled up in her eyes and when he put his arms around her she balled like a child and fell completely apart for the first time since her early childhood. "Yes," she cried. "I did think that, daddy."

"No, no, no," he repeated. "God no, sweetheart," he said and the tears welled in his eyes. "You're mother loved you," he promised. "She would never have wanted to hurt you like this, Emily. I wish you could remember her for the good days she had. In the beginning there were so many good days."

Emily looked at her father, her eyes brimming with tears. "When did her depression set in?" she asked. "Was it after I was born?"

"No," he said. "On the very day that I had met her, she was crying. It was the tears in her eyes that had drawn me to her. Like a fool, I wanted to save her. For a time I thought I had, but then the depression came back to her. For a while we put up a good fight, but I suppose we both wearied of it. I fought harder than she and for a much longer time, but I too had little fight in me at the end. I know now that it was harder for her and that's what's been eating at me for so many years. I never should have given up, but I did, Emily. I gave up after a long time of seeing that she had no will to fight it. We tried the medication, but… She had imbalances," he said after a time. "There's very little understanding of it still, but it had nothing to do with you or even me. I blamed myself for the longest time, but I've given that up now. I used to think it was possible to choose happiness over depression and I believe it still. Perhaps she could not do that, but I think that I can, Emily. And you must believe that you can too. Only you can make happiness for yourself. Only you can rule your own emotions. Don't waste any more of your precious time on grief."

They held on to each other for the longest time and at the end of it they both shared a great sense of relief. With a few words and a simple hug they had purged so many years of guilt and remorse. Emily felt a great weight had been lifted from her and she could now breathe easily. She smiled as a blue jay landed in a birdbath that Robert had added in recent days. The bird fluttered about. His wings were smacking the water playfully. She thought for a moment that she had not been in tune with such things for quite a long time. She wished to see such things again. I want to stop and smell the flowers; she thought and smiled at the lameness of it.

She did not continue to press her father about his writing or about his friend. In time, she thought, he would reveal them both to her. In the mean time it was good that he was writing and that he was seeking companionship with Maria Scapelli. Maria would be good for him, she thought. She only wished that she could call her and tell her how pleased she was for both of them and to perhaps dispel any thoughts to the contrary. In time Aunt Elizabeth, too, would come to welcome her and things would manage to go on much as they have. Perhaps the family would be just a little bigger and that would be a good thing.

In any case, she thought, it was good for her aunt to be preoccupied with other things. Aunt Elizabeth beamed with pride about her classes, she thought. This was exactly what she needed and it was her brother's happiness that had forced her hand. Fear, she thought, could do wonderful things if you will allow it. In time it would all go right.

Chapter Fifteen

"I tried to stay away from you," Robert said. He was sitting on the curb in Prospect Park. His legs were open and his shoulders were hunched in between them very much like a child and his eyes did not help to dispel the impression. He watched her furtively in a peripheral position. He was sulking and as he became aware of this he straightened his posture and drew his breath in silently.

"It's been five days since I've seen you. I wondered if you'd see me again," Madeline said.

"I tried not to, but I can't stay away," he said. He turned to face her and as he feared she was as beautiful as ever. "I shouldn't be with you."

"I thought you loved me."

"I do," he said shakily.

"Then why shouldn't you see me?"

"I'm frightened of you. You overwhelm me, Madeline."

"Why, frightened?" she asked.

"You've turned my world upside down," he said more audibly than he wished. He looked around to see if anyone had heard him, but they were quite alone. "If I go with you, I fear that I shall never return to my life."

"Is the life you have without me so much better? Is it a life; a world that you prefer to live in?"

"No," he said truthfully. "I'd much rather stay here with you. I'm very happy here with you."

"Then stay here with me forever," she said and smiled seductively.

"You tempt me like a devil," he said. He looked at her closely. His eyes traced over the lines, curves and contours of every inch of her body. His breath diminished in his chest and the struggle to maintain it left him nearly panting. He ached to touch her and like two people of one mind, she reached out and took his hand and placed it on her thigh. He trembled at the feel of her skin against his fingertips. "We don't belong in each others worlds," he said. He went to withdraw his hand, but she held it and he did not attempt to resist.

"We do belong in the each others world," she said simply.

"There are others to consider," he retorted.

"Do they need all of you, Robert? Can't I have just a little bit of you from time to time?"

"I don't know," he said. "I'm afraid that I'll just run off with you and never go back to them."

"That won't happen," she promised. "We won't let us go that far. We'll steal away from them for a little bit at a time and they never need know."

He turned to her sharply and his eyes narrowed. "Can we do that? Is that really possible?"

"We'll just have to be strong," she said. "We'll not allow ourselves to be swept so far away."

She smiled at him and he thought how indulgent her mouth looked to be. "How can I trust you when I can't trust myself?" he asked weakly.

"I want you," she said and he could feel her grip on his arm. "I want to be with you. Must that be so difficult?"

"But it is difficult."

"Than I'll go away," she said. "I'll go and I will never come back to you, Robert Montgomery."

"No," he erupted. He turned and saw that there were people now and that they were watching him.

"Don't look at them Robert," she said severely. "Look at me. Don't let strangers come between us."

"I've never been one for a scene," he whispered. He looked up to see if he was being watched, but the few that were nearby had lost interest in him. "As I said before, I tried to stay away from you, Madeline. I tried very hard, but I'm here now because I could not. I love you and I very much need you. I had hoped that you would leave me, but I really don't want that. To have you for a little bit of the time would be wonderful," he said.

"Then we shall have each other for a little bit of the time," she said. "Let's walk. Let's just walk and talk for a while and not think about being apart."

It was early in September when Elizabeth received her certificate. "It's official," she said to no one as she opened the letter. "I can start to work now." She knew that she could be frightened if she permitted herself to be so, but she declined that emotion. She was determined to be elated and so that was the way she would play it out. She immediately picked up the telephone and called Mr. Drake to give him the good news and to ask how she should proceed. He told her to come into his office on the following morning and that they would work out the details. "Perhaps you can come in at eleven and then afterwards we can see about lunch," he said.

"Lunch?" she nearly yelped. Then more controlled, "lunch" she repeated.

"Yes," he said with a slight stammer. "I know a place where we can go and… Unless it's impossible for you," he said offering her an out.

"No," she said. "It's not at all impossible for me. Lunch would be delightful." She hung up the phone and wondered about her use of the word 'delightful' and thought it might have sounded excessive if not a little too desperate. "I'm not that," she said to no one with an air of dignity that rang false to even her. She straightened up a little and smiled. "He wishes to have lunch with me." She immediately exchanged her smile with a frantic look of determination and went quickly to her rooms to see about an outfit that would do her justice and hopefully a little more than that.

* * *

"I had entered an entirely new world of my own making, Toby. I had begun to run out on the life I had led for so many years. I knew this and yet I didn't. I did not see that I was abandoning Elizabeth," he says despairingly. "I was doing it to her again, but she'll forgive me that," he says. "I know in my heart that she will forgive me. It is Emily who will be left to suffer in my withdrawal. It is Emily who will ultimately pay the price. It's just that more than anything else I wished to have this," he says hopefully. "I was willing to gamble away everything for this last chance at happiness and I'm afraid that she will never understand or accept this.

"Was it so very wrong of me to surrender myself to Madeline?" he whispers. "Yes," he says finally. "It was wrong. I should have resisted her in the beginning when it was more possible to do so. It did not take me very long to fall in love with her, Toby. I fell very much in love and no matter the consequences; I cannot retreat from my path. They will have to understand. It is as simple as that," he says with resignation.

"Elizabeth is doing rather well," he says as though the old man has just inquired about her. "She's been working. I don't know how this change in her life had begun," he says shaking his head. "One morning I came down from my rooms and saw that the breakfast table was set for one with a note about my breakfast and some detailed instructions on how I was to proceed. I believe that Elizabeth fears that I would die of starvation in her absence," he says smiling fondly. "I've been so fortunate to have her in my life. I suppose without really thinking, I'd taken her for granted. She has a lot to offer the world. There are very few like my sister.

"In the beginning she was missing for a few hours a day two or three times a week and before I knew it she was gone all day every day. I made a mess of that too," he says regretfully. "When she told me that she'd taken a job, I told her that I was glad for her and truly I was. I promised that I was fine without her; that I could manage rather nicely on my own. It wasn't true, but I made a rather good show of it and without realizing it, I'd diminished the whole of her life. I seem to have a talent of mucking things a bit," he says thoughtfully. "I only wanted her to do as she pleased without the restraints of guilt. I didn't want to lose her, but I did not wish to hold her back. Can you understand that?" he asks.

"It was Emily who had come to see this, you see. She pointed out the mess that I had made and now I need to put it right. I'll do that," he says with some conviction. "I have so many things to put right. I hope to see her soon and to do that. I have to do that properly."

Robert walks away from the old man and down to the rivers edge. He stands there stone faced for a while and then a smile breaks his face and his body relaxes and his eyes glaze over and his mind travels off on its own.

* * *

"Can't we go away from here?" she said. "Just the two of us for a little while," she pleaded.

"Where to?" he asked.

"Don't you have any ideas?" Her face was cast down, but her eyes looked up at him seductively.

"I do at that," he said grinning like a wolf. "I want to take you out into the wild and have my way with you."

"Is that right?" she said. "And where in the wild are you thinking?"

"A campground," he said. "I've bought myself a car this morning. I haven't had a car in years. I never really needed one until now."

"You bought a car?"

"I did," he said. "It isn't much really, but it's clean and as I understand it has been well maintained. Do you know what else I purchased this morning after picking up my car?"

"I'm almost afraid to ask," she said gingerly.

"I bought a tent and a double sleeping bag. I also purchased a lantern, the type that requires a battery and not kerosene. I would not want to be responsible for a forest fire," he said. Madeline laughed and cuddled closer to him in his bed.

"No," she agreed. "We would not want that. Isn't it getting a little cold for camping outside in the open?"

"No," he assured her promptly. "I have a means for keeping us warm."

"Does it require batteries?" she asked playfully.

"No not batteries," he said, "but there's an idea in there somewhere."

She laughed shyly and kissed him softly. "And how shall we eat out there in the wild? Will you hunt down wild animals and cook for me over an open fire?"

"Possibly," he said. "Although I've downloaded a list of promising restaurants in the area and thought it might be more pleasurable to have others do the butchering and cooking on our behalf."

"Well that might be nice," she said. "It's not much like Hemingway though. I was envisioning the green hills of Africa and a safari under Kilimanjaro."

"You shall be the Memsahib," he said. "Instead of tracking and hunting lions, buffalo and bears, we shall track box turtles, deer, rabbits and birds and we shall photograph them."

"No broken lava rock country or salt flats?"

"No, but we can skip flat rocks off the Delaware."

"We can have an adventure," she said excitedly. "We can make our camp under the skies and stars of Africa and from beneath our mosquito netting and nestled in our sleeping bag we can recollect our day's journey. Can we have an open fire?"

"Yes," he said enthusiastically. "There are fire pits at every tent site and this time of year should allow for us to have some privacy. I thought we might go up this weekend. There's a path along the river where trains used to run. The tracks are long gone, but the path remains. We can rent bicycles and ride for miles and miles. The leaves will be turning in the coming weeks. If we like it we can go back all through the fall and even into the winter. They offer a great deal of lodging throughout the area on either side of the river."

"It will be our private world," she said. "Every trip will be a new adventure for us. Oh Robert, you've made me so happy."

"I hope to, Madeline. I love you."

"Hello my child," Elizabeth said to her grandniece at the door and hugged her tightly. She looked beyond Shannon and towards Emily down at the curb. Emily paid the driver, turned and smiled at her aunt and came up the steps.

"Hello, Aunt Elizabeth." She stopped in her tracks and surveyed the woman before her. The hair was different and the dress was one she had never seen before. "You look absolutely stunning," she said to her aunt.

"Oh, stop," said Elizabeth blushing bright red. "Come in, come in, dears." She looked at her watch anxiously. "Why didn't you tell me that you were coming in this evening?"

"It was a last minute thing," Emily said. "We were having pizza and thought we'd come by with some dessert," she said holding up a little bakery box. "Were you on your way out?"

"Well actually yes," she said. "I can try and cancel, but I think it may be too late. You see," she continued, "I'm to be picked up in a few minutes. I'll just cancel when he gets here," she said uneasily. "He'll understand."

"No don't be silly," Emily said. She handed the box to Shannon and sent her off to the kitchen for some milk and plates for the pastries. "He?" she said to her aunt with an exaggerated raise of the eyebrows. "Is this man a romantic interest, Aunt Elizabeth?"

Elizabeth blushed again and like a schoolgirl she gushed that it was. "George and I have been seeing one another for a little more than a month, love."

"You've been seeing a man for a little more than a month? And why have you been keeping this from me?" she asked on the sly.

"It's really not such a big deal."

"Of course it is," Emily retorted. "Tell me everything at once or I will grill this man the moment he walks in the door."

"No, no, you mustn't do that, Emily. I don't want you scaring him off. His name is George Drake and he was the man to hire me."

"You've mentioned Mr. Drake several times and never once let on that you were seeing each other. Why have you kept this from me?"

"I didn't want to keep it from you, dear. It's only that I wanted to tell you in person and now I have such little time," she said looking down at her watch.

"I'll come back tomorrow," Emily promised. "You can tell me everything then. Don't worry, though. I won't come too early."

"Don't be fresh now Emily," she said and gave her a mock slap on the arm. "I do hate to leave you, though. I wouldn't, but George is taking me to the theatre this evening. I would hate to disappoint him. He was so excited with the seats he had managed to get and..."

"Go and have a wonderful time and tell me all about it tomorrow. We'll just have a quiet visit with daddy."

"Oh," said Elizabeth with dismay. "You're father is away this weekend. Didn't he tell you?"

"No, he didn't. Daddy doesn't tell me much of anything these days. He's so tight lipped about his… About his everything," she said finally. "Where did he go?"

"I really don't know, love. Ever since he bought that car he seems to be off nearly every weekend."

"Is he still writing?"

"I really couldn't say. I'm out at work all day and on the weekends he's always running off."

"Does he go on his own?"

"Perhaps, but I don't think so. He bought some camping equipment and I noticed that he had provisions for two," she said. "At first I though it was he and Henry that were going off, but then one Saturday morning Henry happened by looking for him. It was apparent from our conversation that they hadn't done any camping together."

"Henry didn't know anything about daddy going camping?"

"No."

"What did he say?"

"Oh, I didn't come out and ask Henry Grifhorst anything about it, dear." She cast a duplicitous face at Emily and lowered her tone. "I have a way, dear, of talking that gets me answers without asking direct questions," she said.

"Yes, Aunt Elizabeth, I know all about that. Did you forget that I was a teenager in this house?"

Elizabeth narrowed her eyes. "You knew that I was doing that with you?" Emily laughed, but before she could answer Elizabeth grabbed her sweater from the coat tree behind the door. "He's here Emily, but I'm not prepared to have you meet him. Let me run down to him and we'll all have a nice get together real soon. Give my love to Shannon and we'll see each other tomorrow?"

"Yes," she said. "I'm so happy for you, Aunt Elizabeth."

"So am I, dear," she said with a smile bigger than Emily had ever seen on her before. "And I love you." She turned and quickly made her way down the porch steps and onto the sidewalk.

"Do you think he's going off with Maria, Aunt Elizabeth?" Emily called from the doorway.

Elizabeth looked up from the curb. "I'm certain of it, dear." She ran to the approaching car and jumped in before George could get out and open it for her. Emily watched as the car went off and then pushed the door closed with her back as she faced the staircase. "Can you put the tea kettle on for me, Shannon? I'll be right down," she said and hesitantly made her way up the stairs and to her father's rooms.

She walked into his den and opened the laptop and turned it on. She immediately saw the icon that was her father's story. She opened it up and was surprised to see that he had over a hundred thousand words in the file. She logged into her email account and with an enormous sense of guilt and betrayal, she sent the file to herself. She logged off, thought for a moment and then wiped the history. She turned off the computer and as casually as she could went down to her daughter and split a cannoli with her in the kitchen and drank a cup of tea.

Robert walked up to bar at the Hearthstone Pub and exchanged a few friendly words with the bartender and then asked for the usual. Louis Armstrong was singing *La Vie En Rose* in the background. The room was dark, lit only by the few spots that beamed down over the bar, and the small candles that floated on water in the center of each table. He moved to a table in the back of the warmly lit inn and took his seat across from Madeline. A minute or so later the barman dropped two cocktail napkins down on the table and placed the drinks accordingly. "Let me know if you need anything else," he said and patted Robert affectionately on the shoulder.

"I like it here so much," Madeline said brightly. "I'm so glad that we found this place."

"I like to think that it found us," he said. They lifted their glasses and toasted without words. Each knew what the other was thinking. "You're absolutely beautiful," he told her.

"I am so happy when I'm with you," she said. "I wish we could always be together like this."

He stirred in his chair and again he thought about his daughter, granddaughter and Elizabeth. "We have now," he said with strained confidence. "We've had these past several months."

"Yes," she agreed, but he could hear the discontent in her voice. He struggled with the conflict in his mind and with sheer will he pushed it aside. "Thanksgiving is only three weeks away. We can't be together then?"

"No," he said softly. "I need to be with my family. Emily and Shannon will be coming. I need to be with them."

"Of course," she said.

"I want to be with you always," he said. "But I have to go back to them sometimes too." There was a tone of finality in his voice. "What shall we do tonight?" he asked her. He needed always to redirect the course of their direction. He could not give in to her or to himself and he could never allow himself to forget this.

"It's so beautiful outside," she said cheerfully. "Let's walk some more before it gets too cold to walk too far."

"Yes," he agreed. "Let's walk together some more. The air feels so good, but I'm afraid that there will be very little to see at this hour."

"It doesn't really matter. We'll see in our minds what we saw this afternoon. The red, gold and yellow leaves that still hang on to the trees and the quickness of the river flowing over the rocks after the heavy rains that kept us in all of last week."

"Yes," he said and thought about the heavy downpour of rain and the cold winds that blew from the north driving the rain against the windowpanes in the room of the bed and breakfast where they had stayed. He had lit a fire and kept it fed all of that weekend and they stayed beneath the blankets talking, cuddling and making love. They read the Sunday paper and worked on the crossword puzzle and only left their room to eat.

Today they had gotten there early and had walked much of the afternoon and stopped only to peruse over the titles in a little bookstore. Robert came across an old copy of Edmund Gosse's *Father & Son* that he had sought for some time. The copy he had found was a paperback version that had been printed in nineteen seventy-three. Of course he probably could have come by it much sooner if he had searched for it on the Internet, but he had always found it to be more of a delight to come upon these rare finds on his own in a little bookstore such as this.

Tonight Madeline and Robert would walk well into the evening. They could not get enough of each others company, and the demand for more time than he felt he could give lay heavily on him. He did not wish to refuse her, but he felt he must. He knew that he would eventually have to lose himself completely to be with her in the end and that he must fight that off, but he also knew that he would be so utterly lost without her. Dear God, he thought to himself. What is happening to me?"

Emily lay in her bed reading the pages that she had only just printed out. She was mesmerized by the words that her father had so passionately written. He had written a love story that was completely honest and utterly detailed. He so clearly revealed the pain and joy that he knew so well. She was wracked with the guilt of her treachery as she passed over each word, but she could not put down the pages. Her father was exposing himself to her whether it was his intent or not and what she learned filled her at once with joy and sadness. He had had such sensibilities and had to learn to live without ever truly expressing them. Through his written words she could see that he was a romantic man at heart and took a playful and tender approach towards his sexual desires. He could love and be loved with great confidence, if only in his mind.

His story, too, was filled with great adventure. It took place a hundred years in the past and its main protagonists, a man and woman, traveled to the Dark Continent in search for answers of earlier civilizations. Emily read on, gripped at times by the perils that the hero and heroine encountered and captivated by the discovery of their deep and profound love of one another. The man in the story was in so many ways very unlike that of her father and yet it was he. She could see him there so very clear in her mind. He was the man her father wished to be.

The love that the man and woman shared was pure and unselfish and a more skeptical Emily would have dismissed it as pure fiction, but she could not dismiss it so quickly now. There was something here that was too sincere to just put away. There was something here that she too, longed for. She thought then about Maria. Had Maria inspired these feelings that her father put so eloquently into words? Had Maria brought her father back to life? She wanted so much to speak with her, but for now she could not. She would have to be content with the knowledge that her father had found his happiness. She was certain of this through the pages she had read.

When the very last page had been laid down beside her, she thought that she could easily sell this material. She felt so proud of her father in that moment. He was accomplishing something of great importance. Emily relaxed her body and pushed the pillows aside. For the first time that evening she had felt the heaviness of her eyes and with the realization of the time, she turned off the light and gave way to the sleep that had been drawing her in. It's all very good, she thought and cuddled under her blanket and drifted off.

Chapter Sixteen

"Hello stranger," Henry Grifhorst said as Robert entered Farrell's. It was a Monday night and the barroom was fairly quiet. The few people that were there were neither loud nor quiet. Robert sat on the stool beside his friend and without asking, received a pint and nodded his thanks.

"Hello Henry," he said.

"That's it? Hello Henry."

"Am I forgetting something?"

"Fill me in," Henry said. "I don't mean kiss and tell stuff; I just mean what's been going on with you?" Henry pulled his glasses from the inside pocket of his jacket and studied them.

"I've fallen in love." Robert looked thoughtfully into the mug in his hand and put it down without drawing from it.

Henry looked at his friend curiously. He retrieved a handkerchief from the right hand pocket of his trousers and rubbed at his glasses with meticulous care. "Have you?" he said.

"Yes."

"Do I finally get to meet her?"

"No," he said, "no, not just yet."

"Am I still invited for Thanksgiving?"

"What a question," Robert said. "You're family. It wouldn't be Thanksgiving without you."

"And Madeline?" he asked.

"Madeline?"

"Will it be Thanksgiving without the woman you love?" Henry put on his glasses and watched him carefully. He was not sure what it was that he had sought, but he knew that something was amiss.

"Madeline will not be there."

"I see," he said. "Is she a married woman?"

"No," he declared firmly. And then more softly he said, "No she is not married."

"I understand that you only talk with me because I don't push, but why do you talk with me at all?"

Robert looked at him and smiled grimly. "To tell someone, Henry, makes it all the more real."

"All right. I won't ask for more than you want to give, but don't let me get cut down in the crossfire between you and some jealous guy. I've survived too many direct hits to get cut down at this stage of my life."

"There'll be none of that, I can assure you," he said with a smile. And then he turned the stool towards Henry and his mood brightened. "We found a new place this weekend."

"In Hunterdon County?"

"Bucks County," he said. "It's just across the river in Pennsylvania. It's a beautiful little place and we had a room on the top floor and a view of the river from a rather cozy little balcony. I should think that the view of the river will get better as the trees continue to thin out," he said. "The room has a gas fire and a big sunken tub. I don't normally go in for baths, but we added the salts and the bath feels rather good after the long walks. I really ought to invest in a good camera. There are some spectacular scenes that unfold with each season. We've seen the summer and fall. I can only imagine the winter. I do hope that we get some snow. The icicles on the faces of the rock supposed to be something to see. And then of course the spring," he said dreamily. "This will be the first spring in many a year that I will welcome and not at all dread."

"It sounds like you don't dread much at all, Monty."

"Only my time away from her," he said with no hint of amusement.

"Thanks a lot."

"Oh, I didn't mean any…"

"Forget it. I'm just breaking your chops. If I had a woman as good as all that, do you think I'd be sidled up on a stool next to you?"

"It's just that I love her, Henry. I feel complete when I'm with her."

"Don't get all corny on me, Monty."

"Love does that," he said. "I thought I was far beyond that point in my life, but it can sneak up on you at any age, I suppose."

"Are you going to ask her to marry you?" Henry asked with a sidelong glance.

Robert smiled and began to nod, but stopped short of it. His face darkened and his eyes gave the appearance that he was searching his mind with bewildered fury. "Marry?" he said. "No. I don't think I'll ever do that."

"Why not marry her?" Henry was grasping for anything.

"It's too much."

"Why is it too much?"

"Too far; it's going too far," Robert said.

Henry let out a sigh. "It's all right to love again. Nobody would think it wrong, Monty."

"Thank you for listening to me, Henry. I'm very grateful to have you as my friend." He looked up at the television screen. "Look at that," he said. "The Giants are playing tonight."

Henry laughed. "You really are in love," he said and slapped the bar. "Two more," he called out. "And let's order a few pies," meaning pizza, "for anyone who swears their loyalty to the Giants, on me."

Elizabeth punched in Maria Scapelli's phone number to ask her about Thanksgiving dinner as she always had. If Robert and Maria were not going to be forthcoming about their relationship, Elizabeth would have to carry on as if it there was no relationship in the know. Besides, now that she and George were getting on rather well, she had far less concern about what Maria and her brother were up to and Thanksgiving, she felt, would be an appropriate time for all of them to meet as couples.

"Hello?" Maria answered. Of course with her caller ID having already identified as to where the call was coming from, her questioned 'hello' was more about the why the call was coming than about whom the call was coming from.

"Hello Maria, this is Elizabeth. I'm so sorry that I haven't called you sooner," she lied. "It's just that I've been so busy and time just seems to be getting away from me all the more these days." Of course, she was thinking, you could have picked up the telephone yourself for once.

"Hello Elizabeth," Maria said fighting back the discomfort in her voice that ached to get out. "It's my fault really. I've been meaning to call for some time to see how you and Robert were getting on."

Elizabeth rolled her eyes and shook her head, but her tone did not betray her thoughts. "Well dear, I'm only glad that I got a hold of you now. Dinner of course will be served at five and starters will begin at two. I am, of course, so looking forward to your cinnamon apple crumb pie," she said. The look of her detest on her face did not transcend over the phone line.

"Oh," Maria said in that drawn out way that people use to stall while their brain searches for something to say. "I really should have let you know sooner, but I won't be able to make it this year."

Elizabeth's eyes narrowed. "Not able to make it?" she questioned. "I don't understand, Maria. I can't remember when you weren't here on Thanksgiving. Robert will be absolutely crushed."

"Will he?" Maria asked hopefully.

"Of course he will." Elizabeth was quite taken aback. This was not at all what she had expected. "Has something happened between you and Robert?"

"Happened?" Maria said cautiously.

"Did you have a fight or something?" Elizabeth asked forgetting herself.

"Why should you think such a thing? We've had no fight. I just can't make Thanksgiving, is all. I'm very sorry for not saying so sooner. I've always been very happy in your home and I think the world of your family." Maria's voice began to break with her last words and the tears began to stream in her eyes. She suddenly felt very much alone. "Give everyone my love Elizabeth," she said in a high-pitched voice and then abruptly put the phone down.

Elizabeth held her ear to the silenced phone and sat down heavily in the chair closest to her. She could feel Maria's despair as if it were her own. She knew with certainty that now it was all over between Maria and her brother and there was no pleasure to be gotten from that. She thought of George and what it might feel like if he were to leave her now. The pain, she thought, would be too much for her to bear. She understood in that moment what love truly meant. It wasn't just the pleasure of being together, but the dread of forever being apart. She hated herself for wishing that upon them. Her brother and Maria were two good people and they deserved to be happy.

Elizabeth squeezed the phone in her hand and pushed aside her grief in exchange for an air of determination. She called Emily and explained the gist of her conversation and let it be known that it was now Emily's difficulty to remedy and that she expected favorable results. Emily readily agreed and was pleased that it had been Elizabeth to initiate such action. Emily decided to go to the school and discuss the matter with Maria instead of taking up any such action with her father.

It had been quite a long time since Emily had last walked these halls. She was not at all a tall woman, but still she felt bigger than she actually was. She had remembered these lockers, which lined the corridors, being larger than they now appeared to be. The water fountains had not been changed, but they too seemed to be lower to the ground and the walls themselves felt as they too had been closing in. She stopped and carefully studied her surroundings and came to the conclusion that nothing had changed and yet it was not quite the way she had remembered it.

She stopped at the school office and asked where she could find Maria Scapelli. After explaining that she was the daughter of Robert Montgomery, she was greeted warmly and directed to Maria's classroom. She hesitated at the door for a moment and then peeked in from the back of the room and waved brightly to Maria.

"Class," Maria said. "Why don't we leave off here and let you use the last remaining minutes to get started on this evening's assignment." She exited the room through the front door and walked slowly down the corridor to where Emily was standing.

"Hello Maria," Emily said.

"Emily," Maria said mirroring Emily's smile. "Is everything all right? Is your father all right?"

"Yes," Emily said and held up an assuring hand. "It's you I wanted to see. I'm sorry to interrupt your class. I can wait a bit if you need to get back in there."

"No," she said. "I have a free period after this and the bell will be ringing momentarily. Why don't we go to my office before it does go off?" she said and started on her way before Emily could speak. In truth, Maria wished to be done with this meeting as quickly as possible. She supposed that Robert would never have mentioned to anyone how he had rejected her, but she could not be so sure. At the very least, Emily might have come to insist on her being present for Thanksgiving dinner out of pity. "And how is Shannon?" she said turning towards Emily as they walked.

"Very well, thank you. She made the honor roll in the first marking period and she's to be the second lead, as she puts it, in the school play."

"That's so wonderful," she said as she opened her office door. "You must be very proud. Please come in," she said and gestured her to take a seat. "Would you like some coffee or tea?"

"No. No thank you, Maria." Emily sat down and Maria sat behind her desk more for security than necessity."

"What can I do for you?"

"Well," Emily said hesitantly. She had been determined to come and speak, but she had not thought of what she might say when she got here. "Aunt Elizabeth said you were not coming for Thanksgiving this year."

"Oh," Maria said softly. She broke eye contact with Emily and struggled to keep her face from reddening, which made it all the more crimson. "I am sorry about not letting you guys know sooner, but I had made other plans."

"I just want to let you know that you will be missed, Maria. I have always thought of you as family. I may not show it in that I never call, but that's just one of my failings and I want to apologize for that."

"Please don't," Maria said waving off the apology. "I don't make the calls myself and…" Maria broke off and turned away as the tears accumulated in her eyes.

"Please confide in me, Maria. What's happened?"

"Why do you say that? Did your father say something?"

"My father is a very private man. He's a good man, though."

"Yes," Maria said. "He is a good man."

"Do you love him?"

Maria faced Emily no longer caring about the tears. "Why do you say that?" she asked almost pleading for the right answer.

"I know that you've been seeing my father."

Now Maria was confused and her face showed her puzzlement. "You know that I've been seeing your father?" she asked. "That's not true. I haven't seen Robert since his retirement party."

"But my father had been seen coming from your apartment late in the evening and then there were all those weekends away in the country."

"Your father came to my apartment to work with me on some things, some school programs, that he had hoped would change the boards' minds on his forced retirement. This school was everything to him as you know."

"Forced retirement?" Emily's face showed her shock.

"I am sorry, Emily." Maria reached across the desk and took her hands. "I thought you knew that. I didn't think he would keep that from you," she said in earnest. "Your father thought he would die without his work."

"He never told me," Emily nearly whispered.

"Robert really is a very private man." Maria thought of Robert's pain then. It was the first time she had allowed herself to think of him with sadness and not anger since he'd rejected her.

"But what about all those weekends?" she said.

"I don't know about any weekends. I haven't spoken with your father since the end of spring. I didn't even speak with him in the last weeks of the school year," she admitted.

"But why not?" she asked. "You were always such good friends."

"Because I wanted more than friendship," she replied. Maria looked up and the tears ran down her face. "I did love your father, but he didn't love me. He didn't want me, Emily. I loved your father for years and years and I blamed him for never wanting me. I've ruined my life by only wanting men who never want me back."

Emily hadn't the words to brush such things aside. It would be demeaning to try and so instead she walked around the desk and hugged Maria and allowed her to have a good cry. She could not insist that she come for Thanksgiving dinner and she could not offer promises on her father's behalf. She could do nothing, but offer this hug and hold her until she was cried out. And as Maria cried, Emily's mind raced. Her father had been forced to retire and he was off on his own or with someone else nearly every weekend. She needed to know more.

After leaving Maria's office she went directly to office of the principal, John McEntyre. "Come in," he said greeting her at the door. "It's good to see you again, Emily."

"Hello John," she said.

"And how is your father?"

"He's doing very well, thanks. He writes everyday and is off nearly every weekend to the country."

"That's wonderful," McEntyre said. "I'm so happy he's filling his time so well. I had hoped that he would come around to see us once in a while. I have to say that I hated to see him leave. He was the best teacher this school has ever known."

"Than why did you make him leave, John?"

McEntyre's face turned grave. "It wasn't my decision, Emily. I fought very hard to keep your father on."

"I don't understand any of this. My father isn't all that old. There are faculty members on your staff who are older than my father. Are you just humoring me by telling me that he was the best?"

"Not at all," McEntyre said fighting to keep the anger from his voice. "I loved your father and that's the truth. He was the best, but you have to understand the bureaucracy."

"I don't understand the bureaucracy," she said. "Why some people can stay and others can't. If I had known, I would have put some very good lawyers on this and sued for discrimination. I'll go and talk with my father about this," she said haughtily. "If I can get him to agree, you'll hear from my lawyers." She began to storm from the office, but John took her hand gently.

"You can't do that to him, Emily."

"To him?" she retorted.

"You actually want him to go through a competency hearing?"

Emily let go of the doorknob weakly. "Competency hearing?" she said and shook her head in disbelief. "What are you saying?"

"Surely you've seen the signs?"

"What signs?" She blinked and shook her head again. She looked up to him and waited.

"I said nothing about it, but others began talking. The board came to me, Emily. I couldn't hide it, but I did try."

Emily stood there, but her knees went weak. McEntyre took hold of her elbow and sat her down gently. "What are you saying?"

"I'm sorry, Emily. I assumed you would know this better than anyone else. Robert was getting lost."

"Lost? How do you mean, lost?"

"Forgetful."

"I get forgetful," she said.

"Not like that," he said. "Sometimes I would find your father standing in the hall and I would have to prod him to go to class."

"Standing in the hall?" she repeated dumbly.

"His mind would drift. This isn't something new, Emily. It started a few years back, but last year it had gotten worse. I would find him in his office during class and he would be off in another world. A few of the students confided in me about this, not because they wished him harm, but because they loved him and worried. For the most part he was dead on in his lectures and did far more good than harm, but there is very little leeway in these matters when it comes to city employees, especially where children are concerned."

"Why didn't you speak to me about this?"

"Truthfully I assumed you knew."

Emily turned away, not in anger, but in shame. "I should have known, but I never saw any hint of it. I don't get to see my father all that often. Truthfully, I don't make it a point to see him all that often. I've been pretty wrapped up in my own world."

"Most of us are," he said. "I should have spoken to you about this, but I felt a little uneasy about it. I have great respect for your father and I wished him to go out with some dignity. His illness isn't shameful, but I know from personal experience that some people feel humiliated in the early stages."

"Illness," she said. "I don't understand, John. I talk with my father at least twice a week. He's seems as sharp as ever to me. He's been writing," she said enthusiastically. "His work is good. I don't say that as an adoring daughter, but as a professional. I know good work when I see it. He writes with such clarity and confidence. It's not the work of a man who is lost."

McEntyre pressed his fingertips together and methodically tapped away at his chin. "Believe me, Emily, I know all too well that your father is and always has been a very sharp and intelligent man. He's wandering off, though. I believe he's aware of it. I saw it in his eyes and heard it in his protests when he was fighting to stay on. He never pushed me as to why he was being let go and I never brought it up."

"Do the others know?"

"You mean the faculty?"

"Yes. Do they all know why he's been let go?"

"Yes, I believe so. There are the whispers in the staff lounge. Most felt that the board was being unfair and that your father was well, but truthfully I know the signs."

"A parent?" she asked.

"My mother," he said.

"Did Maria Scapelli ever say anything?"

"She's been your father's biggest cheerleader. She's always contended that he's a bit absent minded, but still the sharpest knife in the draw. I think she believes that, Emily."

"I think you're probably right."

"My father has been driving out to New Jersey and Pennsylvania nearly every weekend," she said.

"He shouldn't be driving."

"No," she said. "If what you say is true, he certainly shouldn't be driving." Emily stood up and took McEntyre's hand and shook it firmly. "Thank you for your time, John. I'm sorry to have blown up at you the way I did."

"Not at all," he said. "And I am sorry. I think the world of your father. I thought it was a mistake to retire him just now. He still has so much to offer."

Emily turned at the door. "He certainly does," she said. "I tend to agree with Maria, in any case. My father is off starting his life over again and he is filled with such promise. In his case, life began at sixty. Goodbye, John."

"Hello Henry," Emily said from the door as she entered Farrell's.

Henry turned on his stool. "Emily," he yelled across the room. He stood up and gave her a hug. "I don't know that you've ever crossed that threshold," he said.

"I did a few times, but that was a long time ago and before it was legal for me to be in here," she said.

"And is it legal now?"

"Unfortunately," she said with a sigh. "Legal and then some and more some than I care to admit."

"I won't listen to age complaints from a child. You can cry about your lost years to some high-school kids. I'm sorry, but your father isn't here today. He hasn't been around much of late."

"I know, Henry. Actually I came to see you."

"Me? What about? Is everything all right?"

"I hope so, but I thought you'd know better than anyone."

"Oh," he said. Henry led her over to a little table against the wall. "What can I get for you?"

"White wine," she said.

"I'll be right back." Henry pushed his beer away and ordered a scotch for himself and a glass of white wine for Emily and went back to her. He took his seat across from her gingerly. "And what might I know better than anyone?" he asked.

"Has daddy been himself lately?" she asked getting straight to the point.

"How do you mean?"

Emily looked at him expectantly and waited.

"He's been a little different, Emily. His world has changed and he's decided to change with it, is all. I should think everyone would be pleased," he said, "most of all, you."

"I am pleased about certain things. It's just that I want to know that he's safe."

"Why shouldn't he be safe?"

"This is in confidence, Henry."

"Of course," he said.

"I spoke with John McEntyre today. He said that daddy was forced into retirement because his mind was beginning to wander."

Henry looked at Emily thoughtfully for a while. "He was forced?"

"Yes. Have you noticed that his mind had been wandering?"

"We're not kids any more," he said. "All of our minds wander off here and there, Emily."

"I said the same thing, but John pointed out the differences. Be honest with me Henry and be honest with yourself."

Henry looked at her sharply. "Maybe a little, kiddo," he said. Henry took a long draw on his scotch and began to motion for another, but then thought better of it. "He does get lost a little here and there, but he comes right back. He doesn't say strange things or forget who people are and his mind is always so sharp in his recollections that it amazes me still. He just tunes out for a few minutes here and there."

"Why didn't you say anything to me?"

"I didn't think it was such a problem, for one thing. It seems more like attention deficit. Also, I assumed that you and Lizzie would have picked up on it by now. I wasn't looking to embarrass anyone."

"This isn't a shameful thing, Henry."

"Of course it isn't. It's just that I'm not of your generation. I'm from an old world, Emily. I'm constantly attempting to make upgrades, but it's hard to get past the old ways."

"It's hard for me too," she admitted Emily sighed heavily and gripped his hand. "I'm scared for daddy."

Henry placed his free hand over hers. "He's fine," he said. "Actually he seems better these days than I've seen him in ages. His mind rarely drifts when I see him now and he's so happy and enthusiastic about his life. My theory is that your father fell into a routine that offered him comfort and stability, but no challenge. He was stagnant in his life and now that it's been turned upside down, not of his own doing of course, he's had to fight back and adapt to the changes. He seems sharper than ever before, Emily."

"He does," she said brightly. "He really does. I think you may be on to something. You can't tell him this, but I've read his manuscript."

"You have?" he said. "He won't tell me a thing about it."

"He wouldn't tell me anything either. I snuck up to his room and forwarded a copy to myself. I feel horrible about doing that, but let me tell you, it's great."

"Can you send it to me?"

"That would be really horrible," she said. "I'll think about it, though." She sat back and sipped her wine. "He just needed a challenge," she said quietly. And then her eyes narrowed. "Where does he go off to, Henry?"

"His weekend excursions, you mean?"

"Yes. Aunt Elizabeth thought she knew, but she was wrong."

"I can't say," Henry said. "It's only that I promised your father that I would never say anything."

"I'm worried, Henry."

"You really needn't be," he said, but there was something in his eyes that Emily read.

"You think there is need for me to worry?" she said.

"No," he said.

"I don't believe you, Henry Griffhorst. You're worried, aren't you? What is it?" she said. "You can't leave it like this."

"There's really nothing to worry about," he said.

"Is there a woman involved?"

Henry answered without speaking. "I didn't say anything about a woman," he said.

"Do you know her, Henry? Do you know who she is?"

"No," he said

"Aunt Elizabeth was sure that it was Maria Scapelli."

"Maria is crazy about your father," he said. "Monty never paid her any attention, though."

"Where do they go?"

"Hunterdon and Bucks counties," he said. "They camp out under the stars," he said with a wry smile spreading over his lips. "They've retreated to some bed and breakfast since the weather had gotten colder."

"Does he love this woman?"

"He believes so," Henry said without looking her in the eye. "He says he does, but..."

"But what?" she pleaded.

"No," he said shaking his head. "I made a promise to your father and I've broken it. I can't say anything more." He lifted his hand and gestured for another scotch and then went on over to get it himself. He took the drink and took a long draw on it and then, reluctantly, went back over to where Emily waited patiently.

"I can see that you're concerned, Henry. I am too and I'm probably the only person in the world who loves daddy more than even you and Aunt Elizabeth. I don't want to hurt him," she said and turned Henry's face to hers with her fingertips. "I just need to make sure that he's all right."

"There's no reason why I should think that he's anything but, all right." Henry put his hand around Emily's fingers and rested his head upon them.

"What is it?" she said.

"It's just that I can't understand his secrecy," he said. "At first I thought maybe he was worried about Lizzie."

"Why?" she asked.

"I let my mind think further down the road, Emily. If Monty were to fall in love again, where would that leave Elizabeth?"

"Daddy would never leave Aunt Elizabeth. She would stay with them, of course."

"And how would Lizzie feel about that?"

Emily drank down the remainder of her wine and exhaled sharply. "I don't know," she said finally. I guess she'd feel unwanted. I suppose that's why she's working now."

"That's what I believed at first, Emily."

"You think there's more?"

"Yes," he said. "I do think there's more, but I can't put my finger on it." Henry slapped his palms down on the table and then pulled them up leaving only his fingertips on edge. He drummed them quietly while his mind raced behind his eyes. "There's something else, but he won't say. I try prodding him along, but he just puts me off."

"Does he tell you about her?" she asked.

"A little bit at a time," he said. "He tells me a little thing here and a little thing there and I try to piece her together."

"What can you tell me, Henry?"

"Why don't you go and ask him for yourself?" he said nearly pleading with her. "I don't feel right about this."

"Please Henry," she said. "It's easier for me to talk with you."

Henry looked around as though he was on the lookout for spies and then he leaned in a little closer to her. "She was a student of his," he began. "Not of recent," he quickly clarified. "She must be in her mid to late forties now. It's all very proper now," he said. "Perhaps that's what bothers your father. Maybe even after all of these years, he's still thinking of her as his student. He says she's quite beautiful and that they have a great deal in common. They apparently go on at great lengths about the same books and enjoy being out in the air for long walks and bicycle rides along the river. He describes her, but I don't think that makes much difference."

"Did he ever mention her name, Henry?"

"Yes," he said. He looked at her and his face showed that he was about to betray his closest friend in the worst way. "Her name is Madeline," he said without looking at her.

"Madeline?"

"Yes. His dear Madeline," Henry said. "I'm afraid your father will never trust me again. I wouldn't blame him."

"Do you know her last name?"

Henry looked up at her. His face said that she was asking too much, but then he lowered his eyes. "It's a French name," he said. Mar something or other."

"Marceau?" she said faintly.

"Yes," said Henry. "Marceau. You know her, Emily?"

"Sort of," she replied. Her face was white and Henry moved around the table and quickly took her arm in case she might fall down.

Chapter Seventeen

"I'm not at all angry with Henry for telling Emily about Madeline. I never, for even a moment, felt betrayed by Emily for reading my manuscript. I suppose I could," he said. "It's no good, though, to harbor such thoughts. I'm rational enough to know that their only motivation for unmasking my behavior is love and concern. I'd been quite unpredictable for the first time in my life and that, I'm sure, was a bit unnerving for them. I was having fun," he says with a wry smile. "And that my dear Toby, was not at all like me."

Robert turns up the collar on his coat and stares at the spot on the river where the sunlight has broken through the clouds. The day will be over soon and then it will be night. "How I dread the night, Toby. How can you stand it here?" he says, still looking at the reflection on the river. He feels a sharp tug on the back of his coat and turns quickly to find that the old man is scowling at him. "What is it?" he asks. Toby throws the small sack of nuts at Robert's feet and motions for him to pick it up.

Robert bends down and retrieves the bag and finds that it is empty. "All gone," he says. Toby stares back at him sharply, expectantly. "I've nothing for you, Toby." The old man gets up stiffly and walks off toward the residence. Robert follows him with his eyes until the door is open and then he sees Emily coming out. He turns away from her path. He does not wish to see her today. He wants more time, but he knows that there is little left. It will be best to tell her now, he thinks. I should tell her now when it is still possible to explain it.

* * *

"Robert?" Elizabeth called from the bottom of the stairs.

He came out of his study and walked to the banister. "Yes?" he called down to her.

"Telephone" she said.

"Who is it?" he asked.

"Emily is on the phone, Robert. Come down and pick it up."

"Tell her I'll call her back. I'm in the middle of something here," he said. He turned to go back into the study, but Elizabeth called him again.

"No," she said. "You've put her off all week, Robert. Come and speak with her now," she said with a tone of finality.

He trudged down the steps with hesitant reluctance. "All right, all right," he muttered. There was annoyance in his voice, but guilt was in his heart. "I'll take it here," he said and picked up the extension on the little table at the bottom of the stairs. "Hello sweetheart," he said wincing before she could reply.

"You've been avoiding me, daddy."

"No dear," he said somberly. "I've just been so busy of late."

"You've been writing?" she asked.

"As a matter of fact, yes I have."

"Are you going to let me see it any time soon?"

"In time," he said.

"What's going on daddy?" she asked.

"Whatever do you mean? I'm just writing as you had wished," he said allowing the irritation to come into his voice.

"I feel like you're shutting me out."

"You're being ridiculous," he said a little impatiently. And then catching himself he told her that he loved her and that he was only a little tired and that she should not worry herself over him.

"I thought I could come by this weekend," she said. "Maybe we could just talk and catch up a little."

"This weekend is bad for me, Emily."

"Shannon would like to see you," she said. "You haven't been around for her much lately either," she said coldly.

"Don't ever do that to me Emily. I've always been here when you were not and I never laid any guilt out at your feet. I have plans for this weekend. I can hardly change them now."

"No," she said. "I wouldn't want that. I'm sorry, daddy."

He tightened his grip on the telephone and rubbed at his temple and forehead methodically. "I'm sorry. I did not mean to snap at you. I'll see you and Shannon next week for Thanksgiving," he said. "I am very much looking forward to that."

"So am I," she said brightly. "I love you very much." The tears began to run down her face, but she did not let her father hear them. "So, where are you off to this weekend?"

"I'm staying at a little place in Bucks County. I've just purchased a new camera and I've been taking quite a few pictures. It's a digital camera, Emily. I've been getting quite a bit of use out of that computer. This morning I bought a new wide-angle zoom lens. It was very expensive, but the way I've been using this camera of mine, I thought it well worth it." He sat on the bottom step as he continued to talk. His mood had brightened considerably and Emily could feel that he wished to confide or at the very least share what was going on in his life.

"What are you photographing?" she asked.

"Mostly just the landscapes," he said. "Lately I've been capturing birds and deer as well. It's a little bit like hunting without the bloodshed and destruction of life," he said comically. "The world is really quite beautiful if you stop to look at it."

"I'd like to see it with you," she said. "I think I've closed my eyes to that part of the world for some time. Can I come with you?"

"Yes," he said. "Yes you must come with me one day. We can make a vacation of it. There are plenty of things to do. Shannon will love it as well," he said. "Perhaps the three of us can go hot air ballooning. It looks to be quite terrifying, but that has never stopped you."

"I'm not all that daring anymore," she said.

"I often wonder if it was becoming a parent or just getting older that had made me more fearful."

"I think for me it's a little of both," she said. "I'd love it for us to go, though."

"Hot air ballooning and all?" he said.

"Yes," she said.

"Do you still like to climb trees?"

"I think I might," she said. "It's been such a long time. I don't know that I can do it any more."

"Anything is possible," he said. They were both silent for a time and then he spoke. "I miss you, Emily."

"I miss you too."

"I don't ever want to lose you," he said solemnly.

"Why so serious?" she asked with less than playful intent. "You could never lose me. Maybe we can go with you this weekend," she said with little hope in her voice.

"No," he said. "I'm afraid not this weekend."

"Who are you going away with, daddy?"

He rested his elbow on his knee and cradled his head in is hand, but never let the phone falter from his ear. "A friend," he said.

"Who is your friend?"

"Just a friend," he said. "Nobody you know."

"Does your friend have a name?"

"Not now," he said. "I need a little space and privacy, Emily. Please give me that, sweetheart."

"Of course," she said dryly. "You can't lose me daddy, if you don't leave me. Please don't ever leave me," she said.

"I'll see you at Thanksgiving," he said with forced energy. "Goodbye Emily."

The trees had lost most of its leaves, but the temperature was unseasonably warm as Robert and Madeline walked alongside the river. He held her hand in his and thought about Emily and Shannon and wondered if he would ever have to choose. It would be much too painful, he thought. He wished it could go on as it had, but he felt a net coming down around him and knew that his time was limited. "I love you," he whispered.

Madeline smiled her sweet smile. She had her golden hair tied back with a black ribbon and she wore the pearl earrings that he had given her on her birthday. Her wide green eyes gazed happily into his and her hand gently squeezed her assurance of her love for him. "Be in this moment with me," she said. "Let go of the outside world."

"It's hard for me."

"I know it is, but it's your only chance for happiness."

"I'm happy," he said.

"I know when you're happy and I know when you worry. Just let go of everything else for now. You can go back to all of that tomorrow."

"Yes," he agreed. "I can let all the rest of it go for today." His mouth smiled, but there was panic in the eyes.

It was the Wednesday night before Thanksgiving. Elizabeth was rolling out the crust for her apple pie shell when the doorbell rang. She quickly ran her hands under the faucet and dried them on her apron as she ran to answer the door. "Just a minute," she called as she made her way. On the other side of the door was a very pale George Drake. His palms were sweating and his heart beat heavily in his chest. "George," Elizabeth said with surprise. "What ever are you doing here? You know that I have much work to do tonight."

"I'm sorry to bother you, Elizabeth."

"What is it?" she said. "My god George, you look like death warmed over. Is everything all right, Love?"

"We need to talk," he said gravely.

"All right," she said opening the door wider allowing him to enter. George walked on through and went on into the living room. "Should I put on some tea?" she said.

"No, no," he said waving his hand in protest. "This is all very difficult for me, Elizabeth."

"Relax, dear. I'm afraid you're heart will burst in your chest. Please sit down and breathe."

"I don't think we should see each other any more, Elizabeth."

Elizabeth took a step back and sat down on the edge of the sofa and kneaded her fingers. "I see," she murmured.

"I am so sorry, but I can't."

"You can't what?" she asked and slowly looked up to him for an answer.

"I've never committed to anyone, Elizabeth. I'm not a young man and I can't just change my way of life. I'm a loner," he said as if that would explain everything and then wiped the perspiration from his forehead. He looked into her eyes and saw that they were filling with tears and he quickly turned away from her. "You can do much better than me," he said. "I'm not good enough for you." He attempted to keep a certain amount of coolness in his voice, but it was not to be.

"Apparently not," she said.

"I should go," he said. His face was white with red blotches and his knees were weak. "I'm sorry," he said, his voice breaking, and walked out of the front door.

Elizabeth jumped up and ran to the door, but stopped short of opening it. Her body trembled and shook and her breaths were shallow. She held onto the doorknob for support. Her life was flashing through her eyes as she stood there. There were images of her father and of her mother and of a very young Robert. There were the faces of the kids in school that had been cruel to her and then the bell rang startling her back to the present. She opened it, without thinking to ask who it might be, and there was George. He threw his arms around her and held her tightly. "Marry me Elizabeth," he whispered into her ear. "Save me from myself and stay with me forever. I will try to be good enough for you."

"Yes," she said and clung to him. Their faces were pressed together and their tears commingled on their cheeks. "It will take quite a bit of work on your part to be good enough for me, but I think there is hope for you yet," she said.

George pressed his lips against hers and they fell back in the doorway and nearly onto the floor. "I love you," he said. "I could never live without you, Elizabeth."

Thanksgiving Day was as gray and dreary a day that Robert could ever remember. He thought of his childhood walks along the canals of Birmingham during the fall and winter seasons and how it had seemed to him to never brighten. Of course it wasn't true, but he could still only envision it as it was today. It was cold on this day as well, but not unseasonably so. He was walking in Prospect Park very much alone realizing that his guests were arriving as he did so. Elizabeth had told him on that morning that George Drake had asked her to be his wife. Robert was a little stunned, but did not show it. He hugged his sister and congratulated her profusely and asked her of her future plans. How she responded was still unclear to him now as he walked the hills.

He looked around as though he were expecting someone to appear, but the park was virtually empty but for a few determined joggers and the occasional man or woman walking their dog. In a sense he felt a little freer now that Elizabeth would no longer depend upon him, but the freedom itself came with mixed feelings. What exactly was he free to do?

He thought, then, of Elizabeth in the kitchen keeping a close eye on the clock on the wall. She would want to be taking out the stuffed mushrooms and the pigs in the blanket to put out on the buffet and she would wonder where he was and then to have to call on Henry to mix the drinks. He could almost smell the turkey as he walked on and he could picture Kathleen gutting it of the bread stuffing and putting it into a serving bowl and slapping at any hand that reached for it. He could see Emily with her hair tied back into a ponytail sneaking a chocolate drop cookie from a tray that was wrapped in cellophane and he could see her skipping off without the least bit of guilt.

"Happy Thanksgiving," a man said as he passed Robert with his dog.

"And to you," Robert replied. He stopped in his tracks and watched as the man moved on. Nearly an hour had passed before Emily came along and took Robert by the arm. He turned and smiled at her and then they walked for a while without saying a word.

Chapter Eighteen

A small branch drifts slowly down the Delaware River. Robert watches as it bobs along with the current, skipping over the rocks where the water is shallow. He waits to see if the branch will get hung up, but it does not. The branch moves steadily on until he can no longer see it. "We're all meant to do that," he says.

"What's that?" Emily says hesitantly. She did not know if he was aware that she was standing behind him.

"Drifting along," he says jovially and makes his hand ripple along the air. "Just drifting along and hoping not to get hung up along the way."

"Did you feel that you had gotten hung up along the way, daddy?"

"Only a little," he says. "If anyone ever said otherwise, they'd be lying." He turns and takes Emily's hand. "You've always helped me to keep moving along."

"I hope so," she says.

"Have you come to take me away from here?" he asks without a trace of hope in his voice.

"I was hoping that you would like it here. You've been spending so much time in this area."

"I appreciate that," he said. "I really and truly do appreciate that, but I'd like to leave. I want to go home."

"I was thinking that maybe you'd come and live with me and Shannon for a time."

"Until what time?" he asks.

"I spoke with Dr. Hurley."

"So have I," he says.

"And?" she says looking at him hopefully.

"Why can't I just live my life, Emily? Why does it have to matter what I do or with whom I do it with?"

"I read your book again."

Robert says nothing to this. He begins to walk, but doesn't let go of Emily's hand. "It's all right," he says. "You shouldn't fear for me."

"Tell me about your friend, daddy."

"We knew that you would try to keep us apart, Emily. We wanted to tell you about us, but we knew that you would never understand."

"Is her name Madeline? Is it Madeline Marceau, daddy?"

Robert looks around, but not at Emily. He inhales the clean air that moves with the river. The air always makes him feel good and helps to relax him. "I do love it here," he says.

"Henry told me that you talk with her from the phone in your study."

"So I do," he says simply.

"That phone hasn't worked since I was a child. I checked and it still isn't working."

Robert narrows his eyes. "It does work some of the time," he says quietly; reluctantly.

"No, daddy, it never works." Emily bites down hard on her lip to keep from crying. She's prepared herself for this talk for some time, but still it is hard for her.

Robert turns to her and smiles weakly. "I know it some of the time," he says. "I don't know it all of the time, but I know it some of the time."

"Do you know it now?"

"I do," he says.

"Can you hold onto that?" she pleads.

"I've tried to fight it," he says. "I get down, Emily."

"I don't understand."

"I get down," he repeats. "All of my life I have gotten down, but I always get right back up because I have to. Your mother got down, but she stayed down and never really got back up. I hated her for not getting up, Emily. I hated her for it, but that wasn't fair."

"We all get down," Emily said. "We all do, but then we get back up. That's what we do."

"Yes," he said. "I know that. It's never been all that hard for me to get back up, but now it is hard. I keep getting slapped down and when I get back up the rungs don't climb up as high as they used to." He turns to Emily and takes her face into his hands the way he did when she was just a little girl. "There's very little for me to get up for," he says clarifying himself.

"There's me, daddy." Emily brakes down and Robert puts his arms around her. "There's Shannon and Aunt Elizabeth too."

"I know that," he says. "You all love me and I love you, but none of you need me. Oh Emily," he sighs. "I'm tired. I just can't fight it any more. I tried to fight and I did for a very long time, but I just can't do it any more." He turns away and bends down and picks up a flat rock and walks closer to the rivers edge. He wraps his index finger along the edge of the rock and rocks his wrist back and forth a few times and then releases the rock skipping it off the water. "That wasn't bad," he says pleased with himself.

"Emily," he says with all seriousness. "Madeline is good for me. She saved me," he says. "I kept falling and with each fall I was getting deeper into an abyss. I know that sounds melodramatic, but unless you've been there I must say there is no better way to explain it. I felt like I was surrounded by darkness and I wished to be dead," he says. "I had only just begun to understand Kathleen," he says looking away. "I'm sorry. I shouldn't hurt you like that."

"It's all right, daddy."

"Madeline came into my life just in time. She lifted me out of that darkness when I couldn't do it any more. And now when I get down, she comes to me and saves me and now I don't get so far down any more because I know that she's out there and that she will come."

"But she's not there, daddy. She's just a story that you've written. It isn't real life..."

"Don't," he interrupts sternly. "Don't do that to me, Emily. I've been hearing those very words for my whole life."

"What are you saying?" Emily makes fists of her hands out of her deep frustration for her father's words.

"It's only words," he says. "My mother would tell me that my stories were only words and not real life. What did she know about real life?" he says. "What do you know about it? No," he says shaking his head and walking off a bit. "No, it is real life. It's my life now and I won't have it taken away from me."

"But you said you knew that it wasn't."

He turns to face her again. "I said that I do some of the time. When I'm with her she is very real to me, Emily. My life with Madeline is as real and true as this very moment. And there's no grief in it," he says pleading for her acceptance with his eyes. "I suppose that I know that I should fight it, but I don't really want to. I want to be happy, Emily. Come and we'll sit down," he says taking Emily by the hand and leading her back to the bench. They sit for a while in a welcomed silence.

"I've decided to go with her," he says calmly. "I know that you don't believe in her and to you she is only some words on a page that I've written. I understand that and I won't try to dissuade you from your beliefs. But you have to respect me in this, Emily. I have faith in Madeline. I know the feel of her touch against my skin and the softness of her hair against my cheek. I can see the depths of her soul through her eyes, Emily. I wake each morning with her scent still lingering in the air around me and on my clothes. I can recall the sound of her laughter at any given moment and it lifts my spirits in an instant." He tilts his head and looks into her eyes. "I can't just let her go. Can't you understand that?"

"Yes," she says. "I suppose that I can." Emily looks at her father and sees that with her simple words, she has given him his peace. She does not pursue the argument. She does not tell him that Max Spellman of the delicatessen had asked to see if he had gotten the briefcase that he had left in the door on the porch. She does not mention seeing the barman at the Hearthstone pub just down the road from here who had liked Robert so very much. The man thought it was sweet how he would come in and order two drinks. One for himself and one for, he assumed, his late wife. She decided that it would not matter now. "You're book is very good," she says.

"Is it?"

"Yes," she says. "It is beautiful."

"Can you publish it?"

"I think I can," she says. "I think that it would do quite well."

"That would be very good," he says. "I'd like others to know about Madeline. She deserves the company of others besides me," he says in earnest. "I have to go, Emily. I've been avoiding her and I'm afraid she'll go on without me. I think that I would most probably die if I had lost her."

"I love you, daddy. We'll you still see me?"

"Yes, of course. You come and see me when you can." He kisses Emily on the cheek and then gets up and takes Madeline by the hand and together they walk off.